MUSEUM MURDER

BOOKS BY KATIE GAYLE

The Kensington Kidnap

KATIE GAYLE

THE MUSEUM MURDER

bookouture

Published by Bookouture in 2021

An imprint of Storyfire Ltd.
Carmelite House
50 Victoria Embankment
London EC4Y 0DZ

www.bookouture.com

ISBN: 978-1-80019-342-0
eBook ISBN: 978-1-80019-341-3

CHAPTER 1

At least she had the kittens.

It was hard to feel down with three fluffy balls of squeaking cuteness staggering around like little drunks. Pip sat down on the floor, scooped them up and bundled them against her chest. 'Group hug!' she told them as they squirmed and mewed in outrage. She released them onto the carpet and arranged them in colour order, lining them up from darkest to lightest, and took a quick picture in the nanosecond before they started to disperse.

Fully awake now, the kittens headed for their mum, nuzzling into her, looking for supper. The purring from Most was loud enough to be heard across the room.

Pip checked the photo on her phone. Amazingly enough, she'd got the shot: three furry little sausages: a black one, a tortoiseshell and a grey, their funny triangle tails sticking straight out behind them. She posted to Instagram, noting that this was her twelfth consecutive kitten picture, and about the hundredth kitten picture she'd posted since they were born. She knew she should go and take a picture of flowers or sunsets or something for variety, but she was too low.

The kittens were about all she had going on for her, now that she'd lost the job at Boston Investigations. Being a private investigator had seemed like a dream, which, really, she should have known from experience, was a sign that things were about to go wrong. She had excelled in the training and started off well. Not even the hard work and long hours had been a problem. She'd had a job at last, and a regular salary cheque. No more wondering where the rent was coming from. No more begging for handouts from Mummy. Best of all, it had been a good job that she really liked and thought she could be good at. After almost a decade of, frankly, disastrous attempts at Finding Her Life's Purpose, or at least steady employment (yes, there'd been some adventures and a lot of fun, but at the end of the day things always seemed to fall apart) she'd thought that she'd finally got it.

But of course, it had all gone wrong. And this time it wasn't even her normal brand of spectacular mess-up. Just one background check, where she'd spelt Marc with a 'k' instead of a 'c', which honestly could have happened to anyone. A teeny, tiny problem – except that unfortunately while Mark-with-a-k had a clean record, Marc-with-a-c most certainly didn't. Which wouldn't have mattered, if it wasn't for the fact that they'd been doing checks for the Palace, and now Marc-with-a-c had been allowed sight of some top-secret security plans. It had all imploded after that, when Doug Bradford had decided to do his own background checks on Pip. Honestly, he was the one who should feel like a fool for not having done them earlier, especially when he'd already known that she'd basically committed identity fraud to get the job. It was a bit rich, him getting all worked up about the so-called theft (actually, the rescue) of Most-the-cat from the vet where she had been temping. And as for the incident with the tractor when she'd been working at the bee farm – she had only been trying to help, and who could have known the thing would be so unwieldy to manoeuvre? So here she was, once again without a job or purpose in her life.

The sound of Tim's key in the door gave Pip a little flutter of pleasure. Her flatmate's appearance even more so, although he looked pale and tired after a long day at work. His nice blue cotton shirt – Pip's personal favourite – was rumpled, with a small stain on the pocket. Possibly coffee, thought Pip, who was finding it hard to give up on the idea that she was a detective.

'How are the kids this evening?' Tim asked, bending down to inspect the bundle of cats. It was a little joke between them – that they were the parents, and the kittens were their kids. It was funny, but squeezed Pip's heart a little. When would she be in a real relationship? Maybe even one with long-term potential?

'They're in fine fettle. Most is a really good mum, isn't he?'

'He really is.'

'Not many blokes are so devoted.'

'Or manage to feed their young so well.'

Another little joke between them – the three-legged cat had been a male. Until, of course, a bellyful of kittens had proved otherwise. Pip's relationship with Tim was a bit strange. Their conversation had recently taken on the air of a comfortable couple, but there hadn't been any coupling, so to speak. They were just roomies with a bit of a tingle between them.

'You look as tired as I feel,' said Pip. 'I've just been sitting here on the floor with the cats, too exhausted to move.'

'Thank God it's Friday. It's been a long day for me. A long week,' said Tim. 'We've been working on this job, trying to hack into a particular system that was...'

Thereafter, a lot of technical muttering floated by Pip. Firewall... Server... Once Tim got going on computery stuff, it was best to just nod and wait until he'd finished. His recent revelation that he actually worked as a hacker – but for the goodies, he claimed – had had the unfortunate effect that he, no longer trying to keep his profession a secret, shared his work with her in mind-numbingly tedious detail.

Pip picked up a sleepy kitten in each hand and popped one on each shoulder, their little wet noses pressed into her neck.

'Look, epaulettes,' she said. Which made Tim laugh and lose track of whatever he'd been saying about phishing and encryption.

'So how was your job search?' he asked, looking at her fondly. Or, Pip hoped it was fondly. Tim was also her landlord, so his interest in her job search wasn't exactly entirely altruistic. 'I don't understand how someone who stands out like you isn't snapped up immediately,' he added, with a twinkle in his eye.

That was another thing about Tim – he had this odd way of maybe-flirting that confused and flustered her. Did he mean she was noticeable for being attractive? Or for being an awkwardly tall person with odd mannerisms? Or perhaps for some other, even worse attribute, that she was unaware of?

'I'm trying,' she said with a sigh. Well, it wasn't entirely a lie. She'd even got up the courage to phone Sharon at the temp agency today, although when Sharon had heard her name she had started screaming something about the cat and Boston Investigations and then slammed down the phone. Pip had a sneaking suspicion that this kind of thing happened to her more than it happened to other people.

'You've had some bad luck, Pip. But you'll get there. I know you will.' And with that, Tim disappeared into his own room.

She'd get there. But where was 'there', and how would she even start? She looked down at the kittens for inspiration, but they seemed fresh out of ideas, too.

CHAPTER 2

Pip surveyed what was indeed a very fine costume on an admittedly *very* buff bare-chested mannequin, and turned to her sister.

'This gladiator get-up would be just the thing for a young man trying to make an impression down at the pub.'

'Oh, he'd get noticed all right,' said Flis. 'And you'd feel quite secure having him walk you home. What with that sword, or whatever that thing is dangling from his belt.'

'Don't you think it's odd that gladiators had bare chests, and wore skimpy little loincloths?' Pip asked Flis. 'They wore sandals and then had these random bits of armour on the arms and legs. I mean, what were they protecting? What does it say about their priorities?'

'Their wives were probably shouting after them, "Take a chest-plate, Magnus, you might need it!"' Flis said.

'And he'd shout back, "I've told you a hundred times, Octavia, I am invincible," before stubbing his toe on the way to the arena.'

That was one of the nice things about a sister: you always knew how to keep each other's jokes going.

Pip let her fingers linger a moment on the shiny curve of the gladiator's bare chest. She wondered what dishy Tim's chest would feel like under her hand. Warmer, hopefully, than the gladiator's. And less plasticky.

'No touching, please ma'am,' said a polite voice behind her.

Pip pulled her hand back and turned to see a young guard in a blue uniform with 'Museum of Movie Memorabilia and Vintage

Costumes' embroidered on the pocket, and 'Gordon Tshuma' on his name badge.

'These are valuable items, miss. That one there was worn by Michael Douglas in *Spartacus.*' Pride lit up the guard's remarkably chiselled face, as if he himself had worn the costume. Which was not an entirely displeasing mental image.

'Michael Douglas?' Pip asked in surprise. 'I'm pretty sure he's not old enough…'

The guard continued regardless. 'It's magnificent, isn't it? A collector would pay a good few pounds for this one, that's for sure. I have to keep an eye. A sharp eye.' To illustrate his point, he closed one brown eye and rolled the other about, tapping his forefinger against his temple in what was, all in all, a rather confusing gesture. 'So, no touching of the display items, if you please, miss,' he repeated.

Pip apologised. She had to admit, she wouldn't have minded touching *him*, but she was almost sure that was against the rules, too. It so often was. The guard smiled graciously at her and moved along towards a tableau of aliens and space explorers: a mishmash of *Star Trek, Doctor Who* and *Star Wars* figures gazing up at where the Milky Way might be, if they weren't in the ground floor of a London building.

'Gosh, he's nice-looking, isn't he?' Flis whispered, loudly. 'Like that Trevor Noah. Only hotter.'

'Is he? I didn't notice at all,' said Pip. And the sisters laughed.

'But d'you see what I mean, Pip?' said Flis, as if they were in the middle of a conversation. Flis often did this, and Pip knew to nod and agree until she'd figured out what they were talking about. 'This stuff is really valuable. Collectors' items. It's very big right now. Part of this whole retro-vintage-heritage thing. It's all about recycling, upcycling, downcycling…' Flis gestured at the gladiator, narrowly missing hitting him in the chest.

'I don't think downcycling is a thing.'

'Upscaling. Downgrading. Whatever you like to call it. It basically means that people are reusing and rewearing. I've got a new content partner on my blog – big sponsor – and they're all about vintage clothing, high-end stuff. Celebrities are wearing vintage and heritage items, even on the red carpet. It is all the rage. Especially if it has a history, like this stuff here.'

Flis had garnered a huge following on her various social media platforms. What had started as a 'mummy blog' with an eco edge was now a top-rated lifestyle blog that was big on Instagram, Facebook, Twitter; you name it. And Flis, in a mind-bogglingly unlikely turn of events, was now a recognisable 'influencer'. Just the other day, they'd been in Tesco buying toilet paper, and someone had stopped them and demanded a selfie – including the toilet paper. Lucky for Flis, it had been a one hundred per cent recycled brand.

'It's all about lifestyle trends,' Flis continued, waving her arm in a wide, vague sweep to illustrate the broad and rich lifestyle that encompassed vintage clothes, movie gladiator armour and bizarre conglomerations of space travellers. 'I knew I was right to check this out. What better place to get a taste of it than at the Museum of Movie Necrophilia and Vintage Clothing?'

'Memorabilia,' corrected Pip. 'It's the Museum of Movie Memorabilia and Vintage Costumes. Otherwise it would be really… terrible.'

Flis looked annoyed. 'That's what I said, Pip. Really, must you always repeat everything that I say? Anyway, I told you it would be fun, didn't I?'

To be honest, Pip hadn't been eager to leave her cats and her flat on a Saturday morning. She had wanted to stay at home, contemplate how everything had turned pear-shaped, play with the kittens and possibly spot Tim coming out of the bathroom in just a towel. These were the little things that kept her motivated these days. But Flis had insisted that it would do Pip good to get out. She'd said that Pip would love all the movie costumes, that it would take her mind off the job situation. And that afterwards, they might have a drink at a nearby café by the bridge, and pretend the Thames was a country river. And when Flis insisted on something, it was rather hard to argue. And to be fair, she'd been right: so far, this strange museum had cheered Pip up quite a bit.

Pip and Flis moved away from the gladiator and made their way around the room, until they came to an open doorway, and went into the next room.

And then they saw it.

'OMG!' Pip squealed. 'Do you see what I see?'

'Do you think that's…?'

'I think it most certainly is.'

The signage confirmed: 'Worn by Julia Roberts, *Pretty Woman*, 1990.'

In the centre of the room, on a raised dais, was a gown of perfect, fiery red: form-fitting in the bodice, off the shoulder, with a little plunge at the cleavage and a gather below the waist intended to set the full, silky skirt swishing when the wearer moved.

'"Pretty woman, walking down the street… Pretty woman, the kind I'd like to meet…"' The two women started to sing the theme song from the film they must have watched dozens of times in their early teens, bringing the good-looking guard scurrying into the room, an expression of worry on his face. He was closely followed by a well-dressed older woman.

'We also have the dance dress worn by Jennifer Grey in *Dirty Dancing*, if you like eighties movies,' said the woman, almost shoving the guard out of the way. 'It's just in the next room. Let me show you.'

The two sisters, however, stood rooted to the spot. They had no interest in any other gown just yet.

'It's magnificent. Best movie ever. Best dress,' said Flis to Pip.

'No contest,' Pip agreed. Then, turning to the unknown woman: 'Is it the real thing? As worn by Julia Roberts?'

'Yes. And the other dress is the real thing, too. Visitors really love to see it. Iconic. You really should come through,' the woman continued, quite insistently, as if the *Dirty Dancing* dress had a dentist appointment and might leave at any moment. She even pulled slightly at Flis's arm.

Pip wasn't listening. She was deep in thought. Julia Roberts's actual shoulders had emerged from that silky bodice. Richard Gere's actual hand had cupped the slim waist. And now here it was in London, before her very eyes. The real thing. It gave Pip a thrill, just thinking about its history.

'Do you work here?' Flis asked, shaking the woman's hand off her arm.

'Yes, I do. Arabella Buchanan. I'm the manager,' said the woman. She was older than them, and very stylish. She could have been an exhibit herself, dressed in a fifties-style pencil dress that looked like something Jackie O might have worn, her hair in a sleek black bob.

Flis was suddenly more interested in her, now that she was more than an arm-pulling distraction. 'I'm Felicity Bloom-Green. I'm doing a story for my blog, *EarthMomma*,' said Flis. "This is my sister, Epiphany."

Arabella Buchanan's eyes widened in recognition – Flis had this effect on people these days.

'The museum is really cool,' Flis continued. 'I'm interested in vintage trends and celebrity culture. I want to do something on it for the blog. Can I chat to you for a bit?'

'Of course, I'd be happy to talk. Vintage clothing is my passion. Shall we sit down over there?' said Arabella eagerly, gesturing to a grouping of two chairs and a sofa in the foyer by the entrance, below a large box frame featuring Elizabeth Taylor's tortoiseshell hairbrush.

Pip told them she'd be perfectly happy to wait while they chatted. In fact, she was rather keen on taking a break. She moved over to a little velvet sofa where she could sit and rest her feet, admire the killer red dress, and also check her phone messages and maybe catch up on a bit of celeb gossip. They had done a great job of the display of the dress, though, she thought; it was hard to tear her eyes away. The elbow-length white gloves. The diamond choker necklace that Edward (had Richard Gere ever been more gorgeous than in that film?) had presented to Vivian (had Julia Roberts ever been more captivating?).

Pip remembered that scene frame-for-frame. As a teenager, she'd practised her favourite lines in her bedroom mirror. Looking at the dress now, she murmured – in her very best Julia Roberts accent – the words that Vivian said to Edward in the lift as they set out on their date: '"If I forget to tell you later, I had a really good time tonight."' She loved those words. Pip wished she could feel some of that optimism for herself, some day.

Her phone beeped. A message from Tim! Perhaps with Pip out of the flat, he'd realised how empty his life was without her, and had decided he couldn't wait another minute to tell her so. Her heart hammering, she opened the message.

> 'I don't mean to put pressure on you, but the council tax is due tomorrow. Any chance you could pay at least some of your rent?'

Pip felt her eyes prickle with imminent tears. This was not what happened to movie stars and Insta-celebs and influencers. What *was* she going to do?

Flis and Arabella got up from the sofa and came over, chatting and laughing together. 'Can you believe it, Pip? Arabella knows our cousin, Jane. They went to school together, back in the day. What a strange coincidence – quite splendiferous.'

'Why is it splendiferous?' Pip asked Flis.

Flis looked confused. 'You know,' she said. 'When something happens, and then another thing happens. It's splendiferous.'

'Serendipitous?' Pip suggested, with an inward sigh.

'Yes, that's what I said,' said Flis, not quite meeting Pip's eye. 'Anyway, Arabella was just telling me how they're looking to update the museum, to focus on some recent movies and TV shows.'

'That is a fabulous idea. There's nothing like that around. It would bring in a younger crowd, too,' said Pip.

'And Arabella was telling me how she's looking for someone who knows that celebrity and TV world, to source new pieces.'

Pip sighed. 'Oh, that sounds like a wonderful job for some lucky person.' If only she could get a lovely job like that, Pip thought, miserable again. Life just wasn't fair.

Arabella looked at Pip. 'Your sister says that you know a lot about popular culture and stars and so on, and you're friends with all sorts of celebs,' she said, her perfectly plucked eyebrows raised in an inquiring arc – which was quite a challenge, given her Botoxed forehead.

Flis gave Pip a meaningful look. 'I told her all about how you're basically best friends with Madison Price, ever since you found her missing son.'

'Not best friends, exactly,' said Pip with a modest shrug. 'Just friends.'

It was true, though, that after Pip had found Matty Price, Madison had messaged her and called her and sent her gifts for weeks. Pip had been for dinner at the Prices' Kensington townhouse twice, and met all sorts of interesting people. And it was true that Madison had hugged Pip warmly when she saw her, and her husband, Ben, had looked at her with big, grateful, puppy-dog eyes. Pip never thought she'd say this, but sometimes she wished that the Prices were slightly less grateful.

Flis was doing weird things with her eyebrows, as if trying to communicate something. Pip had no idea what. She could see why speech had been invented.

'Wait,' said Arabella. 'What about *you* for the job?'

'Who, me? What job?' Pip had somehow lost the thread of what they were talking about. It happened a lot, with Flis in the mix.

'As a buyer for the museum. If you know all about movies and TV, and you've got access to celebrities. You might be just right for the job. Buyer-slash-curator-slash-stylist,' said Arabella. 'I was just working on a job description and some notes on the ideal candidate.'

Flis had stopped doing the eyebrow thing and was nodding enthusiastically.

Arabella handed over her phone, and Pip glanced down through the notes she'd typed: *Creative vision... Sourcing original items... Curation... Intimate knowledge of celebrity culture...*

It was starting to sink in, what Arabella was saying. And it made a lot of sense. Pip had had her heart set on the detective job, but that had fallen through after the misunderstanding. If she couldn't be a sleuth, she supposed there were far worse jobs than buying expensive dresses for a living. Maybe this was the job for her – clothes and celebs and buying stuff and rubbing shoulders with people. She glanced towards Arabella, who was smiling, showing a lot of gum. Worst-case scenario, it would pay the blasted rent.

'So,' said Arabella. 'Would you like to come in for an interview? I'm on my way to a meeting now, but how would Monday at nine thirty work for you?'

Pip took a deep breath, and tried not to look like she might wet her pants with excitement – which wouldn't be the first time.

'I'd love that,' she said to Arabella. 'I really would.'

CHAPTER 3

Monday was strange from the word go. Pip had had an awful night's sleep, tossing and turning, wondering what Arabella would ask her in the interview, and trying to think up brilliant answers and ideas which, knowing her, she was then bound to forget under pressure. It was vital that she didn't mess this up. Whatever she did, she mustn't mention how she'd stolen Most from the vet, even though it had been perfectly justified. Employers tended to react badly to that story.

All in all, she only managed a couple of hours of shut-eye. Up early, she went to make tea and check on the kittens, only to discover the fluffy grey one was stuck behind the fridge, mewing pathetically, while Mummy Most stalked anxiously in front of it, miaowing pitifully back. Pip got Tim up to help her move the fridge without squashing the kitten. Between the two of them, they lifted the fridge carefully. The kitten scampered out, and for a brief, glorious second, victory was achieved. But a fridge, even a small one, is a remarkably unwieldy thing, being wide and slippery and heavy. Pip felt her grip loosening. The appliance tilted forward and the door opened, spilling milk and eggs and a hundred glass jars of mystery condiments and sauces onto the kitchen floor as the cats hurtled to safety, their tails like bottle brushes.

Pip and Tim looked at each other, pushed the fridge back into a standing position and, without a word, bent down to pick up the shards of glass, the eggshells, the nameless goop, the lids and cartons that had landed at their feet. The kittens scrambled about, trying to get at the milk, tracking egg yolk across the floor, putting themselves in imminent danger of laceration. Fortunately, Most lay down comfortably on the far side of the kitchen and let out a throaty chirrup that drew the kittens away to breakfast. As they fed, Most gazed at Pip and Tim implacably through blissfully half-closed lids. *Humans*, she seemed to be thinking. *What odd creatures they are, randomly throwing their groceries all over the kitchen for no reason.*

Once the fridge crisis had been dealt with, Pip dashed for a shower, then scoured her wardrobe, putting together a stylish-yet-professional look – not the look of someone who had recently scraped red pepper hummus off a kitten. She kept remembering how smart Arabella had looked on Saturday, but eventually, with a deep sigh, accepted that someone of her own height would never channel Jackie O.

When Pip arrived at the museum, Arabella was waiting outside the big double doors, chatting to a security guard – not the hot youngster, Pip noted, this man was a bit older and not nearly as good looking. He didn't look particularly friendly, either. Arabella looked Pip up and down, surveying her outfit – slim-fitting black trousers and a gorgeous embroidered green jacket she'd picked up in a market in Kashmir.

'Nice jacket,' Arabella said. Pip had obviously passed muster. 'What a coincidence that you and Felicity should have come by just at the right time,' she continued. 'Ever since I suggested to Henrietta, the director, that we appoint someone, I've been absolutely stumped as to where to find the right person for this job. Henrietta was most impressed with my vision. Most impressed. Before she disappeared off to Morocco, that was.' For a moment, Arabella looked like she'd smelled something bad. Pip hoped it wasn't the red pepper hummus.

'Anyway,' Arabella said, after a moment. 'It's like you've fallen into my lap, isn't it? The answer to my problems.'

Pip wasn't accustomed to being the answer to anyone's problems, but she wasn't going to argue.

The guard opened the doors and stood back, allowing Arabella and Pip into the dark museum. Arabella turned on a set of side lights that gave the empty reception a gloomy, eerie feel. The two women walked through reception and on into the main museum, arriving at the room where the red dress stood on display, catching a ray of morning sun.

'Let's just sit here,' said Arabella, indicating the small sofa where Pip had sat and looked at the red dress on Saturday. 'I have a small office – which you will share with me, if you get the job. But I'm always happier out here, in the museum, surrounded by our beautiful things.'

She looked at Pip as if she expected an answer, but Pip couldn't work out what the question was.

'You have a remarkable collection,' Pip said, after an awkward pause. 'Wonderful.'

'Oh, I'm so glad you think so,' said Arabella, as if she hadn't suggested it in the first place. She then looked down at her hands and seemed to suddenly realise that they were empty. 'I really should get something to make notes,' she said to Pip. 'You wait here, and, um, think of what ideas you would bring to the museum.'

Arabella clearly had no idea how to interview a prospective employee. Pip had been to lots of interviews, and she knew that the clueless interviewers were the worst. Although in fairness, they were also the most likely to give her a job.

Being asked to come up with ideas on the spot always made Pip nervous. Fortunately, she had a lot of ideas this time – the ones that had kept her up till four that morning. She just had to try to remember them.

Pip looked at the Julia Roberts dress again, trying to calm herself with its soft lines and the good memories it brought, wanting to recapture the way it had made her feel when she'd first seen it on Saturday. She'd been full of ideas then. And the way the sun caught it now made it stand out amongst the shadows. Odd, though – it didn't look quite as she remembered from the film. She got up to examine it more closely. Hadn't there been a bit of a deeper cutaway at the back? In that scene where Vivian and Edward walked through the theatre, Pip had always wondered how the dress stayed up. And had it been *quite* that dark a red?

She must be wrong. She took her phone out of her bag and typed 'Pretty Woman red dress' into Google Images. Up came multiple pictures of Julia Roberts. Using her thumb and forefinger, Pip zoomed in on one that showed a back view. The back of the dress in the picture did look deeper cut, but it could just be the angle. She looked at another photo, examining where the skirt was gathered at the front. It was a double pleat, centred. The dress in front of her had more of a gather, positioned slightly off-centre, to the left. It was definitely *not* the same dress, whatever Ms Arabella Buchanan, manager, had said. Now that she'd seen it, she couldn't understand how she'd ever been taken in.

Scrolling down further, Pip found a slew of ads for knock-offs of the famous dress. Off-the-shelf versions as well as dresses individually made to fit, from £179.99 plus delivery. Pip felt like someone had punched her in the solar plexus. Was nothing sacred? Was nothing true? Did people just buy a bunch of knock-offs now and call themselves a museum? Well, she wouldn't be working here, in this fake museum of fake fakeries, that was for sure – rent due or not. Arabella could take her interview and shove it.

'Should we get on now?' came Arabella's voice. She was back in the room, armed with a notebook and pen.

'It's not the real dress,' Pip blurted out, pointing at the red dress in front of them. 'This one's a fake.'

'Of course it's the real dress,' said Arabella quickly. 'Of course it is.'

'It's not,' Pip said, holding the phone with the pictures of Julia Roberts in front of Arabella's face. 'Look at the back here. And the gather there. You know what, I was so excited about this job and this place. I should've known it was too good to be true. I've done some dodgy things in the past, but I draw the line at deliberate fraud. I really do. I can't work here. It wouldn't be right. I bet *everything* in this stupid museum is a fake. You should be ashamed of yourself.' She turned to go. Another opportunity, dead before it had started.

'Wait...' said Arabella. 'It's not like that. They're not all fake. It's just that one.' Pip turned back. Arabella looked shocked at her own revelation – had covered her mouth, like someone in a bad movie. But it was too late, the truth was out.

'So you think that makes it okay? Because it's just the one? You lied, *lied*, to fans of perhaps the greatest romantic comedy ever made.' Pip was uncontained in her disdain.

Tears pooled in the corners of Arabella's eyes. 'It's not like that. No one, absolutely no one respects and loves classic movie dresses more than me. It's my life. And this film in particular... This dress... Julia... Richard... It's just... It's very complicated.'

The tears spilled over. Ordinarily, Pip would have felt sorry for her. But not today.

'Complicated? Spit it out, then,' she said roughly. 'What's the story? What is so complicated about being a scam artist?'

Arabella clutched her notebook to her chest. 'I'm not a scam artist,' she said. 'The truth is, the real dress has been stolen. I came to work two weeks ago – and it was gone. There was no sign of a break-in, or forced entry. The dress had just disappeared. I didn't know what to do. So I bought a replica off the internet and put it here until I could work out what to do. No one noticed until now. No one.'

'I do have an eye for this type of thing,' Pip admitted, starting to feel a little bit sorry for Arabella, despite herself.

'That's why you'd be so perfect for this job,' said Arabella, eagerly. 'You have a good eye. Listen. Forget about the interview. I was going to hire you anyway, I just thought I had better do an interview. If you want it, you've got the job. As long as you don't mention the fake dress to anyone.'

Pip thought about it. If Arabella was telling the truth, then it wasn't like she'd deliberately set out to mislead people. And Pip did love the sound of this job.

'Actually, I've got an idea,' said Arabella shyly, squirming a little. 'Didn't your sister say you found Madison Price's kid when he was missing? Maybe you can help me figure out what happened to the dress and get it back, before Henrietta finds out.' Arabella's face brightened, as if she'd just convinced herself. 'You can help me find the dress, and you can help me bring the museum up to date. And then everything will be okay. Absolutely okay.'

Pip looked at the woman like she was crazy. 'Why do you need me? Surely the police are investigating already?'

Arabella, looked down at her feet. 'Oh, that. Well, I haven't reported it.'

'Why on earth not?' Pip thought about it, and could see only one explanation for the dress not being reported stolen. She sighed. 'Just tell me the truth, Arabella. Were you lying to me? Was there ever really an original?'

'Yes, there was,' Arabella said, sounding offended. 'But if I tell the police, I'll have to tell my boss. And if I tell my boss, that's the end of my job and the end of the museum. I know I was wrong, but it's more complicated than it sounds, believe me. So I didn't go to the police. And by the time I decided maybe I *should* report it, it was a week later – and how was I going to explain that?'

'You need to tell me the whole story,' said Pip. 'And when you've finished, I'll decide if I'll take this job and help you with the dress. Or whether I'll go to the police myself.' It was quite satisfying to be calling the shots like this, Pip had to admit. She'd almost say that the interview was going better than she could have hoped.

CHAPTER 4

Arabella motioned to the front of the museum. 'Emily will be here by now,' hissed Arabella. 'We need privacy, and she's a bit of a nosey one. Let's go and talk somewhere else.'

Arabella seemed to pull herself together and stand up taller. Pip followed her to the small reception area of the museum, where people bought tickets and the few sad postcards that were available for sale. Arabella had a word with the elegantly dressed younger woman behind the desk – Emily, presumably – telling her she was heading out for a few minutes and to phone her if she was needed.

'It's not like it's ever that busy, really,' she explained to Pip, as they walked across the street to a little café. The café, in contrast to the museum, was all wood and glass and black-painted metal, in the style that seemed ubiquitous this year. Potted ferns and aspidistras provided the only relief from the stark planes and sharp angles. They ordered coffee. Pip wondered if she was the only one regretting that it was a tad early for wine.

The words spilled out of Arabella. She seemed relieved to finally tell her story. The red dress had been stolen at some point between the Saturday afternoon and the Sunday morning, two weeks previously. The museum closed at three on a Saturday. Arabella had popped in on Sunday morning, as she often did, to enjoy a silent walk around the place, 'imbibing the atmosphere of the glory days of cinema,' as she put it. When she'd opened up, the dress was gone. The alarm had not been triggered, and when Arabella came in, it was set. Whoever had taken the dress had done so without setting off the alarm. There was only one entrance to the museum, and no signs of forced entry.

'That dress must be worth a fortune. And apart from that, it's an important part of movie history. And yet you didn't go to the police?' Pip said.

'I should have done. I meant to, I really did. It's just that I got scared.'

'Of what?'

Arabella sighed, and reluctantly began to speak. She seemed to have decided to tell the whole story. 'This museum is owned by Henrietta Powell. Of the Powell family?'

Pip looked at her blankly.

'They were very rich and very famous,' Arabella said, with clear disapproval of Pip's ignorance. 'Henrietta's paternal grandfather was Baron Powell. He wasn't an actual Baron – he changed his name from Brian when he made all his money. He invented a particular thing, for, um, drains, I think. Was it the S-bend? Or no, maybe… Was it the original valve for the flushing loo? Henrietta doesn't like to talk about it, and I don't recall the specifics. Definitely toilety. But it was very important. A very important piece of toilet equipment. And her father built her grandfather's original company into an empire. A toilety empire, based on that thing for the toilet. What was it…?'

'It doesn't matter exactly what it was,' Pip cut in hurriedly. 'I'm sure it was very important. Carry on.'

'Well, Henrietta's mother, Charise Adderley, was a great beauty, and a Hollywood actress. She never made it to the real A-list, but she was enormously stylish and loved fashion. She was dressed by all the most famous designers and never threw out a single one of her gowns. She kept the pieces she wore on the movies she'd been in, and even took other bits and pieces, if wardrobe would let her. That's how we got the gladiator suit, I think.'

Pip took a sip of her coffee. This was interesting, but Arabella did seem to be one of those people who could make a short story long. What did any of this have to do with why Arabella hadn't reported the theft to the police?

'To cut a long story short, Charise married Henry, the heir to the plumbing dynasty. Or toilet-widget dynasty. Baron's son.'

'That would be Henrietta's father?' Pip said, trying to move things along. It was like one of those endless historical novels where you had to keep looking at the character list at the front to see who was married to whom in the sixteenth century.

'Yes, exactly. Henry is Henrietta's father.'

'Henry and Henrietta. That's pretty narcissistic,' muttered Pip. 'Seems to run in the family; must come from Baron Brian.'

Arabella looked mildly affronted by Pip's lack of respect for the Powells, but continued her story. 'Anyway, Charise met Henry when he was on a business trip to the States. They fell for each other, and she married him and moved to London. A Hollywood star, even a rather minor one, was a big deal in those days. Not like now, when there are Americans all over the place, and anyone who's been on *Strictly Come Dancing* for five minutes counts as a celebrity. Henry adored Charise, and was delighted to have a bit of star power around, so he was more than willing to indulge her clothes habit. Now she had money, there was no stopping her on that front. She started collecting movie clothing and accessories quite seriously.'

'So the stuff in the museum was all hers?' Pip asked.

'Most of it, yes. Henrietta has added to the collection with some more contemporary, iconic pieces. But most of it was from Charise. That red dress? The one that is, um, missing? It was the pride of the collection. Charise had tried to get her hands on it for years, and finally managed to acquire it. It cost a fortune, and it was the last piece she bought before she died. It was the main reason

Charise started the museum just before she got ill, and moved the collection into this space and opened it to the public. Henrietta was particularly proud of that dress – because of the movie, and because it meant so much to her mum.'

'I still don't understand why you didn't tell Henrietta and the police about the theft.'

Arabella glanced at her notebook, as if it might give her inspiration, or perhaps courage. 'Because this dress is so precious – both financially, and in sentimental terms – it's one of the few pieces that the museum insures,' she said.

'Well, thank goodness for that,' said Pip, wondering why she'd needed to hear the entire history of the toilet baron just to get to the point that the dress was insured. 'At least you know that if you don't find it, insurance will cover it. Sorted.'

Arabella looked at Pip. 'I forgot to renew the insurance,' she said. 'I was so busy and there's so much to do here, and it just slipped my mind. And I didn't think it actually mattered really. We've *never* been robbed. Before now.'

'So, the dress is *not* insured…'

'No. Henrietta doesn't know. She was already in Morocco when it happened. And if she finds out, she'll fire me. I've no doubt.' Arabella looked like she might start crying again.

'So you bought a fake?' It was all starting to come together now.

'I didn't know what to do. I went online and found a knock-off – turns out there were quite a few made, and luckily, someone was selling one in Brighton. I was lucky because the Monday was a bank holiday, so we were shut. I went down to Brighton to fetch it, and by the time we reopened at 10 a.m. on Tuesday, I had installed the new dress. I didn't mean to deceive anyone or cause any trouble. It was a temporary fix. I thought I could get the real one back somehow; that it would turn up. Things do, you know.'

Maybe car keys, thought Pip. *Not priceless iconic dresses.*

'Is there much of a market for that sort of thing?' Pip asked. 'Would it fetch a lot of money?'

'Oh, absolutely. The value is hard to pin down, because obviously we don't know what the dress would actually sell for on an auction. Charise bought it from a private dealer, and the price was confidential. So we don't even have a clear starting point. The Marilyn Monroe halter neck, the dress that blows up over the grate? That was sold by auction for nearly five million dollars, a while back.'

'Five million dollars? Good lord.'

'I know, it's crazy. That red dress wouldn't be worth quite that much, of course. But it is worth a lot, hundreds of thousands even. Last year, it was insured for £50,000, and Henrietta kept muttering about how the people at the insurance place were idiots and had undervalued it, but that at least it kept the premium lower. But now it's not insured at all, because of me. And if it's *not* going to just turn up, then I need to find it,' said Arabella. 'Henrietta has been abroad looking at racehorses, but she's coming back next week and she's bound to come into the museum soon after. My big worry is that she'll notice that it's a fake. And then I'll have a whole lot of explaining to do.'

'I guess I can see how it all happened,' said Pip. 'I'd be lying if I said I've never slipped up in a job, so I do see how you could forget about the insurance. Such a bore, paperwork.'

'So will you help me find it?' asked Arabella, looking at Pip.

The more Pip thought about it, the less bad this suggestion appeared. She would take the job, and help Arabella find the dress. She wouldn't have to beg snippy Sharon for another temp job, or Mummy for a handout. She could pay her rent to Tim. With no signs of forced entry, it sounded like an inside job. How difficult could it be to figure out who had stolen it? Maybe this was a sign – a sign that she was meant to be a sleuth after all, despite everything that had happened with Boston Investigations and Marc-with-a-c.

After all, she'd found an actual human – how hard could it be to find a frock?

After the interview, such that it was, Pip and Arabella agreed that she would start work the very next day.

'Take today to think about the dress and what could have happened,' said Arabella, as if an answer would just come to Pip out of the air. 'Then tomorrow, when you start, I'll just introduce you to everyone as the new buyer-slash-curator. The staff can't know about the, um, replacement dress. Someone would tell Henrietta, for sure. And besides, if you're just one of the staff, people will be more likely to let slip something that might be useful.' Arabella paused for a moment. 'They don't share gossip with me,' she said. 'They know that I'm above that sort of thing.'

In Pip's experience, nobody was *above* gossip; some people were just excluded. But she nodded; the plan was sound.

She left Arabella and the museum full of energy. Out in the road, she immediately phoned Flis to tell her the good news about the job.

'One door closes and another door slams,' said Flis happily. 'That's what they say, and look at you. Walking right through that door and into a whole new window of opportunity.'

'Right,' said Pip, trying desperately to untangle what Flis was saying. 'But it's all a bit complicated.' She quickly filled Flis in on the story of the Julia Roberts dress.

'I can't believe it,' said Flis. 'Oh goodness, I hope that you can figure it all out for that poor woman. Get her out of the frying pan and into the fire. That's what you need to do.'

'I think she's hoping for the exact opposite,' Pip told her sister. 'Anyway, I have a feeling it's not going to be so easy. It's a real mystery. No forced entry. The dress simply disappeared. I just hope I can find it, that's all.' She was starting to wonder if she'd bitten off more than she could chew. 'I'm not a real investigator,' she added, glumly.

'You found Matty Price,' Flis pointed out. 'Everyone knows teenagers are much more difficult to find than clothing.'

'I got lucky once, but I don't know if I can do it again.'

'Of course you can! Don't be so hard on yourself. And didn't you do that special training before you left BI?'

Pip liked the way Flis said 'left BI', as if Pip had left for greener pastures, rather than with Doug Bradford shouting that 'Mark with-a-k has a CRIMINAL RECORD FOR INTERNATIONAL FRAUD…' It was kind of her.

'A month's training, that's all, and it was pretty basic. How to follow someone. How to stalk them online. Believe me, I've been doing that for years. That's not detective work.'

'Now, Pip,' said Flis, in her Big Sister tone. 'I don't want to hear any more of this negativity. This is an opportunity. Carpet them, as they say in French! Get out there and go find the dress.'

'Carpe diem. And it's Latin,' said Pip. But she said it softly – Flis had a point.

CHAPTER 5

By the time Pip arrived at the museum on Tuesday morning, she'd calmed down a bit. She would get started sleuthing right away; gathering more information and meeting the staff. If it was indeed an inside job, the staff were the first place to start. The people at Boston Investigations might have thought she was a bumbling fool, but even she could put two and two together and reach a number somewhere around four.

Arabella took her through some of the paperwork relating to her new employment, and Pip felt the familiar fizz of excitement of starting a new job. She knew that fizz well – after all, this wasn't her first rodeo. Literally, this wasn't her first rodeo – that job had ended terribly when she'd left the gate of the paddock open and the bull had got to all the cows.

Once the paperwork was done, and Pip's email set up, Arabella turned her gummy smile on Pip. 'So,' she said. 'How do we find the dress?'

'Well,' said Pip, hoping she sounded more confident than she felt. 'Tell me about the museum. Who owns it now?'

'Henrietta is co-owner with her father, Henry.'

'So he's still around?'

'Oh yes. He's still going strong, but he's not involved with the business any more. My uncle was quite a bit older than Charise.'

'Your uncle?'

'Oh yes, didn't you know?' Arabella said this as if it was all quite obvious, and that Pip should have known this straight off the bat. 'Henry is my uncle. My stepmother's half-brother.'

Pip tried to rewind through the convoluted conversation that they'd had before, to see if she had said anything rude or inappropriate about the family. She soon gave up trying to untangle her memory, and listened to the rest of Arabella's story.

Arabella explained that Henrietta, Arabella's cousin-ish, had inherited her mother's love of fashion and a good party.

'To give her her due' – a phrase that always managed to sound like an insult, or precede one, thought Pip – 'Henrietta is genuinely fascinated by clothes and collectibles, and is quite knowledgeable for an amateur.' This sounded like very faint praise. '*I* have a degree in the history and sociology of fashion,' Arabella continued, 'so *I* have a deeper understanding and a more professional interest in the field. I worked at a top fashion magazine, you know. But a love of fine and memorable vintage wear is something Henrietta and I share. Anyway, she's the one who runs the show.' Arabella stopped talking suddenly, like she'd said more than she meant to. Pip made a mental note of that.

'Is she involved in the day-to-day running of things?' Pip asked.

'Not like she used to be. She was the hands-on manager in the beginning, but when I came on board, I gradually took that over. At first, she still came in to work quite regularly, every second day or so, but it's dropped off. Now she comes in once or twice a week, just to say hello and have a look around the place. And she looks at the financials every month. Not that there's much to see on that score. This is really *not* a money-making operation, as you can imagine.'

Pip nodded.

'We talked about plans for the museum recently,' Arabella carried on, 'and she was sounding like she might give up on it. So I suggested that we update the whole place – hire someone – you – to source more modern items. She liked the idea, and is letting me try, but if it doesn't work, I don't know what will happen. She might close the whole museum. And then what will happen to me?'

'She'd close it, even though it was her mother's special place?'

'I don't know. But the last few months she's been travelling so much, we barely see her. Like this trip to Morocco to look at racehorses. She's horse-mad,' Arabella said this with a sneer, as if horses were a ridiculous interest. 'She might close the museum and open something terrible and horsey that I know nothing about. I don't know what to do. I need this job. Unlike some people, I don't have a rich father.'

Pip wondered if the rest of the staff shared this fear of Henrietta closing the place. Someone scared of losing their job might decide to steal and sell a valuable piece to have some money in the bank before the axe fell. Arabella certainly was scared, and the rest of the staff might be, too. The disappearance of the dress might be that simple. Not everybody was as adept at losing and finding jobs as Pip.

Pip asked Arabella about the rest of the staff. It was a small team, it turned out. Emily was the assistant administrative manager – 'a lovely girl, very loyal, she wouldn't have had anything to do with this' – and the only other staff members were the two security guards, who rotated shifts. Emily came in at ten, when the museum opened. Philip, who was on duty now, would be here until two, when the shift changed and Gordon arrived. Pip remembered Gordon, of course.

'Well,' said Pip. 'I think that it's time for you to introduce me to the staff, don't you?'

'Oh absolutely,' said Arabella. 'As the new buyer.' She executed a very unsuccessful 'discreet' wink.

'I *am* the new buyer,' Pip reminded her. 'If I manage to find out something about the dress, that's just going to be lucky, okay? I'm here to "source and curate".' Pip was keen to establish that her job was not dependent on finding a dress. She wasn't at all confident that she could. If the sleuthing didn't work out, at least she would have the curating.

Arabella nodded, and winked again, leaving Pip feeling even more unsettled.

*

Arabella took Pip around the museum, introducing her to the staff. First, Emily Marvin at the front desk. Emily seemed deeply suspicious of Pip.

'Since when were we hiring a buyer-slash-curator? I could be a buyer,' she said to Arabella. 'I'd be a great buyer. I could curate. I *do* curate.'

'Yes, yes, of course. But you didn't fit the requirements,' said Arabella, vaguely. Emily seemed to be waiting for more, but Arabella wasn't giving it.

'It's great to meet you, Emily,' said Pip. If she was going to get information out of her co-workers, they needed to like her. 'Arabella has been telling me what a wonderful fountain of knowledge you are. I'm sure that you'll be able to help me learn the ropes.'

Emily preened slightly. 'I do know ever so much,' she said to Pip. 'And I have a great eye.'

'Wonderful,' said Pip. 'I can't wait to pick your wonderful brain.' She stopped talking before she could say 'wonderful' again.

'I'm petrified that her great eye will spot the fake dress,' muttered Arabella, as they walked off. Unless it was Emily who took the original dress in the first place, thought Pip.

After meeting Emily, Arabella explained that the security guards spent some time inside the museum – especially if there were guests, and some time outside the museum – checking for suspicious characters, she said. Pip was taken outside to meet Philip Bastion, where he was eyeing an unfortunate dog walker on the other side of the road. Philip was the same guard that had let them in for the interview. He had one of those bland faces that could put his age anywhere between thirty and fifty. He was slightly balding, and stood hunched over, like the weight of the fashion world was too much for him. He said a terse hello, and promptly turned his back on them, showing absolutely no interest in her at all. Clearly, a man who kept himself to himself. Usually Pip liked this in a person, but not when she was hoping to get information out of them.

'He's always like that,' said Arabella, as they returned to the museum. 'Dark horse. Don't expect any info from old Philip.'

Back at her desk, Pip spent a happy hour online researching memorabilia for sale, before she asked Arabella if she could take a tea break.

'Sure,' said Arabella. 'Emily and Philip drink litres of tea.' She said this as if it were an inexplicable habit.

'Um, okay then,' said Pip. 'I'll just have a quick break. Back soon.'

The kettle was in the small kitchen at the back of the museum. There was also a microwave and an ancient fridge that made wheezing sounds. Although the wheezing might have been coming from Philip, who was standing sipping at a cup of tea, his back against a counter.

'Hi again,' said Pip, filling up the kettle, which involved an awkward manoeuvre around Philip, who didn't move. 'Gosh. First day on a job always makes me thirsty.'

Philip grunted.

Pip changed tone, going for new-girl banter. 'So, tell me about this place. How's the boss; how's Arabella?'

'She's all right. Doesn't give me any trouble. Keeps out of my way.'

'Emily?'

'Don't know her well. Keeps out of my way.'

'What about Gordon?'

'Nothing to tell. He's okay. Keeps out of my way.'

It would seem that keeping out of Philip's way was a company policy. *Giving him enough space to steal the dress?* Pip wondered.

'I'm looking forward to meeting Henrietta. I believe she's back next week.'

'She's all right.'

'Keeps out of your way?' Pip asked, hoping for a hint of a smile, at least. But… nope. This was going nowhere fast. Maybe if she'd made it to Module Two of the stupid BI training course, she would be better at this. She busied herself making the tea while she considered her options. She had an idea, but it was a risky one. Still, she had to try something.

'Listen,' she said. 'You're a security expert, right?'

'I am.'

'Good, good. And you're in the know about the museum, right?'

'Yes.' Philip wasn't sharing much, but he'd stopped staring at his mug and was watching Pip. She had his attention.

'The thing is,' she said, dropping her voice and improvising wildly, 'I am a very anxious person.' She said this as if it was a great secret that she was sharing with only him.

'Sorry to hear that,' Philip said, slurping at his tea. 'Tough one, anxiety.'

Pip was encouraged by a sentence that didn't refer to keeping out of his way. 'Philip, it is absolutely awful,' said Pip. 'I am a slave to my anxiety. A slave.'

Philip grunted again.

'What helps me,' said Pip, hoping to move things along, 'is if I feel safe. That's where you come in.'

'Me?' Philip looked anxious himself at this suggestion.

'You,' said Pip decisively. 'You are the security expert. You can explain how the systems work. And then I will feel a bit less anxious. I'm sure you wouldn't want me to suffer with my terrible fears.'

Philip looked at her, as if assessing whether or not this was true. Perhaps he didn't particularly mind how much she suffered.

'Fine,' he eventually said. 'What d'you want to know?'

Pip let out a small sigh of relief. 'Okay then,' she said. 'Just tell me how the museum security works, with the guards and so on. I'd feel so much better knowing.'

Philip started to speak in short staccato sentences. 'Well, there's me and there's Gordon. We do eight hours each. Six in the morning till two in the afternoon, and two till ten at night. Studies show that a place like this is most at risk just before it opens, and just after it closes. So that's why we come early and stay late, see? Then whoever's doing the late shift puts the alarm on before they leave. Whoever's opening up turns it off. The alarm's not exactly state of the art, but it's got your basics – access control on the doors and windows, beams in the main foyer area. Nobody's going to break in with that alarm on.'

'And the alarm links to the police?'

'Yes.'

'And who has the alarm code and keys to the front door?'

'Me, Gordon, and Arabella. Henrietta doesn't keep keys because she loses things a lot. We had to change the locks seventeen times before she decided it would be easier if she didn't have a key. There are also keys with the people who own the building. This place belongs to the old man's company.'

'Mr Powell?'

'That's him.'

'Are there security cameras?' asked Pip, realising that this would solve all her problems at once.

'For a little museum like this? Don't be daft,' said Philip. Perhaps thinking that this was a bit harsh, he added, 'Just goes to show how safe we all feel, eh?'

'What about weekends?'

'Gordon and I take turns. Whoever is on duty here on Friday also does Saturday, until we close at three. And then locks up and puts the alarm on, same as always. But you won't be here on a weekend, will you, so you mustn't worry about that.' His last comment sounded almost kind.

'I just get the shivers thinking of the museum standing empty. What if things were stolen? Imagine walking in… and finding everything was gone.' Pip tried to make this sound truly frightening.

'Never happened so far,' said Philip. And then, with an uncharacteristic moment of pride: 'Five years I've worked here, and not one single thing has ever been stolen.'

Ha, thought Pip. *That's what you think.*

'So it's safe, you say?'

'You're safe here. Never had a problem. You really mustn't worry.'

Pip smiled at him. 'Oh, Philip,' she said. 'I'm feeling so much better already. You're such a brave man, being a security guard.' Pip looked at him with her eyes as big as she could make them without actually spraining some lesser-known eye muscle. She fluttered her eyelashes. This had worked on many men, but not Philip.

'Have you got something in your eye?' he asked.

Pip stopped the fluttering. He was surly, Philip, but did that mean he had something to hide? Or was he just monosyllabic by nature? She wasn't sure. But she was certain she was getting nothing more from him. She wanted to work out which guard had been on duty the weekend that the dress had disappeared, but she'd just have to ask Arabella.

'Ah well,' she said, with a look at her watch. Or where her watch would have been, had she remembered to put it on. 'Time to be getting back to work.' She hoped he hadn't noticed that she'd apparently just told the time from her bare arm. 'I've loved chatting to you, Philip. I think we're going to be great friends.'

Philip looked at her. 'I'll keep out of your way,' he said, putting his mug down at the sink, and walking out.

CHAPTER 6

Pip got a chance to chat to Emily a little later. She'd checked in with Arabella, and discovered that Philip had been the guard on duty on the day that the dress disappeared, and then tried to focus on some ideas for the museum exhibits. Pip kept glancing out of her office all morning, waiting for Emily to appear. Finally, just as she was beginning to conclude that Emily was one of those annoying people who never eats, drinks or uses the bathroom, she came sauntering into the main section of the museum. Pip followed her to the kitchen, where she sat down at the small table. She opened up a brown paper bag, from which she started to pull various lunch goodies – an apple, a yoghurt, a small health bar.

Pip was a bit taken aback by the early lunch – she'd expected Emily to maybe make a cup of tea, but she gamely fetched her own lunch – leftovers of a family-size Marks-n-Sparks salad – and went to sit next to her.

'Mind if I sit with you?' she said.

Emily shrugged. 'I guess,' she said, not making eye contact.

Just as they both took their first bite of food, Arabella came breezing past the kitchen. 'Just off out for some lunch,' said Arabella.

'Bye,' said Pip. 'Enjoy.'

Emily said nothing.

As soon as she was out of earshot, Emily muttered, 'Too good to bring her own food, that one. Always off to some coffee shop or something for lunch.'

Pip felt extremely relieved that she'd remembered to bring something from home. 'So,' she said. 'What's the actual owner like? What's her name again? Henrietta?'

'She's amazing,' Emily said, perking up. 'Just an awesome person.'

'In what way?'

'Her look. Her style. She's just, like, so cool. I mean, for someone her age, obviously… It's amazing.'

Henrietta's great age was late thirties, from what Pip could work out – just a few years older than Pip herself. Emily looked as though she was a few years younger, in her mid-twenties, perhaps.

'And she's very kind. She gave me a Balenciaga handbag once, one of hers. I said it was really cool and she just, like, scooped out her wallet and stuff and gave me the bag. And it was very amazing of her to give Arabella a job, even though Arabella is, like, nearly fifty and she's not even a proper cousin. She's a half or a step or something.' Apparently, eating loosened Emily's tongue, but didn't seem to bring out her kind side.

Pip practised one of the techniques she'd learned in training. She kept quiet, cocked her head slightly, and looked at Emily expectantly, waiting for her to go on. Not more than ten seconds of awkward silence went by before Emily leant forward and continued: 'For all her airs, Arabella's not nearly in Henrietta's league. You know, socially. They hardly knew each other growing up, you know. So it was really amazing of Henrietta to take her on after she got into all that trouble.'

Cocked head. Expectant air. Extraordinary, how the trick worked! Pip listened as Emily spilled the beans on 'all that trouble'. An ill-advised fling with a government minister had lost him his job, and Arabella hers. She had been art director at a top fashion magazine, and because her dalliance had taken place on company time and, from time to time, on company desks, out of the door she'd gone. This story was related with barely controlled glee from

Emily. Arabella had been, apparently, 'on the bones of her bum' when Henrietta had given her the job of managing the museum. Emily had clearly preferred it when Henrietta was running the place herself, with only Emily by her side.

'Of course, Arabella is great really,' Emily said unconvincingly, as if realising she'd rather overstepped the mark, dissing the boss. 'Those pretty frocks she wears. Amazing. Of course she doesn't have Henrietta's flair – I mean, who does? But she is quite... diligent... in her work. I do wonder about her a little. I'm surprised that she's not more appreciative, after all that Henrietta has done for her. If it was me... But really, she's great, and she can't help what she is. Scorpios, you know. *Vipers.*' This last word was said with unexpected venom.

Pip was no astrologist, but she was fairly sure Scorpio wasn't a snake. Not that she was going to have that conversation.

'Do you and Arabella have personal issues, would you say?' she asked Emily. 'Conflict at work?'

'Personal issues?' Emily sounded amazed at this misconstrual. 'Oh no, nothing like that. I wouldn't say a word against her. Don't you tell her I did.'

It was a while before the security guard shift change, when Pip would get a chance to talk to Gordon. She went back into the office, determined to do some work on the job of sourcing great finds for the museum. But the Mystery of the Red Dress was nagging at her. She took her notebook from her bag to jot down some thoughts.

The notebook was a ridiculously unprofessional thing. Its cover featured a dolphin leaping out of a wave and through a rainbow, with the word 'SHINE' embossed across the top. Her friend Jimmy had given it to her as a joke, after she'd conducted the entire Matty Price investigation using a pink shiny notebook with a kitten and the word 'GRREEEEAT' across the top and on every page.

Pip stared thoughtfully at the first page of the notebook. Arabella was scared for her job, so she'd replaced the dress. Or had she? There was still the possibility that she had stolen the dress herself. She might have needed the money, after the debacle of her previous job and with the fear of losing this one if the museum closed. But she really did seem to love the museum and the work. And why would she have hired Pip? To keep an eye on her? She'd only hired her once Pip had noticed the fake dress. Might be a case of wanting to keep her enemy close. Pip wrote Arabella's name with a question mark next to it.

Next, she wrote down Philip's name. Philip was a dark horse, that was for sure. He was very reluctant to talk, and had given her the absolute minimum of information. He had been on duty on Saturday, so he would have had the opportunity to leave the alarm off for the thief. Or perhaps he'd forgotten to put it on. Or maybe he *was* the thief? Pip knew from trawling through job sites that security guards didn't earn much; he could probably use the money.

Number three on the list was Emily. Emily, well... she was an odd one. Arabella had enthused about what a lovely girl she was, but the feeling was certainly not mutual. She was jealous and dismissive of Arabella, yet adored Henrietta. Could she have stolen the dress to set up Arabella for a fall? With a view to taking her job, perhaps? And again, the dress was worth a pretty penny. If Emily had caught hold of the idea that the museum might close, she might also have wanted some financial security. Judging by her resentful mutterings about Arabella's lunch habits, she didn't seem to have much of a financial cushion to fall back on.

While Pip mulled over these problems and waited for two, when Gordon would appear at work and she could put the last member of the team in place, she felt her phone vibrate on her desk.

She looked at the screen before answering. *Mummy.* Pip felt her stomach drop. Mummy was in South America with GeeCee

– short for Gentleman Caller, a nickname Pip and Flis used out of his earshot, in preference to his real name, which was Andrew McFee. The trip was the fulfilment of GeeCee's lifelong ambition to visit the Galapagos and see the blue-footed boobies. Why was Mummy calling? There was no way she would pay international call rates unless there was some disaster. Pip hit the green button.

'Mummy? Are you all right?'

There was a horrible delay on the line which caused them to begin talking over each other.

'Yes of course. Why wouldn't I be? Just a small—'

'How were the blue-footed boobies? Everything Andrew hoped for?'

'Marvellous, marvellous. They were so… blue. Their feet. Very, very blue.'

'Good. Why are you ph—'

'Speaking of animals, I've sent you some l—'

'Mummy—'

'Llamas—'

'What?'

'I've sent you—'

'I thought you said something about llamas?' Pip realised belatedly that she needed to wait to account for the delay. She took a deep breath, closed her eyes, and let her mother speak.

'I said: I… sent… you… some…. llamas,' her mother enunciated slowly, as if the main problem with the sentence was its articulation. When, in fact, the problem was its utterly nonsensical meaning.

'I have kittens,' Pip said, a response almost equivalently nuts.

'Don't be silly, darling,' her mother said. 'I don't expect you to keep the llamas in your flat with the kittens. That would never work. It's just that I had to send them over… Did I mention that Andrew and I are starting a llama farm? You know I've always loved them. Anyway, we are – and the shipping company needed a recipient before they'd send the llamas. So fussy, really. I didn't want to send them to Flis – you know how funny Flis can be about things, and I knew you wouldn't mind.'

Pip's heart dropped. The last time Mummy had sent her something from abroad, she'd spent three hours in a holding cell. And llamas? Well, surely that could only end worse.

'Mind? Of course I mind! I want nothing to do with the llamas. Do not put my name on that form!'

'I'm just putting your name on the form, that's all,' said Mummy, in direct contravention of Pip's instructions. 'It's just in case they phone. We'll be back long before the llamas actually arrive; they are travelling by boat.'

Pip imagined the ridiculous beasts in sun hats, drinking cocktails in deckchairs and gazing out to sea. She sighed. Her life was stressful enough right now. Did she really need this added level of lunacy? No. She did not. But it came with the territory. There was very little point in trying to resist the force of nature that was Mummy.

Her mother's voice called her attention back to the phone. 'I can't be chatting, Epiphany. This is costing me a fortune,' she said, as if Pip had asked her to call.

They said goodbye and rang off. Feeling too rattled by Mummy, Pip decided to find out a bit more about Emily. Take her mind off the llamas, and give her a chance to calm down before she spoke to Gordon. She typed 'Emily Marvin' into Google. Pip was an old hand at this, both in her personal capacity as a nosey parker, and from her recent training as a would-be PI. She hit up Twitter, Facebook and Instagram, scrolling rapidly through Emily's feeds.

In her Instagram bio, Emily referred to herself as a 'Fashionista, stylist and influencer, sentimental old soul, vintage lover'. She also claimed to be manager of the museum, dropping the less grand "assistant administrative" from her actual job title. There were lots of pictures of clothes. Street-style shots. No fancy locations – just everyday street scenes. Could Emily need money to up her Insta look?

A little more digging revealed that Emily got into quite a few online spats for a 'sentimental old soul', and seemed easily riled. She seemed to have only two modes – a right bitch, or all sweetness and light. In right bitch mode, her comments were either eye-rolling and sneering ('I don't THINK so' and 'What even IS she wearing?'), whereas her other persona was all gushing and sucking up ('You're *so* amazing' and 'Oh my heart'). One thing was for sure – between the lie about her job title and her schizophrenic personality, the woman could not be trusted.

Pip put down her phone and stared at her notebook, adding the final name to the list. *Gordon, Gordon, Gordon*, she wondered, not without some desperation. *Will you be the one to give me a clue?*

CHAPTER 7

Pip found Gordon outside, at the door of the museum, leaning against the wall and watching the passing traffic. Gordon was the polar opposite of Philip. He was charming where his colleague was surly. Chatty where Philip was terse. And he was pretty darn cute for a man in head-to-toe navy polyester. Not everyone could pull that off. It helped that he was so well-proportioned and that the uniform was perhaps just half a size too small, showing off his form. And the colour set off his dark skin.

'So, new girl,' he said, giving Pip what she half-hoped might be a seductive look. 'Philip tells me that you're the anxious type.'

Pip was thrown by this. She would have bet her last kitten on the fact that Philip wouldn't have shared their conversation with anyone. Pip looked at Gordon's eyes – the colour of polished oak – and the way his muscles rippled under the polyester. She didn't want Gordon to think badly about her, and she'd vowed never to get caught up in a fake identity situation again after the whole Matty Price search debacle. But there was no going back, really.

'Yes,' she said, with a sigh. 'Anxiety. I'm a slave to it.'

'My dear Aunty Lottie, back home in Zimbabwe, suffers with her nerves,' said Gordon. 'It's a terrible thing.'

Pip did not want Gordon to put her in the same category as Aunty Lottie and her nerves, no matter how exotic the setting. 'It's not my nerves,' she said, firmly. 'It's just a sort of anxiety thing. Nothing to worry about really. Definitely nothing like your aunty, I'm sure.'

'Well, anything I can do to help...' said Gordon.

'That's very kind,' said Pip. 'I just wish I knew more about the people I'm working with, you know. Familiarity breeds...' Pip faltered for a moment. 'Familiarity breeds contempt' was not going to serve her purpose. 'Familiarity breeds security,' she said decisively, feeling a bit like Flis. She continued, 'Is there anyone I should be careful of? Anything I should know? You must know so much.'

The big-eyed look seemed to work a bit better on Gordon than it had on Philip. His rather shapely chest expanded a bit more. Pip was awfully tempted to touch him, just to see if he was real.

'There's nobody you can't trust here, I promise you that.' Gordon roared with laughter. Pip wasn't clear why this was funny. Gordon seemed quite easily amused.

'Ha, ha, yes, of course,' said Pip. 'Trust. So important.'

'But you want to keep an eye on what that Emily tells you,' said Gordon, leaning towards Pip.

'Emily? Really?'

'She's a bit of a fibber, is all I'm saying,' said Gordon. And then, maybe thinking of his Aunty Lottie's nerves, added, 'Not dangerous or anything.'

'Well, like what?' asked Pip.

'Well, just for example, just last week she took Wednesday off with a so-called cold, although she was fine the day before and the day after. Not even a sniffle. I don't think she was sick. Fibs, I tell you.'

Pip nodded. In spite of his easy charm, Gordon was clearly one of those people who would shop their neighbours to the Stasi for some genuine American Levis. However, this did not seem the sort of information that would help her at all. 'Do you know Emily outside of work?' she asked.

'We've been for drinks after work a couple of times,' he said.

'I see...'

'Nothing like that,' he said quickly. 'Emily wouldn't go for the likes of me. She's got her eye on bigger fish, I'd say.'

Pip wondered if she'd uncovered some unrequited office crush. But even if she had, how would that help her find the dress?

Just then, passing on the other side of the street, Pip saw a gaggle of young women, dressed to the nines in outlandish combinations of trendy vintage gear. One of them waved and mouthed a flirtatious hello to the good-looking Gordon, sending her companions into giggles. She was dressed in a look that reminded Pip of photographs of Japanese schoolgirls – ankle socks and buttoned shoes, a pleated skirt and a tight-fitting collared T-shirt. Her hair was black at the roots and silver white at the tips, with a pair of huge sunglasses on top. She looked great. Pip wished she could carry off something like that, but she was too tall for outlandish outfits or strange hair. She'd tried it at times in her life – a short-lived attempt at dreadlocks when she'd had that job on a sailboat in the Caribbean, but she'd looked like a long-handled string mop.

'Those are some of our regulars,' Gordon said, gesturing towards the cool kids. 'They're from the fashion school; they like to pop in and see the clothes. That one, Maisy, or maybe it's Daisy. Or possibly Annabel. But she's a friend of Emily's. She helps with the displays. They're changed quarterly – we take down some items and bring out new stuff from the storeroom to show.'

'Like the red dress? The Julia Roberts one?'

'No, that one's a drawcard. It's always on display.'

'Where's the storeroom? Is it here on site, or somewhere else?' Pip was wondering if perhaps the dress had just got moved to the storeroom by mistake. If so, she could find the bloody thing in no time and get on with the business of having a job.

'In the basement. There's a load of stuff there. Historical items, vintage clothing, some movie costumes, a whole collection of fake guns and swords from film sets. Really cool things. I've got keys – I can show you sometime, if you like?'

'That would be amazing,' said Pip. 'Can we look now?'

'I can't leave my post,' said Gordon, swelling with self-importance and putting serious strain on the blue polyester. 'But maybe tomorrow, if I have time. Or another day.'

'Oh, that would be jolly interesting,' said Pip, feeling more and more like a character in a play. Maybe something by Enid Blyton, involving spiffing adventures and bottles of ginger beer.

'No problem. Anything you need, I'm your man.' There was something in the way that he said this that sent a shiver down Pip's back. She could think of a few uses for the good-looking Gordon.

Keep your eye on the ball, Epiphany, she told herself. *No distractions. Remember what happened with the pet grooming business and Antonio's marvellous biceps.*

Pip looked back at the museum, wondering what had happened on that Saturday. Who had taken the dress? And why? She surveyed the big wooden doors and sturdy brickwork as if willing them to give up their secrets, or at least send her a clue. Which of course, they didn't. Buildings didn't hold clues, or give them up to inexperienced part-time investigators. Or maybe they did…

'Bloody hell, how could I miss that?' Pip asked herself out loud, to the surprise of a passing jogger. On the building two doors down over the road, there was a security camera. And it was pointing right at the front of the museum.

CHAPTER 8

Pip joined the flow of office leavers and stood underneath the security camera, staring up at it. The way it was angled, she felt pretty certain that if she could get the footage from two weeks ago, she could see anyone who had entered or exited the museum between the time Philip had locked up on Saturday, and the time Arabella had arrived on Sunday to find the dress gone.

The sign on the front of the building said: 'ADVANTAGE PROPERTY SERVICES'. *No time like the present*, thought Pip, and she walked up to the huge front door and rang the buzzer.

A voice that could cut glass came through the intercom. 'Hello?'

'I'm from the museum across the road,' Pip said into the intercom. 'I need to talk to you about a security issue please.'

She was buzzed in. A small, older woman sat manning the large reception desk in the foyer, looking rather out of place, and not like the owner of a glass-cutting voice. When she spoke, however, it seemed that she was.

'Good afternoon.'

'Hello, I hope you can help me?' said Pip, in what she hoped was her most charming manner. 'As I said, I'm from the museum across the road. We've had a small security incident, and I notice you have a camera. I'd like to speak to someone who might be able to help me source security footage.'

'Well, I can't just give it to anyone,' the woman said, looking at Pip sourly. 'I haven't seen you around, and I'm often at the museum. Who did you say you were?'

'Epiphany Bloom,' said Pip. 'I'm new. The new buyer. And I'm just helping out on this, um, incident.'

'Well, it's odd that Henrietta didn't come and ask me herself.' The elderly receptionist sounded a bit miffed.

'She's abroad,' said Pip. 'Morocco. She'll be back next week, but she's asked me to look into it for her. So here I am.' Pip gave the smile she'd been taught at her Finishing School for Young Ladies. It often worked on this type of person. And… bingo.

'I suppose I could find out.'

'That's very helpful of you, thank you, um…?'

'Sylvie. What date are you looking for footage from?'

'Saturday fourteenth and Sunday fifteenth.'

'Oh, well. I can't help,' said Sylvie, settling back into her seat, looking almost pleased to be of no use. 'We don't keep more than a week on the system on-site. The rest is backed up off-site. I'd have to speak to the security company. Probably best to wait for Henrietta, anyway.'

'It's rather urgent.'

'I'm about to leave for home now. But if I have a chance tomorrow, I might give them a call for you. In the meantime, you get Henrietta to phone me or send me an email requesting the footage. And don't try fob me off with that Arabella woman. I know full well that it's Henrietta who's in charge there. So get Henrietta to let me know I can hand it over.'

Pip thanked her, even though she'd been less than helpful, frankly, and Pip knew there was no way she could get Henrietta to give the required green light given that she was a) in Morocco and b) unaware of the theft. She headed for the door.

Outside, she examined the notice affixed to the wall beneath the camera. The company name, 'CCTV Specialist Services', and a phone number were printed in the bottom corner. Pip photographed the number, quickly lowering her phone when Sylvie emerged. She pretended to be sending a text.

'Have a good evening,' said Pip, popping the phone into her bag, before turning sharply away and setting off down the street.

It was Tim's turn to cook, thank goodness. When Pip got home, she was off-duty until it was time to do the washing up. That meant she could settle down with a glass of wine and go through her notes. After a bit of kitten therapy, of course.

She fed Most a nice big bowl of gourmet Free-Range Pheasant and Organic Spelt Cat Food with Extra Calcium for Lactating Cats. While Most ate, Pip entertained the kittens in the sitting room. She lay on the carpet and put them on her chest, letting them crawl all over her and each other. Then she arranged them on their backs and blew on their fluffy tummies. She took a few pictures but there was nothing worth posting to social media, just blurred tails and legs.

She heard Tim's key in the door and his footsteps heading towards the sitting room. She popped the black kitten on her head.

'Look, a fascinator,' she said, turning her head to the side and giving Tim an exaggerated smile as he entered, like someone posing for a picture. After a few glasses of bubbles, perhaps.

'Fascinating,' Tim said with a grin, scooping up the other two kittens and kissing them in turn. He really was a nice bloke, that Tim.

He turned back to her. 'Speaking of fascinators, I've been meaning to ask... Would you like to come to my cousin's engagement party? As my date... I mean my plus one... What I meant was, my partner... Which is to say, my friend... or...' He ground to an embarrassed halt, blushing, and ran his hand through his hair.

Pip gawped at him in disbelief, and almost dropped the kitten. Was this actually happening, or had the excitement of her day gone to her head? She stumbled over her answer in a most inelegant fashion. 'I, um, well, I guess... Uh, when?'

He jumped in quickly: 'If you think it'll be at all awkward, then, no pressure. Really. You don't have to. I absolutely understand. Forget I asked. Terribly sorry. Foolish of me.'

'No, no, I'd love to,' said Pip, finally recovering a modicum of composure. 'Yes, of course. I would like that.'

'Really? Great!' Tim beamed. 'It'll be fun having you for company. I can't vouch for my family, but I can tell you the food will be good. My cousin, Amy, is a big foodie, and she's having it at some fancy spot overlooking the river. It's this coming weekend. I'm sorry it's such short notice. I've been wanting to ask you. I just didn't want to make assumptions, or make everything weird, you know… Spoil things between us. Our friendship, I mean.'

'I get it,' said Pip. 'No weirdness, no assumptions. Just one question.'

'What is it?' he looked nervous.

'What on earth has that got to do with fascinators?'

'Weddings. Isn't that where they wear them? Fascinators? I dunno. What do I know about strange headgear?' he asked. He put a kitten on his head and gave Pip the same exaggerated photo face that she had given him.

CHAPTER 9

'That's more like it,' Jimmy said, watching Pip pummel the punch bag, one-two, one-two. 'Last week you were down in the dumps. Looks like you've got your mojo back.'

'Oh yeah,' Pip said, panting as she bounced on her toes. 'I am all mojo now. One hundred per cent mojo.' She smashed the bag. 'Mojo and me, we're as one. I got a job!'

She took a moment, hands on her knees, breathing hard. She had left straight after work for a workout at The Glove Box. Arabella had told her to keep her own hours, and this was part of her plan for a New Improved Pip – healthy, happy, fit.

'That's great, Pip! What is it?' said Jimmy, looking genuinely thrilled for her. She'd originally met Jimmy when he himself had been a clue to the mystery of Matty Price, but he'd been such a big help that they'd become friends. Working out at Jimmy's gym was part of her New Improved Pip plan, sure. But it didn't hurt that it involved seeing Jimmy.

She told him about her new job briefly, ending with, 'So I took the job, and now I have to find the dress.'

'Brilliant news!' said Jimmy, grinning. 'Another investigation job for Epiphany Bloom. You know, if you ever need a trusty sidekick with muscles…'

Jimmy did look a bit like a street fighter, Pip thought – sharp-eyed, tough and wiry, tattoos snaking up his arms – and he had been a bouncer in his younger days. He was a sweetheart and a good friend. In fact, there was something rather sexy about the whole Jimmy package, but Pip tried to ignore that thought whenever it cropped up.

'Actually, now you mention it... Jimmy, how would you intimidate someone into giving you something?'

'Like what?'

'I need to look at some CCTV footage. The camera is in the street, outside a private firm. The receptionist is a little sticky about handing it over to a random stranger.'

'Seems reasonable.'

'Anyway. I figured from your days as a bouncer, you might have some experience in persuading people to give you things. You know, secretly intimidating body language. Something like that.'

Jimmy looked at her like she was slightly crazy, but she was used to people looking at her like that.

'Several problems with that, Pip,' he said.

'No secret bouncer tricks?'

'Well, that. But the bigger problem would be that nobody actually has video tapes of security footage any more. You can't intimidate them into handing over the entire internet, can you?' he chuckled. 'They'd have to download it and it's a process – not really a "hand it over now" situation, is it?'

'I guess not,' said Pip, feeling foolish.

'Yup, everything's digital. So I'd say your best bet would be to go that route.'

'What route?'

'Digital. Get yourself a hacker.'

Pip smiled. As it happened, she had a hacker in her back pocket, so to speak.

'I know just the guy.'

As Pip left the gym, she called Tim and found him at home. He worked from home some days – work mobility was just one of the convenient aspects of hacking into computers for a living, she supposed. Striding down the road, her kitbag over her shoulder, pumped from the boxing, her body coursing with endorphins – or serotonins or whatever, she always forgot – Pip felt ready to go out and conquer. She'd found the camera, and with a bit of a reality check from Jimmy, she knew what her next step should be. She'd have this case solved in no time.

Ignoring the weak nudging of New Improved Pip, she avoided the many purveyors of smoothies, gluten-free granola and kale-based meals that had sprung up with the gentrification of the neighbourhood, and found a bakery. She always conquered better with carbs inside her. Was there any better smell than the smell of fresh bread? Maybe the smell of kittens, she decided, but you couldn't eat those.

She bought two croissants – plain for her, almond for Tim. This was what it would be like if they were an item, she thought. Coming home from the gym with treats. Knowing what flavour the other one liked. Helping each other out in work matters – not that she could envisage a scenario in which Tim would require her help with his job as a white hat hacker.

She still didn't know what to make of the invitation to the engagement party. In her mind, she ran over what had happened the previous night, remembering distinctly that during the course of the somewhat excruciating conversation, he had referred to her variously as a friend, a date, a plus one, a partner and company.

Did he like her? Of course, they got on really well and he clearly enjoyed her company. But as she and Flis used to say when they were kids, did he *like* like her? And, for that matter, did she *like* like him? Or was she just in the habit of thinking that she *like* liked him? It was like being fifteen again! She didn't have the time or the energy to think it through. She needed all her brain power to find the red dress.

Back at home, Tim was pottering about the kitchen. The kittens were gathered around a saucer, eating.

'Oh hi,' he said. 'I've just fed the cats. Wasn't sure how long you'd be and they were starting to look peckish. Didn't want them to start on my toes.'

Was he not just the most sweet and thoughtful guy? Pip got out two plates, and handed him his croissant.

'Yum. Almond, my favourite,' he said. 'You remembered.'

Pip smiled and put the kettle on for tea, then gave him a brief outline of the case of the missing red dress, and the potentially helpful CCTV camera across the road.

'I need to get permission to have the footage handed over, but obviously I can't get that, because the owner is abroad, and she has no idea that the dress is missing.'

'I see how that could be a problem.'

'So, it's all digital now. Backed up off-site.' She pulled up the picture of the sign with the name of the security company on her phone, and showed him. 'Do you think you could help me get a look at the footage?'

Tim thought a bit, munching slowly on his croissant, then said, 'It shouldn't be too difficult. Lots of security firms generally have surprisingly weak systems when it comes to digital attack.'

The words 'digital attack' made Pip quite nervous.

'I'm pretty sure I could get in,' Tim said, with some reluctance. 'It's not legal though. I could get into trouble.'

'Oh, I wouldn't want that,' said Pip. 'I'll figure something else out, if you're worried about getting caught.'

'Getting caught? Someone with my skills?' Tim smiled. 'I never get caught. I'll do it.'

'You're the best, Tim,' said Pip, and for a moment she thought from the intense look on his face that he might hug her or something, but it turned out that he just needed a small burp.

CHAPTER 10

Something was niggling Pip. A thought, wriggling away inside her brain, like a butterfly flitting from flower to flower. Except that whatever the thought was, it was more like a caterpillar – slow-moving and sluggish. She felt sure she was missing something: a clue, or an idea.

She stopped what she was doing – googling when the next online auctions were being held for various television memorabilia – and reached for her notes. Glancing around, she saw that Arabella was looking at some sort of spreadsheet, sighing.

Arabella had quizzed Pip about her progress in finding the dress as soon as she'd got in that morning. 'I'm working on it,' Pip had said. She didn't want to say more, until she had something solid. She didn't want to raise Arabella's hopes for nothing. Or put her on guard.

Pip started to read back over the notes that she'd made, hoping they would jog her memory. Arabella. Philip. Gordon. Emily. The conversations hadn't been very helpful. Gordon had cast doubt on Emily. Emily loathed Arabella. Philip? Well, Philip didn't seem to like anyone, Pip included. And Arabella had claimed she just wanted the dress back. Did any of them seem like a suspect? Did each of them seem like a suspect? Pip didn't know. Her inexperience was showing – she knew that Doug Bradford or one of his agents would have had an idea. But she had zip.

She had put her hope in the CCTV footage, but she didn't know how long Tim would take with that. In the meantime, she needed to find out more about these people. There was always the chance that she was on a wild goose chase – and she had once been on an actual wild goose chase in Alaska, so she should know – and that this was a straightforward break-in by a burglar.

Her thoughts were interrupted by a phone call from Flis, who said she was checking up on how the new job was going. Pip started to tell her, but soon realised Flis wasn't really listening; she was bubbling with her own news.

'I'm making vast strides with my vintage stories. Fascinating. It's a twenty-five billion dollar industry. Or maybe twenty-five million. Or is it trillion? Lots of noughts. Anyway,' Flis continued, 'it's mostly young people that buy the vintage stuff. Generation Q. Or is it Generation Zed? Anyway, the youngsters. Where my demographic is; the younger mums. They want to look hip, you know. When they're not in sweatpants and baby spit. And a lot of them have got money.'

Pip thought about the basement storeroom in the museum, with its vintage items and movie memorabilia. Must be worth a packet.

Flis was rabbiting on: 'I went onto eBay and Etsy; there's loads of stuff there. You need to have a look, for your job as a buyer. I bought myself this amazing fringed faux suede jacket that the seller swore was at Woodstock.'

'That'll wow them in the school car park,' Pip said, distractedly.

'It so will. I got flames, too.'

'Flames? Like a fire?'

'You know, trousers, sort of like bell-bottoms.'

'Flares.'

'Yes. I'm going to take some street photos of myself in my jacket and flames for my Instagram. Maybe with my front door as background, now it's freshly painted. Oh, and you should see the movie stuff. You can get almost anything vintage online. It's a bludgeoning industry.'

'Burgeoning, I think you'll find,' said Pip. But even as she corrected Flis, the Caterpillar of Knowledge stirred in her brain. It was almost definitely metamorphosing into a butterfly. And it was about to make its way out of the cocoon. Vintage. Instagram…

'Listen, Flis, this is all really great. I can't wait to see the flares. But you've given me an idea. I have to go.'

Hanging up the phone, Pip glanced back at Arabella, who was lost in a sea of financials. Pip was briefly tempted to make a sudden loud noise – drop a dictionary, pop a balloon – and see what Arabella would do. Instead, following up on the idea that Flis had planted, Pip brought up Emily's Instagram account again. There was something about it that was nagging at her mind. Emily's feed consisted mostly of selfies. There was nothing spontaneous about these. In each one, Emily was made-up, well-coiffed and wearing very distinctive outfits, precisely and unusually put together. Pip was no expert on hip fashion (was 'hip' even okay to use? Or was 'cool' back? Or maybe some other adjective, so cool-slash-hip that Pip didn't even know it?) but to her eye, Emily looked very one-of-those. Her Instagram posts tagged various people and businesses – all fashion-related, from what Pip could make out. And she had a crazy number of followers. Not nearly as many as Flis, obviously. But a lot.

Pip continued scrolling back into Emily's past. And then she saw it. A picture very like all the others – clothes, pout, locks, lashes – but the background was distinctive. And familiar. Emily was leaning against the big red-painted double doors of the museum.

'Just popping out to chat to Gordon,' Pip said loudly, making Arabella jump. 'I think he might be able to help me with something.'

'Yes, quite,' said Arabella, highlighting a figure in red and frowning. 'You don't need to tell me where you are the whole time, though. I know you'll be off finding the dress and sourcing whatsits and whatnot. I understand. Just keep me in the loop. The second you get a lead, let me know. We need to find the dress, Pip, before Henrietta gets back. It's imperative.'

'That's very trusting of you, Arabella. I won't take advantage of it.' Although even as Pip said this, she knew she probably would.

Gordon was leaning on the front desk, staring at a blank wall. He greeted her warmly.

'Chat a mo?' she asked him.

'Of course,' he said, and beckoned her eagerly into the kitchen. It was pretty slow around here on a Thursday morning, Pip thought; a diversion was probably welcome. 'What can I do for you?'

She showed him the Instagram post of Emily posing against the museum front doors, hashtagged: *#DayOut #AroundTown*. 'Recognise this?'

'Sure, it's our entrance. No day out there,' he snorted.

'Do you recognise any of these clothes?' Pip asked. 'Anything that belongs to the museum?'

'The dress, definitely, it's part of the sixties vintage collection.' Gordon squinted at the screen. 'Not sure about the shoes, they might be her own. That handbag on the floor? Definitely ours. We've got a lot of handbags in the storeroom. Henrietta loves handbags. There was a whole show of them last year. "Bags of Beauty", it was called. Or maybe "Beauty of Bags". Very popular.'

He certainly knew a lot about clothes for a security guard, Pip thought. He seemed to take his job seriously.

'Okay, thanks. Do you follow Emily on Instagram? Or on any other social media?'

'Nope. Not my thing, that, social media. Confuses me.'

'Would you take a quick look at her other photos, see if you recognise anything else from the collections?' She handed over the phone, demonstrating how to move back through time in the gallery.

Gordon swiped through the posts, frowning. 'Yup, yup, no, I don't think so, yes that one, yes the jacket is ours, no, yes, the skirt for sure.'

Pip cut him off. She'd seen enough to know that Emily was regularly helping herself to the museum's collection. 'Does she have permission to borrow them?' Pip knew that she could have asked Arabella, but she didn't really want to get Emily into trouble until she knew what was actually going on.

'Doubt it. It's completely against the rules, and if any item leaves the premises, it has to be signed out by me or Philip.'

'Thanks, Gordon, you've been very helpful. I'm going to go and have a chat with Emily.'

'I should hope so,' muttered Gordon.

Pip walked through to reception, where Emily was now rearranging the postcards. It didn't seem like a very big job, or that there were that many possible permutations for the postcards to be displayed, but Emily looked intent upon her task, regardless.

'Can we chat?' Pip asked Emily, who turned to look at her. 'I'm needing a bit of your expertise. Just to, you know, grasp how everything works here. I'm a bit embarrassed to ask Arabella, and you know so much, really.' Pip hoped she'd hit the right note of a needy sycophant and shameless flatterer.

'Sure, of course,' said Emily. 'I can only imagine how hard it is to know nothing.'

Pip ignored the jibe. 'Can you tell me about the collection and the different displays, how it all works? I'm going to be involved in that, and of course, I'll rely a lot on your experience and input.'

Emily brightened at this. Honestly, this flattery tactic was working out great. 'Oh wow, that's like, the most amazing part of the job. So, we change the regular displays quarterly. That's every three months,' Emily explained helpfully. 'And we decide what to focus on, like for instance, around Wimbledon time last year, we did a whole thing on sports.'

'Got it. So who's "we"? Who's involved in deciding on the themes?'

'Henrietta – she's, like, the creative force behind the exhibitions, but she doesn't have all that much time. She values my input, of course, as a younger member of the team, more on-trend. And Arabella is involved too, I guess, but you shouldn't rely on her too much. She's not a truly creative person, more of an admin-sort at heart. And because she's, like, older, she's not so in touch with what's hot. Her Venus is in retrograde, you know.'

Pip wasn't quite sure what the implication of this last statement was, but it sounded slightly medical.

Emily leant over and said conspiratorially, 'You've probably noticed that Arabella's jealous of me. She knows I've got the eye.'

If anything, Pip had noticed almost the opposite – Emily's own bitterness at being overlooked and under-utilised, while Arabella swanned around being the boss.

'So the ideas are mostly coming from Henrietta. And you, of course,' said Pip. 'What happens next?'

'We go through the storeroom and find pieces that would be, like, really amazing for each concept. That's the part I love, the digging around. You can't believe what we've got down there. So, for the sports theme we found the cutest little bathers from the fifties. Ooh, and Edwardian badminton outfits that had this stripe down the side of the shorts – a bit darker than racing green.' Emily's eyes were misting over with the memory of it all.

'And then?'

'Once we've decided, I set up the display, mostly. I have some friends from the fashion school who help out.'

'When you're down in the store, do you ever borrow items for your personal use?'

'That's against the rules!' Emily said, turning bright red. 'I would never... What would make you say that? Are you jealous of me, too?'

Pip quietly handed Emily the phone with Emily's Insta posts open. 'Does this dress belong to the museum?'

Emily looked to the left and to the right, as if for some sort of magical escape hatch that may have conveniently arrived to swallow her up. Finding none, she bowed her head and looked down at her feet (which today were clad in the weird type of trainers with platform soles that Pip had never understood).

'Oh, fine then,' she muttered.

Pip let the silence linger, waiting for Emily to fill it.

'It was only for the photograph,' Emily said defensively. 'I borrowed it. I swear, that dress never went further than the steps of the museum. You can check the store. The dress is there, safe and sound, not a mark on it.'

'I've seen your Instagram. There are plenty of pictures that I suspect feature items from the collection.' Pip decided not to attribute this knowledge to Gordon. She took back her phone and scrolled through the pictures. 'And some of them certainly left the premises. This one, in the park. And this one, out on the street. Here, on a bicycle.'

Emily looked mortified. 'Yes, okay, I borrowed them. I did take them out. I know I shouldn't have, but I took very good care of them.' As she spoke, she began to leak from nose and eyes, sniffing into her sleeve and smudging her eye make-up. 'I would never let any harm come to a treasured vintage piece, I promise. I love those clothes more than anyone.'

Pip felt embarrassed for her, and fought the urge to look away.

'Every one of them is back in the storeroom in perfect condition. I promise. We can go and look now!'

'We'll get to that later. But why did you borrow them? You must have known you weren't allowed to. This sort of thing could cost you your job.'

'Don't tell! Please don't tell. Henrietta can't know. She trusts me. And please don't tell Arabella, either. She's out to get me for sure.'

The false lashes had loosened from Emily's left eye. They flailed around uncomfortably every time she blinked.

Pip wasn't promising anything. 'Why did you do it?'

'I'm establishing myself as a model. You know, on Instagram? Do you know how super competitive that is? Posting every day, like, many times a day. Looking amazing in every shot. I don't have the clothes or the money or the contacts. But I have – had – this whole amazing store full of clothes, just sitting there.'

'So you just helped yourself?'

'I didn't think it would do any harm. Honestly, I was just trying to build up my following, and it's working. My followers are climbing, I'm getting noticed. I've had some nibbles from brands, even. But I needed more pics, different looks, more often. I just wanted to make my mark… I didn't mean any harm.'

'When do you take the clothes? How do you get them past Philip and Gordon?'

Emily was quiet.

'Well?'

Emily sighed, seemingly wrestling with whether or not to say more, before deciding to 'fess up. 'I have a key. Philip left his lying around and I picked it up. I had a copy made. My bad.'

'Damn right it was your bad. And the alarm code?'

'I've seen both Philip and Gordon putting that code in, like, a million times. The security here is trash.'

'You got the key and the code, and you just let yourself in whenever you liked?'

'It was super wrong, I know. I'm sorry. Please don't tell anyone. I won't do it again. Promise.'

'And the red dress?' Pip asked, finally cutting to the chase. 'Is that how you took the dress?'

'What do you mean?'

'Where is it? What happened to it?'

'It's right there,' said Emily, gesturing towards the room where the dress was kept, and speaking slowly and loudly like Pip was slightly deaf. 'I've never touched it. It's too valuable. And besides, it's not on-brand for me at all. So old fashioned.'

Listening to this, Pip just couldn't decide whether Emily honestly didn't know the dress wasn't the real deal. Another skill they probably taught in Part Two of the BI investigation course.

'That dress is a fake,' she said, watching for Emily's reaction. 'The real one has disappeared. It was replaced with a copy. I'm trying to find the real one.'

Emily looked genuinely shocked, Pip had to admit. Or like someone who was genuinely feigning genuine shock. Hard to tell.

'It's what? What do you mean? Wait. You think I…? No!' said Emily, in apparent horror. 'I had nothing to do with that. That dress, it's worth, like, hundreds of thousands of pounds. I would never… I'm not a thief.' She looked like she might start crying again. Either this was real, or Emily was missing her calling as an actress.

'The thing is, Emily, it looks pretty bad. You've taken items from the museum before. You have a key. You know the system. If you stole the red dress and replaced it with a fake, you're risking all our jobs.'

'I only borrow. I swear to you. If that dress is really a fake, that wasn't me.'

'If it wasn't you, then who was it?' asked Pip. 'Who is it that's stealing from this museum?'

Emily looked at Pip for a moment, as if deciding how much to trust her. 'Well,' she said eventually. 'I can tell you who I'd be looking at, if I were you.'

CHAPTER 11

Emily paused for dramatic impact and then said, in a vicious whisper: 'Arabella.'

Pip sighed. Arabella was the least likely suspect – not that Pip had ruled her out. This didn't seem to be something that was going to lead anywhere concrete. But what could she do but listen?

'So then, tell me about Arabella,' Pip said. 'What makes you suspect her?'

Emily leaned in, all secretive, glancing over her shoulder as if Arabella might be lurking behind them. Perhaps on a postcard.

'Well, she's really lucky that Henrietta gave her this job, like I told you.'

'But if she needs the job and wants to keep it, why would she steal the dress?'

'Spite?' Emily offered, helpfully.

Pip suspected that Emily was familiar with that emotion.

Emily carried on, eagerly. 'Just think about it. She knows Henrietta loves that dress, so she took it to hurt her. Or maybe she just wanted to get Henrietta into trouble with, like, the authorities. Or the family! I bet old Henry would be furious if she lost Charise's favourite piece. Whatever, I just know Arabella would be keen to bring Henrietta down a notch.'

It was true, jealousy was a powerful motivator. Imagine seeing the half-step-cousin swanning about buying racehorses in Morocco while you did all the work.

Pip nodded thoughtfully, and Emily filled the silence with more gossip and theories. 'Or, wait, I've got another idea,' she said excitedly. 'Arabella's got, like, *literally* no money. She lives off her salary here and I know she can't buy any of the gear she wants. She's got, like, *one* handbag. It's pathetic. So maybe she took the dress to sell it? For money? So she can get some decent stuff.'

'Hmmm. Well, you've given me a lot to think about, thank you.'

'You are so welcome, Pip. Come to me any time. I'm like, a very intuitive person. Aries. We just know stuff. It's amazing.' Emily paused. 'Why are you looking for the dress anyway? It's not yours.'

Pip desperately scrambled for an answer. Why *was* she looking for it? Then her phone rang. She'd forgotten to put it on silent, thank goodness. Saved by the bell! It was Tim. He hardly ever phoned. She felt a surge of anxiety. Was everything all right at home? The kittens?

Apologising to Emily, she took the call.

'Hello. What's up? Are the cats okay?'

'Hey,' Tim said. 'The cats are fine. I'm fine too, thanks for asking. And I've got something for you. A little gift.'

'You have?' she asked.

'It's to do with your job and the missing dress. Something you should see.'

'I'm just finishing up here. I'll be there as soon as I can.'

After they had said goodbye, Pip hung up. While she'd been talking, Emily had fished out a compact and flipped it open to use the mirror. She'd been rubbing at her face with a tissue, trying to remove the smudges. Now she pulled the dislodged eyelashes off, wincing, and wrapped them in the tissue, then reapplied her red lipstick.

It was time to wrap this up, Pip thought. Emily was a waste of time. And besides, there were only so many times she could hear the word 'amazing' without going insane.

'You've been very helpful, Emily, I really appreciate everything you've told me and I think we are going to have a good working relationship.'

'Oh yes, absolutely,' agreed Emily. She eyed Pip. 'In fact,' she said, 'there's something that I think we can get working on together right now.'

Pip smiled. 'Sure,' she said. 'What can I do?'

'The next exhibition is on the 1970s. It's going to be amazing. But we don't have enough in the museum – we need some feature pieces. Something amazing. And Henrietta was supposed to work on it with me. But then she heard about a horse in Morocco and left me high and dry,' Emily said bitterly, then gathered herself together. 'We should be getting started because it's set to open in a few months, and Arabella said that I can ask you to help me with the sourcing?'

'I'd love to be involved, Emily,' Pip said. 'Sounds like fun.'

'Amazing!' said Emily, with a big smile. 'We're going to put together a kicker of an exhibition. It will be amazing. Anything else you need to know about anything, just come to me. Any help you need, any inside knowledge, any advice. It would be amazing to help you.'

Pip nodded. 'There is one thing, Emily. We need to keep our suspicions about the red dress quiet. If word got out about the fake, it wouldn't be good for the museum's reputation.'

'Gosh yes, I hadn't thought of that. I won't breathe a word. Not even on Twitter.'

'Not anywhere. And certainly not here at work. I don't want anyone else to know about the dress until I've found out exactly what happened,' said Pip. 'It could be anyone, so I don't want to tell Arabella or Henrietta until I'm sure what happened.' Pip hoped that this would stop Arabella from finding out that she'd told Emily, and Henrietta from finding out anything at all. 'Two birds are a stone,' as her sister Flis frequently commented.

'You don't want the rest of the staff to know,' said Emily, her eyes shining. 'I would be the only one?'

'It's a little tricky, not knowing who might have been involved. Who I can trust? Of course, I know I can trust you.'

'With your life!' said Emily dramatically. 'No one will know but you and me!'

'Amazing,' said Pip.

That evening, Pip opened the front door to a proper welcome: Most lurching slightly on her three legs as she rubbed herself against her, and the blackest, boldest kitten trying to scurry up her leg like a kid shimmying up a coconut tree. Best of all, Tim proffered a proud smile and a warm hello.

'I think you're going to be pleased with your surprise,' he said, reaching into his pocket.

CHAPTER 12

Tim handed Pip a grainy black and white photograph, printed off his home printer. It was an angled shot that caught the front door of the museum, almost side-on, with a couple pressed against it. One figure appeared to be a woman, judging by the curves beneath the tight black trousers and black polo neck sweater. She was facing towards the camera but her head was bent, as if she was looking back at something over her shoulder, her face hidden and her hair tucked into a black cap. The other one – looking back over his shoulder, his chiselled cheekbones catching the street light – was Gordon, and from the angle of his body and arm, he seemed to be unlocking the door to the museum. Pip couldn't be sure, but the angle of his body made him appear furtive, almost guilty.

'Oh my God, Tim! This is fantastic!'

'Anything for my Pip,' he answered. Pip didn't have time to unpack what this meant. 'I've got the video footage for you, but their faces are hard to see. This was the best I could get. Do you know the people in the photo?'

'The man is a guard from the museum. Gordon Tshuma. It's 10.07 p.m. on Saturday, according to the timestamp. He shouldn't have been there at all.' He wasn't wearing his uniform, either, she noted.

'So, who's the woman?' Tim asked.

'I can't tell. Not easy to tell from the angle; she's blocking the view.'

'My apologies,' Tim said. 'I'll remember for next time. Try for a better angle. Although seriously, this was the clearest shot I could get from the tapes.'

She smiled. 'You've done great, Tim. Thank you. I really, really appreciate this. I know it was a big ask.'

'Well,' he said, brushing off her thanks, 'I had a slow patch around lunchtime. I do like a challenge, and it was this or Sudoku.'

'No slow patches for me. I didn't even get to the shops. How about I order up your favourite butter chicken and naan as a thank-you treat? You've really gone beyond the call of landlord duty.'

'Hey, just helping out a friend. I won't say no to butter chicken though. And you can tell me about your latest discoveries while we eat.'

Pip took out her phone and ordered, and the two of them returned to the picture, which now lay on the kitchen table between them.

'Let me talk through the scenario. Hear me out,' said Pip. 'So they're in cahoots, Gordon and Mystery Woman. Gordon's not the brightest, really, so my thinking is that she's the mastermind, and she's got Gordon in her thrall somehow. Maybe they're an item, or maybe she's leading him on because she knows he's got the key and the code. They arrange to meet up on Saturday evening to take the dress.'

'Makes sense so far,' said Tim. 'But who's the woman? Who could she be?'

There were not many distinguishing features. Pip stared at the photograph and tried to focus not on what she couldn't see, but on what she could. 'She's almost the same height as him,' she said. 'He's shorter than me, but not by much. Maybe five foot nine or ten. So she is tallish for a girl, maybe five seven or eight. Looks like she's in good shape. Slim, but not skinny. Got some curves.'

This was grasping at straws, clue-wise, Pip felt. She sighed.

The food arrived, the doorbell startling the grey kitten off Pip's knee. She got up and accepted the warm, spicy parcel, depositing it on the table. Tim got out two plates, two forks, and set two places. It felt cosy and domestic.

'Your reward treat dinner comes with wine included,' Pip said, reaching into the back of the cupboard for the good bottle of burgundy that GeeCee had given her for her last birthday.

'Breaking out the top stuff, eh?'

'Well, I'm grateful. Very.'

The photo pushed aside, they spooned the fragrant curry onto their plates.

Pip continued to ruminate on the stranger in the photo while tearing off a piece of hot naan. 'Who is the woman? Could she be an insider, too? It's not Emily, that's for sure. She's smaller than this woman, and skinnier. Besides, I happen to know she's already got a key and the code – quite illegally of course – so she wouldn't need Gordon. Arabella is more that build, but she's the one who's tasked me with finding the dress. So, it's not her.' She chewed slowly on the bread while a thought formulated. 'Unless it is.'

'What?' asked Tim.

'Unless it *is* Arabella.' Pip thought a bit more. 'I was the one to discover the fake. I confronted her with the switch. And it was only then that she came clean and asked for my help. So perhaps…' Pip paused, gathering her ideas. 'Think about it,' she said. 'She gets me to look for the dress, to cover up that she took it, knowing that if she gives me a job she can keep an eye on me. Keep me busy on other things, or whatever.' She thought some more. 'She can hear where I am in the investigation, maybe even give me bad info.'

'Could be.' Tim smiled at her, and the coriander leaf in his teeth did nothing to detract from his devastating dimples. But Pip would not be distracted.

'Maybe Emily was right. Maybe Arabella *is* Suspect Number One after all.'

'So, whoever it is in the photo, they go in together. Arabella has the key so she wouldn't need Gordon for that, but I guess it would be helpful to have an extra pair of hands to wrangle the mannequin, get the dress off, bundle it out. It's fairly bulky, a dress like that.'

'The later footage did show them both carrying it out,' said Tim. 'So that makes sense. Aren't there cameras inside?'

'Not inside. I guess no one was expecting a heist of old dresses. Some of the stuff is quite valuable, but not the sort of items you'd think would be stolen.'

Tim thought for a bit, with that cute quizzical look he got when he was trying to figure out some tricky piece of code, or whatever it was that white hat hackers figured out. 'Quite bulky, you say?' he said, reaching for the laptop bag hanging on the back of his chair.

'Yes, and sort of unwieldy. Long. Slippery material. And surprisingly heavy.'

Tim pulled his laptop out and flipped it open. 'Let's see if there's a car.'

Tim ran her through the video that he'd illegally obtained by hacking into the CCTV Specialist Services server. It was in black and white and there was really nothing to see in much of it. Random people walking past. Cars passing. To save storage space, they didn't save every frame, so the image had a strange jerky quality that reminded Pip of string puppets. Tim fast-forwarded through a lot of it.

'I've marked the places where anything vaguely interesting happens in front of the museum,' he said. 'Here we go, here's Gordon and the mystery woman.'

He slowed the video right at the point where Gordon and Mystery Woman arrived at the museum and opened up. Just as Pip had suspected from the photo, they unlocked, looking around as they did so, then went inside and closed the door. Frustratingly, Mystery Woman kept her face hidden from the camera the whole time. She was even wearing gloves. Pip could see her long silver necklace. But not her face. This was definitely more than Gordon showing off his workplace to a girlfriend. Everything about the way the two of them entered the museum screamed Crime In Process.

'We need to go back a bit and see if there's a car,' Tim said, fiddling on the computer. The film ran backwards jerkily. He stopped it and played. 'That's her,' he said. 'That's her in the car.'

In the corner of the screen, there was a brief sighting of the side window of a car, a black beanie and sliver of jawline just visible.

'If she would only turn her damn head!' Pip exploded. 'It's just so frustrating. It could be Arabella. There's nothing to rule her out. But nothing to identify her, either. Any idea what sort of car it is? I know less than nothing about cars.'

Tim peered at the little wedge of car. 'I'd say smallish. It's shorter than that Range Rover by quite a bit, see? Darkish colour, maybe a dark grey or blue. Not white or light, that's for sure. Difficult to say just from that glimpse.'

Pip slumped in her chair, surveying the table – the smeared plates, the empty wine glasses, the foil takeaway containers, and the useless picture of Perhaps-Arabella in a Small-to-Medium-Maybe-Grey Car. She sighed.

'Shall we go and see the kittens before we clear the table?' Tim asked. 'It always cheers you up.'

'Yes, let's,' she said.

Rubbing the ears of the grey kitten soothed Pip as much as it did the kitten. An idea popped into her head.

'Tim, how would I go about doing a background check on Gordon and Arabella's financial status? It would be handy to know if either of them was in major financial trouble, or had had a recent windfall. Credit reports. Police records. That sort of stuff.'

'That's not hard. I could help you with that.'

'I don't want to put you to any trouble. Or get you in any trouble,' she said. She felt she'd already taken enough advantage of Tim's good nature and his willingness to help.

'It's pretty basic investigation, as far as I'm concerned.'

'Hacking 101?'

'Not even. I've got access to those databases. I wouldn't even have to break the law. Much. It'll cut into my gaming time, but that's probably for the best. New hobby – Pip's technical investigations assistant. Just send me their full names, plus anything else you have on them. I'll report back to you when I have something.'

'Thanks, Tim, you're the best.'

'Happy to be of service, ma'am,' he said.

CHAPTER 13

Pip decided to start the morning with a visit to Camden. One of Mummy's old friends ran a vintage clothing shop there, and she wanted to have a look. She felt better this morning than she had last night. After all, she thought as she walked, she had made quite some progress. She had two suspects – Arabella and Gordon. Okay, so she didn't have a visual on Arabella. Or on a car. Or any other sort of clue. But overall, she was doing quite well. What she really needed was a plan. A next step. But first, she had to make some progress on her real job.

Looking up at the tinkle of the bell on the door, Marlene greeted her like a long-lost sister. 'Epiphany Bloom! What a lovely surprise, dear girl!'

She always called Pip by her full name, for some unknown reason. Much of what Marlene did was for some unknown reason. But she had spectacularly good taste in clothing.

'What's that jacket? Chanel?' she asked Pip. *How are you?* was always the second or third question Marlene asked, after she had determined the provenance of various items of your wardrobe.

'Mummy's cast-off,' admitted Pip.

Marlene winked knowingly. 'I thought I recognised it. She always could pick an item, and as I always say…'

Pip joined her in her famous stock phrase: '"If you time it right, anything good comes back."'

Marlene was her own best advertisement. She seemed to wear a fair proportion of her stock at any one time. She combined the most unexpected pieces and never looked anything less than head-turningly stylish and spectacular. Today, she was wearing soft black velvet trousers embroidered with climbing red flowers, paired with a tight mustard polo neck. Square-toed black boots added an extra couple of inches to her five foot two inch frame. Over her razor-cut silver-white hair was wrapped – well, Pip didn't know, actually. A bandana, or a scarf, or perhaps some sort of turban. It might even have been a towel. A long silver chain hung around her neck with what seemed to be an actual skull on it, perhaps of a small rodent.

'Is that a rat's skull?' Pip asked.

'Good God, no! Why would I wear a rat's skull?' Marlene asked, wrinkling her nose at the notion. 'It's a stoat.'

Pip did not enquire why a stoat was more acceptable than a rat. Instead, she explained her mission. 'Marlene, I have a new job. A really good one, and it's kind of in your area of interest.'

'That's wonderful news, Epiphany Bloom!'

Pip wondered if the use of her full name was a tradition of Marlene's native Japan, or just a quirk of her own. Either way, it made Pip feel like the first field in a self-completion form.

'A job, at last! I told your dear Mama – "Magnolia, dear," I said – "Don't you worry about Epiphany, she's a good girl. Yes, she makes a lot of mistakes, very many indeed, and yes, there have been many, many disappointments and disasters, but at the end of the day, her many failures add up to a good girl."'

Pip thought that one 'many' would have sufficed, and 'disasters' was perhaps a bit strong.

'"But once Epiphany gets her teeth into something – the right thing,"' Marlene continued, '"she's going to be just…"' She broke off, struggling for the right word.

Marvellous? Pip wondered. *Brilliantly successful?*

'Just *fine*. Absolutely fine,' Marlene concluded with a beaming smile, patting Pip's hand.

Pip did not engage on the disputed topic of her fineness, but continued with her own announcement. 'So, as I said, it's in the fashion world. I'm working at the Museum of Movie Memorabilia and Vintage Costumes.'

'Well, that's fabulous! I know it well. They have a good collection. I knew Charise, the woman who started it. American. She bought a number of items from me years ago. Wonderful eye.'

'We're refreshing the collection, and I'm working on sourcing pieces for a new exhibition based on the seventies,' explained Pip.

'Very big right now,' Marlene said, nodding with approval. 'Seventies is huge. Good call. And of course, Hollywood is your thing. What a star-struck little thing you were in your teens.'

'Still am, a bit. So Marlene, I was wondering what you have in that line?'

'It's a pity you didn't come last month. I had a real treasure – what were very likely David Bowie's gardening trousers. Not certified, but there's a *New York Times* picture of him wearing them.'

'Gosh, I had no idea David Bowie gardened. Hard to imagine,' said Pip.

'Well, I've sold them, so you missed *that* boat. But I have plenty of seventies gear. Let me have a sort through and you can come back in a day or two, how's that?'

'Great Marlene, thank you. I'll pop by.'

As she turned to go, Pip had a brainwave. 'Marlene, the museum is looking for a few nineties investment pieces too. Iconic pieces from movies, that sort of thing. Have anything like that?'

'Not much, to be honest,' said Marlene. 'A lot of it has been snapped up already. It's very collectible. Incredibly expensive.'

An idea was forming in Pip's mind. Perhaps Marlene could lead her to people who would know where to find a stolen red dress. 'Are there any specialist dealers that you know about, that I could chat to, who might have what I need?'

'Well,' said Marlene, seemingly with some reluctance. 'There are people who deal in this sort of thing legitimately, like me, and then there are those who you have to be a bit careful with. Let's just say, they aren't always scrupulous about where their stuff comes from.'

'You mean the items are *stolen*?' Pip hoped she'd packed enough awe and outrage into her question. Awe and outrage were particularly tricky to combine.

'Some of it, yes. Stolen, or fake.'

'That's astounding. I would never have imagined that,' said Pip. 'Second-hand clothing always seems so… wholesome.'

'It used to be just us old-school collectors, buying at second-hand sales and charity shops, working flea markets, little shops. People like me, we got into this business because we love it. Like Charise, who started your museum. She was the same.'

'And now? It's changed?' Pip asked.

'The customers have changed. For a start, there are a lot more of them. Everyone's into vintage now; it's not just a niche thing. It's gone mainstream.'

'Surely that's good for you? More customers? Better prices?'

'Yes and no. The thing is, this vintage clothing business has become huge and profitable – for some, at least – and it's attracted a different sort of person. Buying up brand-name garments, selling off the internet to rich kids from Tokyo or New York or Timbuktu. One-off pieces fetch ridiculous prices. Even designer T-shirts are going for a bomb. People are selling trainers for thousands of dollars. Which is okay, I guess. Times change.'

'But?' Pip sensed there was a 'but' lurking.

'Where there's money, there's greed, Epiphany Bloom. Even crime. Organised crime. There's a huge black market in vintage clothing. Especially the iconic pieces. Shall we have tea?'

This was fascinating stuff, and it might give her a lead that would be helpful in finding the dress. She followed Marlene to the back of the shop, where there was a kettle and the necessaries for tea. Marlene got onto her knees and reached into the very back of a small cupboard that was crammed with bags and boxes. She emerged triumphant with a tin of biscuits, having dislodged an avalanche of shoe boxes in the process.

'I hide them from myself,' she explained to Pip. 'It's a right pain to get them out with my knees the way they are, so I only get one when I'm desperate. Just leave the shoes, I'll sort them out later. Here, have a bicky.'

Pip thanked her, and helped herself to a custard cream. 'So tell me, Marlene, what about the collectors' pieces?'

'There's big money at stake, and so there are lots of fakes. It's not as if many people have the original invoices or can trace the provenance of most of the items. It's almost impossible to prove ownership or theft. There are a couple of very unscrupulous dealers around.'

'How do they do it?' Pip asked.

'They'll see a picture of, say, Marianne Faithful or Mick Jagger in a particular outfit, and then they'll find something similar, or even make something themselves. You'd be surprised what you can achieve with fabric from the right era. Take a label off one thing, sew it into another. Anyway, the bottom line is, they sell the fake off as the real thing. They have the photo for reference, so it's sold as "this dress that so and so wore in that show or that movie – look, here she is wearing it". And once it's changed hands, with the certification and so on, it's as good as real, to all intents and purposes.'

'I would never have thought. And the theft? Tell me about that.'

'It's an ugly secret of our industry, but there are dealers who will steal pieces on demand. So, if there's a collector who's into, say, Broadway musicals of the eighties, or British boy bands of the nineties, and they know where a stash of those items are kept, they'll enlist some thief to go and steal them. There have been quite a few thefts from private collections, and my guess is, that's what happened to them. No different to a stolen Picasso or Renoir, really.'

Could this be what had happened to the *Pretty Woman* dress, Pip wondered? Had someone stolen it to sell to a collector?

'Marlene, do you think you could put me in touch with one of those dealers?'

'Epiphany Bloom! Absolutely not!' said Marlene, outraged. 'I won't be part of any illegal dealings, and besides, those people are dangerous. Where there's money involved, you can be sure they wouldn't hesitate to protect their businesses. With violence, if necessary.'

'I don't want to buy from them, Marlene. I think they may have something I need to get my hands on. Get comfortable. I think I need to tell you a story about a dress.'

CHAPTER 14

Arabella wasn't at her desk, which left the coast clear for Pip to riffle through her papers and find the staff list, with everyone's full name and contact details. She snapped a photo on her phone and messaged it to Tim.

Marlene had given her an idea. If the dress had been sold to a collector, the thief would have received money. And if the thief had received money, there was a good chance it would show up in their bank account. She needed more information about everybody's financial situations, not just Gordon's and Arabella's – and Tim was the guy to find it. If one of the staff had had a massive payment into their account recently, then bingo, she had her thief.

At her desk, Pip pondered what to do while she waited for Tim to come through with the goods. She had two other leads – Gordon and his mystery lady guest, and the information that Marlene had given her (along with a bag full of clothes to wear on her date-not-a-date with Tim, and a promise that she would send some pieces for the exhibition to the Museum).

Pip took out a scrap of paper with the name 'Rosanne Roberts' and a number written on it in Marlene's precise writing. Rosanne Roberts was, according to Marlene, a dealer in collectible seventies, eighties and nineties gear, the go-to-gal for real and iconic pieces, and not terribly inquisitive as to provenance. Perhaps she might know something that would lead Pip to the red dress. Pip was going to call her as soon as she had her cover story straight.

She would also have to question Gordon more carefully. But she wanted to hear back from Tim first. She'd only have one chance to use the element of surprise. She didn't want to show her hand prematurely, and tip him off. Besides, her gut was telling her that Gordon wasn't the brains behind the operation. Although her gut was often wrong, and the feeling could just as easily be the effects of too much butter chicken.

Next problem was: how was she going to handle Arabella? She needed to speak to her without tipping her off that she'd – perhaps – figured out that Arabella had – perhaps – been at the scene of the crime. She'd have to just shoot the breeze… *Hey, what's your favourite Netflix show and, by the way, what car do you drive, and where were you two Saturdays ago?*

Not ten minutes after she'd sent all the details through to him, Tim called with news.

It turned out that there wasn't much to learn about Arabella. 'Arabella is living just within her means and getting by. You'd think by her age, she'd have a little more put away,' said Tim.

Pip felt a bit sorry for Arabella. It seemed she wasn't earning a great salary from the museum, despite being the manager and nearly fifty. There wasn't much left for luxuries after she had paid her rent and basics, and by the last week of each month she was scraping along the bottom of her bank account. Baked beans for supper. Pip knew what that felt like.

'So you didn't see anything unusual?'

'There's literally nothing. No bad debts. No red flags from the credit company. No criminal record.'

'No big deposit, I suppose?' Pip asked hopefully, knowing the answer already.

'Unfortunately for her, no.'

'So,' said Pip, 'if she stole that dress, or helped someone else to steal it, either she hasn't shifted it yet, or she hasn't been paid, or she's hidden the money somewhere else.'

'Like where?'

'A secret account. Or a relative's account. Or it could be in cash, under the mattress. But I think that's unlikely. I bet if she got a windfall, she wouldn't be able to resist splashing it about a bit. It would show up somewhere – in her case, she'd probably be wearing it.'

Only, Pip knew that Arabella wasn't wearing it. Despite the short time she'd known Arabella, she'd already spotted that while Arabella always looked amazing, she actually only had a few items that she rotated and wore in different combinations. Pip sighed.

Emily and Philip, Tim went on to explain, were equally disappointing in their financial habits. 'Nothing to raise any eyebrows there,' said Tim. 'Except that Emily would save a fortune if she gave up her online shopping habit.'

Pip was feeling down. She'd pinned her hopes on finding that someone had received a windfall. But there was still one staff member to go…

'Now, our friend Gordon, he of the late night visit to the museum – well, he's another story,' said Tim, sounding pleased with himself.

Pip felt a flush of excitement. 'Please tell me he got a big fat whack of cash and deposited it with the reference "Stolen Red Dress"?'

'No, but Gordon seems to be significantly more flush than your average security guard, and it looks like he's been getting a bit of a cash injection over the last four or five months.'

'From his address on the staff list it seems he lives in a rented room in a modest house in a not-very-smart part of town,' said Pip. 'I doubt there's family money. I heard him mention that his parents are both teachers. The dad met his English wife teaching at the same school in Bulawayo. So what I want to know is, where is he getting this money? Who's giving it to him, and why?'

'That, my friend,' said Tim, 'is what you are going to find out.'

'The problem is,' said Pip, 'that he started receiving the money before the dress went missing. Unless it was an advance payment, of course. Which could support my theory that he's not the main culprit. I can't confront him until I know who's pulling his strings.'

With the financial questions answered, it was time to move on to the next lead. The fashion dealer, Rosanne. Before Pip could call her, though, Arabella arrived.

'How are things going?' she asked Pip. 'Made any progress?'

'Yes, getting my teeth into it,' said Pip. 'In fact, could we chat a bit more, just for background? I would like to go back over that day the dress disappeared. Starting from the Saturday morning, in as much detail as you can.'

'Okay, I'll try and remember.'

'So were you there at ten for opening?'

'No, I arrived around eleven. Philip was on duty, so he opened up. Emily doesn't work Saturdays usually, so the security guys do the ticket sales too. But that Saturday she came in for a bit because there was a big group of Germans booked to come through.'

'So it was a busy morning?'

'Yes.'

'Anything unusual? Anything at all?'

'No.'

'Anything odd about the Germans?'

'*Nein*. Not unless you count their footwear.' Was it possible that Arabella had a sense of humour? Who would have thought? 'They enjoyed the exhibition. Took lots of photos. They left around twelve thirty.'

'Who closed up?'

'That would have been Philip.'

'Did you leave together?'

'I left earlier.'

'By car?'

'What's that got to do with anything?'

'Just covering the bases.'

'No, not by car. I walked to the Tube.'

'And then you came back on Sunday. You came by Tube again?'

'Yes. I don't know why you are so interested in…'

'Transport. I just am. I have a deep, obsessive interest in, er, transport. Carbon footprint. Emissions. And fashion, of course. And the fashion of transport. Transport of fashion. Riveting.' Pip tried to make herself stop talking. She was sounding mad. Madder than usual.

Arabella looked confused. 'As I said, I sometimes come in on a Sunday, just to enjoy the feel of the place when it's empty. That's what I did on that day, and I came, as I usually do, on the Tube.'

'But you could drive if you wanted to?'

'I guess I could. If I borrowed my sister's car.'

'I'm thinking of getting a new car, myself. My Mini is a bit cramped. What sort of car does your sister have?'

'A Polo. A green Polo. It's fine. Nice.' Arabella sounded irritable. A Polo was smallish, and green was darkish. So, had she borrowed a car on Saturday night, in order to transport the dress? Pip was none the wiser. She pressed on.

'Let's talk about Gordon, shall we? What can you tell me about him?'

'Surely you don't suspect Gordon?' Arabella asked, seemingly in astonishment. Was she protecting her accomplice?

'I don't suspect anyone; I'm just getting background on everyone who works here. As you can imagine, the first place to look in something like this is at the people who have access.'

'Believe me, Gordon would be the last person to do anything like this.'

'Do you know him well, then? Outside of work?'

'I wouldn't say well, no.'

'So you wouldn't see him, say, on a Saturday night or anything?'

'No, but I know him well enough to know that you're wasting your time on him. What you see is what you get with Gordon. Good-looking, honest, not going to set the world on fire. The last guy you should be looking at.'

Pip thought back to the brief training course she'd been on before she'd got the boot from BI. The forensic accountant had told them, 'When you go into a company where someone's been fiddling the books, and everyone says, "The last person you need to worry about is Martha, she's got a heart of gold and she's been here forever," you know for sure it's Martha.' Pip wondered if the same held true for crimes of fashion. In which case, Gordon was her man. Besides, if Arabella had got Gordon involved in her plan to steal the dress, wouldn't she be keen to clear him as a suspect in Pip's mind? Between the security tape and the unexplained money in his account, Gordon was definitely at the top of Pip's suspect list. But who was helping him?

'It's Philip that's the dark horse,' Arabella said. Was she trying to throw Pip off Gordon's trail?

'Well he's a very uncommunicative horse, that's true,' said Pip. 'He was less than friendly when I introduced myself. Hardly got a word out of him.'

'He doesn't mix with the rest of the staff much. Never says more than the bare minimum required. He's an ex-policeman.'

'Strange, going from police to security guard. Must be rather dull comparatively.'

'He wanted a quieter life, as I recall.'

'Can you pull out his staff file for me?' Pip asked.

Arabella pointed her towards a filing cabinet. 'Bottom drawer,' she said. 'Help yourself.'

'*A*, *B*, ah there he is: Bastion, Philip. There we go…' Pip said, riffling through the files. She pulled out Philip's file and popped it into her bag. And just like that, she had a whole new angle to her inquiry. Was Philip a dirty cop? Could he have been the brains in the theft of the dress? But if so, then who was the woman?

CHAPTER 15

Before she looked at Philip's file, Pip had a phone call to make to Rosanne. 'If anyone can help you find a dress,' Marlene had said, 'it's her.' Well, time to find out if Marlene's nose for sketchy dress dealers was as good as her nose for vintage fashion.

Pip hesitated before she called. She couldn't ask Rosanne directly about the red dress. For a start, Rosanne would undoubtedly know Henrietta, and news of the theft mustn't get back to her. Furthermore, if Rosanne had had anything to do with the theft, or knew anything about it, asking about the dress would tip her off. Pip needed to be subtle, which had never been a strength of hers. However, she had an idea.

Rosanne answered almost immediately, a brisk and businesslike 'hello' that sounded as if it was designed to dissuade a telesales person. Pip introduced herself.

'I've been retained by a serious collector to find special pieces for her collection,' she told Rosanne. 'Marlene suggested you might be able to help me source this sort of thing.'

Rosanne's voice warmed up significantly at the mention of the 'serious collector', and they arranged to meet the next morning.

She turned her attention to Philip's file.

New Somewhat-Improved Pip decided to swing by the boxing gym on her way home. When she walked in, Jimmy was smashing a punch bag as if it had insulted his mother. He stopped when he saw her.

'Pip, hi. Good to see you,' he said. 'You change, I'll get things set up.'

She changed into her shorts and vest and strapped on her gloves. Jimmy put her through her paces, correcting her technique, and working her like a demon. She was damp with sweat and wiped out by the time they'd finished. She sat on a bench and took off her gloves, getting her breath back. Jimmy sat down next to her. Pip examined his tattoos, the snaking rose and thorns on his arm, the names of his daughters on the knuckles of his hands – Rose and Lily. She smiled, remembering how she'd first thought that he belonged to some sort of flower-obsessed gang.

'How are things going with the stolen dress?' Jimmy asked, with a hint of a smile. Presumably he didn't consider frocks to be hot merchandise for thievery.

'I've got an idea. A friend put me in touch with a woman who deals in high-end collectible items. I figured if someone stole the dress, they'll try and sell it, right? I'm going to talk to her tomorrow. Pump her for info.'

'Do you want to hear a bit of advice I was given by an old friend, former Mossad dude? About how to get info out of people?'

'Indeed I do. That's exactly what I need.'

'He said: "Don't ask a question, have a conversation. Don't scare them off, keep them talking. Try and get a fix on what the benefit might be for them. What do they want?"'

'Sounds like good advice.'

'And if that doesn't work, your right hook is coming on nicely.'

Pip gave him a soft punch to the bicep and he sprawled to the floor, holding his arm in a pantomime of pain.

'Hey, Pip,' he said, looking up at her from the floor. 'I'm going to the races Saturday after next. Big race day.'

'Horses?'

'Yes, horses. What else, llamas?'

'Do not mention llamas,' she said with a shudder. 'Evil beasts.'

He gave her a bemused look, but pressed on. 'Anyway, one of my clients invited me.'

'That sounds nice.'

'Do you think so?' he asked.

'Yes, I suppose. Day at the races. Should be fun.'

'I wanted to ask you something.'

'Sure, what?'

'So, the races… It's an invitation for two. Private box, champagne, the whole toot. Will you come? As my date – you know, my friend – like, whatever. Will you come with me?'

Pip agreed, experiencing a strange sense of déjà vu. She still didn't know if she was going to be Tim's date or his friend at this engagement party they were going to. She would make damn sure there was no such embarrassing misunderstanding with Jimmy.

She liked Jimmy – his wiry, pent-up energy; his kindness, which was so at odds with his appearance and his history. He couldn't be more different from Tim, who was calm and sweet and kind of nerdy. She liked Tim, too. How could she find them both so attractive? It was weird. The only thing to do was to keep them both as friends and not mess things up with maybe-flirtations and perhaps-crushes.

'I'd love to come to the races with you, Jimmy,' she said. 'Seeing as we are such good friends.' There. That should settle that.

CHAPTER 16

Rosanne was not at all what Pip had expected. There was something about this vintage business that made her imagine everyone in it would be an ageing style queen like Marlene, draped in strange garments. But Rosanne was not much older than Pip, late thirties perhaps, with thick, glossy black hair and full lips painted red. She wore a figure-hugging suit in a black and white check, and extremely high heels that looked positively treacherous to Pip, who was herself so clumsy that she had been known to fall off her trainers. In a random coffee shop full of mums in gym gear meeting after the morning school run, Rosanne stood out like a flamenco dancer in B&Q. Pip wished she'd upped her own game somewhat: worn a bit more make-up or added some statement earrings, at least.

Over cappuccinos, Pip told Rosanne about her quest. Her fictitious quest, that was.

'I'm afraid I can't divulge the name of the buyer,' Pip said, rather enjoying the role of the mysterious go-between. 'Let's just say that she is a serious and very determined international collector, with serious resources to match. She has a significant budget for the right pieces.'

Rosanne's eyes shone with interest – you could almost see the pound signs flickering in them. 'And what pieces is she interested in, specifically?' she asked, with a slight accent – Italian, perhaps, or French. Or maybe Spanish? Whatever it was, it was rather sexy, Pip mused. 'What is her love? Her passion?'

'Her particular passion, and an area where she's prepared to invest quite heavily, is in iconic dresses from movies of the eighties and early nineties.'

'Well, that's an area of passion for me, too!' said Rosanne. 'Your client and I, we are going to get along very well. I adore these movies. *The Breakfast Club. Pretty in Pink.*'

'Exactly! That's the era I'm looking for, even a bit later.'

'Those movies also! *Ghost. Pretty Woman.* I adore.'

Pip's heart skipped a beat. 'Yes, that's it. Exactly that era.'

'Well, it is very collectible these days, very desirable.'

'Right. And what she's really looking for is dresses. Iconic evening dresses. She's very into that old screen glamour.'

'As am I!' said Rosanne, enthusiastically. 'The gowns, the glamour. This is what I love also.'

'Well, it sounds like you are the perfect person to help me,' said Pip.

Rosanne had such a bright enthusiasm about her that Pip felt a little bad at getting her all excited for nothing, even though she suspected that Rosanne might have shown an equal enthusiasm if Pip had wanted to deal in outfits for performing hamsters. But that was all behind her; that hamster job had gone terribly wrong. Although the accident with the hamster onesie could have happened to anyone.

'The thing is, I'm under some pressure to get things moving quickly,' said Pip. 'You know how it is, once a person of, um, let's say, a person of great means, gets an idea that they want something. It has to be now!'

'Of course! I know exactly. I am accustomed to dealing with such clientele,' said Rosanne, with a dramatic roll of her eyes and a flick of her wrist. 'They want what they want, and they want it now. The trouble is, these special and unique items do not come up every day. One has to search for them. Pieces like this are very rare and special, but they do come up from time to time. I personally do not have such an item to hand, but I will investigate with my contacts.'

'You have a network of people who might have access to such items?'

'I do. There are a few…' Rosanne paused, as if considering whether to continue. 'There is one man in particular who might have information about items that do not always come through the regular channels. That might not be on the open market. One has to look for them in other places, not so obvious.'

'Well he sounds like a good start,' Pip said. And he did, in that he sounded dodgy enough to know about or even have access to stolen merchandise. 'See what you can find. She wants early nineties iconic pieces. She's a huge fan of those early nineties actresses – Meg Ryan, Julia Roberts, Sandra Bullock. She mostly collects evening gowns. And Rosanne, remember – as soon as you can, please. She is *very* keen to buy, and she doesn't ask too many questions. Money is no object, you understand.'

'You will hear from me quick-quick. I will telephone my contact. He might have an item that will make your client most very happy. And you and I, Peep, we will be happy, too. Good business all round. I look forward to meeting with you again very soon.'

Back at the office, Pip revisited the scant details in Philip's file, just in case something new might strike her after having read it the night before. Philip felt like the staff member that she had the slipperiest grip on, and she didn't want to leave anything to chance. But no, nothing new had materialised in his file. He was still forty. Still not married. Still no kids. The file still didn't give her much on his past – just that he'd left the police force for 'personal reasons'. He had been at the museum for two years. No disciplinary problems. His file remained a clean slate.

Pip had realised that if she left the door to her office open, she gained a good view of the comings and goings of her workmates. Anyone heading from the museum to the kitchen passed by her door. When Philip took his morning tea break, Pip gave him a two-minute start before picking up her empty coffee cup and following him to the kitchen.

He was sitting at the small kitchen table that was shoved against one wall, a cup of tea at his elbow, his head lowered over the crossword puzzle in the morning paper. Pip resisted her natural urge to jump right in with questions, instead refilling the kettle and slowly rinsing out her mug.

Philip filled in a clue with a satisfied air, scratch-scratching across the newsprint. He looked up and gazed thoughtfully at the wall, presumably pondering the next one.

'Hi,' Pip said. 'You winning?'

'Sort of. It's a long game, a crossword.'

Pip had never really thought of a crossword in this way before. 'Anything worth doing is, I guess,' she said. 'Hey, I wanted to thank you for your help about the security stuff. It's just... There's a lot on my mind. Worries. And problems to sort out. But I felt much better after we spoke and you explained all about it. I feel a bit silly being so anxious.'

What she actually felt was a bit guilty for tricking him.

'That's okay, no need to feel silly,' he said. He paused, and then, to Pip's great surprise, added, 'I've suffered from anxiety myself the last few years. Have you tried yoga?'

Pip's mind boggled as she tried to imagine Philip in the downward dog. 'A bit...' she said, uncertainly.

'Yoga and meditation, that's what's helped me,' he said, unexpectedly kindly. 'Here, come and sit down, I'll show you a breathing exercise that is very calming.'

Pip sat down next to him at the little table. The space was so small, their knees were touching.

'Now close your eyes.'

She hadn't been anxious before, but she was now. She closed her eyes as instructed and then opened them, just a slit, so she could watch him.

'Close them,' he said gruffly. 'I know it's difficult, you might feel fearful, but you are safe here.'

She did as she was told. The impulse to wriggle was intense. The whole thing was embarrassing beyond speech.

He continued: 'Relax. You are safe and at peace. Imagine you are in a field, a big green field.' His voice was unexpectedly low and soothing: it reminded Pip of dark golden honey being poured from a ceramic jar. Gosh, she was hungry. 'You are lying on a blanket under an ancient oak tree, its broad leaves protecting you, the sun warm and gentle, a light breeze on your skin. Your body is heavy and relaxed.'

Amazingly, the stress began to leach from her body. Her eyes stopped swivelling wildly behind her eyelids. Her shoulders drooped. Her limbs felt warm and liquid.

'Breathe in deeply and naturally, the cool, fresh air filling your throat and your lungs.'

She felt the air, smelled the wildflowers, enjoyed the sun and the breeze. Her breath was deep and steady.

His honeyed voice came smooth and soft. 'Feel the peace and love of the world surrounding you.'

Those were the last words Pip heard as she slid from the chair, crashing to the floor. Pain shot through her wrist, her hip bone slammed into the tiles, and her head smacked against the table leg.

Instead of an ancient oak tree with its broad leaves, Philip's face loomed over her, worry etched into his forehead. 'Oh my gosh, Pip, are you all right?'

Her many aches and pains were nothing compared to the humiliation of finding herself lying on the kitchen floor, looking into the face of the security guard/yogi. She struggled onto her hands and knees, with spilt tea dripping onto her shoulders and head. She hauled herself up, using a chair for balance and struggled inelegantly to her feet.

'I am so sorry. What an idiot,' she said, rubbing her wrist. 'I don't know what happened. I guess I just relaxed so much I fell asleep for a second.'

'Don't be embarrassed,' he said. 'That can happen when you've been stressed and holding it all together for a long time. It's actually a good thing, but I shouldn't have done the exercise with you in the chair; you should lie down. Let me see that arm.' He took her hand and moved it gently.

Pip wanted to cry at his tenderness and kindness. 'It's fine, just a bang. I'm such a klutz. What a mess,' she said, reaching for a cloth with her good arm. 'Let me clear all that up.'

She slopped milky tea around the table until he took the cloth from her.

'I can do it,' he said calmly. 'Don't feel bad about being anxious and stressed. I've been there. After a traumatic work incident some years back, I didn't sleep for months. This stuff saved my life and helped me sleep again.'

'That sounds really hard? The work thing?' Pip asked, taking quick advantage of an opportunity to find out more about Philip's past.

'Yeah. I was a copper my whole working life. But a job went bad; a kid died.'

'And you left the force to work security here?'

He smiled. 'I decided there could hardly be a lower stress job than looking after old clothes. Not exactly a hotbed of crime, is it? Not likely to see too much action here, I figured. All I want is a quiet life. My cats, my yoga, my crossword, and a job where no one's going to get killed.'

Pip had to admit, Philip was not at all one of those people of whom one could say, 'what you see is what you get'. Her first impression of him as an unfriendly menace seemed to have been completely wrong.

Back at her desk, Pip searched the web and unearthed the very sad story of Philip Bastion. He had been a policeman for fifteen years, serving the community with honour and dedication, seemingly liked and admired by all. Until one day, tragedy had struck.

According to the newspaper reports, Philip had spotted a gang of young roughs shoplifting from a supermarket, and he and his partner had chased them down the road through an industrial estate. Splitting up, they'd cornered the boys. Philip had set off after one of them, chasing him up a metal staircase at the side of a warehouse. At the top, as Philip had reached out to nab him, the boy – Gavin Henley, fourteen, said the newspapers – had jumped, or fallen, to his death.

The newspapers had told the whole sorry story in lurid detail, over weeks. Gavin had been in the company of his older brother, Doug, who was one of the delinquents. It had been Gavin's first foray into shoplifting – he was a quiet, well-mannered kid, who did well at school and never got into any trouble (unlike Doug, about whom an unnamed source had said, 'It's no coincidence that his name rhymes with "thug."') He'd gone to the shops with his brother, not knowing his brother was meeting up with his mates for a morning of pilfering CDs and chocolate bars. Gavin hadn't been part of the plan, or of the pilfering. He'd run when the rest of the boys ran, and had been so terrified when Philip had caught up with him at the top of the fire escape that he'd ended up dead on the pavement below.

Months later, the official inquiry had given its verdict: 'Policeman cleared in staircase tragedy', read the headline. The article reported that although Philip had been absolved of all wrongdoing, he had resigned from the force. Checking the dates on his staff file, Pip realised he'd gone straight from star cop with a great future ahead of him, to a security guard at the museum.

What a sad tale all round, thought Pip. Tragic for the poor boy, Gavin, who had lost his life. Heartbreaking for his mum, who could be seen in the photographs, weeping into her hankie outside the court. Terrible for his hoodlum brother, who wouldn't have lost his sibling if it weren't for his spot of petty shoplifting. Devastating for Philip, whose actions had contributed to a child's death, however unintentionally. No wonder he was so stern and so unwilling to get involved in anything outside of the narrowest definition of his own job.

What a sweet guy he'd actually turned out to be, Pip thought, rubbing her bruised wrist. No way he could be involved in the disappearance of the *Pretty Woman* dress. Except… What about his mental state? Maybe he wasn't as emotionally healthy and stable as he appeared. After all, he'd lived through a terrible trauma. He'd said he had trouble sleeping. Suffered from anxiety. Maybe he had taken the dress? For what reason, though? For money? Perhaps… A security guard didn't earn overly much, and all that yoga and stuff must add up. Or maybe to get back at someone at the museum? Or as a cry for help? Bitterness at the world? And, Pip thought, she mustn't lose sight of the fact that Philip and Gordon were friends. After all, Philip had even told Gordon about Pip's fake anxiety. Or had he warned him about Pip's endless questions?

She liked Philip, but perhaps she shouldn't cross him off the list just yet.

CHAPTER 17

Pip had hoped to spend Saturday morning preparing for the Engagement Party-Maybe-Date with Tim by putting together various outfit options from her existing wardrobe and the sack of stuff she'd borrowed from Marlene. But time spent with Flis always seemed to move at a different pace to the rest of the world.

Flis had kindly offered to blow-dry Pip's hair so that she looked sleek and fashionable for the party. Flis was very good at hair. At university, she had bought hair straighteners, curling tongs and a set of brushes, and started a side-hustle doing other students' hair for dances, balls and hot dates.

Flis's house had been typically chaotic when had Pip arrived for her hair session. The sound of wailing could be heard as soon as the front door opened. Camelia had lost a tooth and was hysterical that the tooth fairy had forgotten to come and leave the required ten pounds (a ridiculously large amount of money, Pip thought. It had been fifty pence when she'd last lost a tooth).

'I didn't have cash,' Flis hissed under her breath. 'That tooth has been wobbly for weeks; I didn't expect it to fall out last night.'

That would be a good reason to think it *would* fall out, in Pip's opinion. But she kept that to herself.

'Didn't your mum tell you that the tooth fairy doesn't work Friday nights?' Pip asked her niece. 'Everyone knows, Friday's her night off.'

'Oh goodness, you're right,' Flis said, smacking her palm against her forehead in an exaggerated display of surprised remembering. 'It was *Friday*. Of course. Well, that explains it.'

'If you lose a tooth on a Friday, the tooth fairy comes on Saturday night,' Pip explained. It almost sounded plausible, she thought proudly. After all, surely even tooth fairies deserved a break? Camelia gave her a suspicious stare, but clearly decided to go along with it.

'So she'll be here tonight?' she asked, looking at her mother coldly.

'I'm sure of it,' said Flis, shooting a grateful glance at Pip. 'Now, can I get on with Aunty Pip's hair?'

Pip wanted the style that you saw on the red carpet and in all the Hollywood movies these days. Hair hanging off a middle parting, and sort of curled loosely into waves. Flis straightened it first, then went to work with a brush, while the two of them discussed the nature of the assignation.

'But did he say "date"?' Flis asked.

'He said, "It's a date".'

'So it's a date?'

'No, it was said more like, "That's a plan".'

'But it could be a date *and* a plan,' Flis said, furrowing her brow. 'Although it could be a plan, but not a date. Would you like it to be a date?'

The truth was, Pip wasn't sure. She'd fancied Tim since a mutual friend had set them up as potential housemates. She'd thought that perhaps he felt the same, but that neither of them had pursued anything because who needed *that* complication? They had bonded over the Matty Price matter – Tim had been a great help with the online search (aka hacking) and then with her sprained ankle, a souvenir of the scuffle. Oh, and he was a marvellous co-parent as far as the kittens were concerned. But did she really want to be in a relationship with him?

And what about Jimmy? She fancied him, too. Whenever she thought about him, she got a warm feeling in her chest. It was all too much to think about right now.

The hair, when finished, didn't quite look as Pip had hoped. More ringlet than wave. A little too much eighties perm in her noughties slick. It had been a while since Flis's hairdressing heyday.

Flis, though, was confident. 'I have to make it a bit tight or the curl will fall out by the time you go out. It'll loosen up by the time you're ready. If it's still too curly before you leave, just run your fingers through it a bit; that'll sort it out.'

Pip gave her sister a hug. 'Thanks,' she said. 'Sorry I can't stay and chat. Catch you tomorrow? Or supper next week?'

'No problem, you run along,' said Flis. 'Call me tomorrow and let me know how it went. Or text me! If it goes really well. Perhaps it will turn out he's infiltrated with you.'

'Infiltrated?'

'Thinks about you all the time.'

'Ah! Infatuated. But infiltrated works too, I guess.'

'You see,' said Flis. 'I'm always right.'

Pip wasn't going to stay for an argument. 'Don't forget the tooth mouse!' Pip shouted over her shoulder.

'I won't. Oh, and remind me to tell you about Mummy,' said Flis.

That was the kind of phrase that instilled fear into Pip's heart. She stopped. 'What about her?'

'She and GeeCee are staying on another week in Ecuador. I couldn't hear quite why. Something with a boat, maybe? Anyway, she said she'd tried to call you too, but didn't get you. It was a bad line, but she told me to tell you not to worry, she will be home before you have to worry about any dramas. Whatever that means.'

'Who knows? With Mummy there are bound to be dramas one way or another, anyway. Gotta go,' said Pip.

It was already close to 4 p.m. and Pip hadn't even looked at the clothes. She upended the bag from Marlene, sending a shower of fabric and accessories onto the bed – bits of lace and fur, shoes, glitter, velvet. Lots of gorgeous vintage stuff. It was just a question of putting an outfit together. That was where the magic happened, according to Emily, who had been rabbiting on about it to Pip just the other day.

The dresses that Marlene had provided were about three sizes too small. She might have an eye for fashion, but not for dress size. Pip hauled out a few dresses from her cupboard. She figured this was probably an occasion for dresses. Cocktail dresses. She had a nice little black number. Was it too dull? Her other option was silver. Was it too, um, silver?

She unearthed a pair of sheer black stockings – when had she last worn stockings? She pulled them on and looked in the mirror. They made her long legs look fantastic, she had to admit. She slipped the black dress over her head. Boring. Black and black. But what if she added the shrug from Marlene's bag? And maybe the red earrings she had bought in India; those were dramatic. Not boring any more, that was for sure. What about the shoes? She couldn't go for heels, or she'd tower over Tim. You did see girls in Doc Martens and dresses, the vintage types. She tried them on. Too much? She didn't know.

Pip had a good idea. She went onto Emily's Instagram account, and from there found links to a few others devoted to vintage looks. There were loads of tips on putting an outfit together. 'What's your theme?' asked one expert. Pip considered the question, but drew a blank. She just wanted to look attractive, and, if it wasn't too much to ask, cool.

'Don't be afraid to mix vintage and new elements,' wrote expert number two. Okay, well, that she could do. The dress, newish; the shrug, old; the Docs, timeless – or so they said.

'Dress around a centrepiece,' wrote another. Whatever the heck that meant. Pip had always thought that *she* was the centrepiece of her outfits.

'Layering is hot right now,' wrote one glamorous woman, who was wearing one dress over another in the accompanying image. How about that? The silver over the black? The black over the silver? Pip squinted at the picture. The shorter dress over the longer one seemed to be the way to do it, which she supposed did make sense, in so far as wearing two dresses at once could ever make sense.

Pip took off the shrug and pulled the silver dress over the black one. She added the shrug. She took it off again. She pulled a long pink feather boa from the tangle on the bed and tossed it over her shoulders. Put the shrug back on over it. Now she couldn't move her arms. The underneath-dress was sliding up her thighs under the over-dress. The tortoiseshell kitten launched itself at the swinging end of the boa, presumably mistaking it for a bird in distress. Its sharp little claws shredded Pip's stockings and pierced the skin on her calf.

'Aaargh!' she shouted. 'Bloody hell, that hurt.'

Tim knocked and called through the door. 'You okay, Pip?'

'Yes, I'm fine,' she called back. 'No problem. Just deciding on an outfit.'

'I'm sure you'll look lovely,' he said. 'Will you be ready to leave in about ten minutes?'

'Sure, no problem, nearly ready,' Pip said, staring at her bag-lady-meets-eighties-movie-space-alien ensemble in the mirror inside her cupboard door in despair.

'Tim?' she called out.

'Yes?'

'So, what kind of people are your cousin and her friends? Are they a smart and trendy set? Is it a *party* party? Or more, like, a casual thing? I'm just wondering about what to wear. I don't want to look out of place.'

'I'm sure you will look just perfect,' Tim said, popping his head round the door, the better to conduct the conversation. Pip caught his startled expression as he took in her multi-layered, laddered-stockinged, feather-bleeding look. It hovered only fleetingly on his face, to be rapidly replaced with a warm smile.

'Just trying a bunch of stuff on,' she said brightly, pulling off the boa and flinging it onto the bed, kitten still attached.

'That black dress is lovely,' Time said. Although he couldn't possibly see much of it under all the other nonsense. 'Shows you off nicely. You'll look great. And the cousins are great; you'll like them, they'll love you. No matter what you decide to wear.'

'Thanks, Tim,' Pip said, noticing for the first time how absolutely smashing he looked in a suit. 'You look…' she wavered between 'hot' and 'handsome', and ended up saying something that sounded like, 'homhan.' He looked suitably confused.

Shedding a few layers of clothing was a great relief and a big improvement all round. The black dress fell simply and elegantly to above the knee. She didn't own another pair of stockings – bare legs would have to do. She put on the fifties pumps Marlene had given her, and she kept on the red Indian earrings with their little mirrors. The shrug lifted the look to somewhere close to vintage layering.

The remaining problem was her hair. All the dressing and undressing had transformed Flis's careful curls into a frizzy halo of static. Pip poured a few drops of almond oil into her hands, rubbed them together and smoothed the oil into her locks, then ran her fingers back through and gave the whole lot a good scrunch.

She leant towards the mirror, applying lipstick that was, as it turned out, the exact red of the earrings. 'Totally winning at grooming,' she told her reflection. She didn't look like a Hollywood actress. Nor did she look like a fashionable vintage maven. She looked like herself, Epiphany Bloom – on a good day.

CHAPTER 18

Tim was right. The cousins were great. Everything was great. The venue was the kind of place to which Pip would never ordinarily go – it was too cool, to be honest. The champagne flowed and the food was delicious – trays of top-class canapés, tiny bowls of stir-fried Asian greens, salmon on blinis, meltingly good chicken and champagne pastry morsels. The fellow guests all looked like the sort of people who would be perfectly at home on yachts or polo ponies. Usually, Pip might feel intimidated, or wrongly dressed, but this time she felt quite up to scratch, actually.

She was happy here, in her vintage-ish outfit, mingling with the cool kids, a kind and good-looking guy at her side. The whole evening was magical. Tim's younger sister, Claire, had described Pip's outfit as 'sick', which apparently was a compliment amongst sixteen-year-olds. Pip was drifting on a glow of champagne and good cheer. Tim was his usual friendly, charming self, good company with a dash of flirtation – unless she was imagining it? Did he like her or *like* her? Pip couldn't work it out, so decided she was just going to put it out of her mind and enjoy the rest of the evening.

The place was loud. Tired of shouting, she leaned in to speak to Tim, her mouth close to his ear. At the same moment, he leaned into her, turning towards her so their faces were just inches apart. Their eyes met and held. Tiny flecks of gold shimmered in his irises. Their lips were inches apart. Was he coming in for a kiss? Should she? All of a sudden, Pip's head began to swim. She felt dizzy. Floating.

Was this love, she wondered? Or one too many glasses of bubbly? Her heart began to pound, and suddenly she felt distinctly queasy.

Oh dear, this wasn't love. Or even lust. And it wasn't too much champagne, either. She knew this feeling, she thought, her heart sinking. She drew back quickly from Tim – his smooth lips, his shining eyes. He looked surprised. Confused. Maybe even hurt. But she had no time for that.

'Tim,' she said urgently, raising her voice to be heard over the noise. 'Those little chicken and champagne pastry puffs they brought round earlier… Did you eat them?'

'Yes. They were tasty, weren't they?' he shouted back. '*Champignon*, though. Not champagne. *Champignon*, as in French for mushrooms.'

Mushrooms. Could these pretentious foodies not just speak English, please? Pip had eaten mushrooms. And she was allergic to mushrooms.

Pip knew from bitter experience that things would go horribly and quickly wrong from this point on. She leapt from her chair, almost knocking it over, and grabbed her handbag. Tim got to his feet.

'Pip, are you okay? You're as white as a sheet.'

'I'll be fine, stay here,' she said, and made a dash for the door. She needed air. And privacy. And an antihistamine. She scrabbled in her bag as she pushed her way through the throng, knowing there was always a spare pill in her purse. Bingo. Her fingers found it. She grabbed a water glass as she passed a table, tossed the pill into her mouth and slugged it down.

Outside on the pavement, she rested her hands on her thighs and breathed slowly. Her stomach rolled, but at least she wasn't throwing up. Her head still reeled, but her heartbeat was settling down. She'd only had one little pastry, and she'd got that pill down quickly. She should be okay. She stood up and leaned against the wall while the evening crowd streamed by.

The city was buzzing all around her. What a vibe. She really should get out more – just look at all these people, out on the town, having a good time. A gaggle of tipsy women about Pip's age tottered past, following behind a girl in a plastic crown and a sash reading 'The Missus'. On the other side of the street was the male equivalent, a stag do, the guys dressed up, unfathomably, in cowboy hats, heading in the opposite direction. A few tourists blocked up the pavement with their dawdling and gawking, stopping to take pictures of a Typical London Night Scene, while typical Londoners dodged them irritably. Loving couples walked by holding hands. Little groups of friends laughed and chatted. It was a beautiful spring evening, and the cheerful throngs were heading for a night out at the trendy restaurants and clubs.

As Pip focused on her breathing and calming her pounding heart, she watched the entrance of a bar across the street. It seemed to suck in a steady stream of the most beautiful people Pip had ever seen. Beautiful in the way of the rich and privileged and effortlessly cool. Every time the door opened to let them in, the sound of cool jazz escaped, and she caught a glimpse of a lanky fellow in black bent over a double bass. Then the door closed and the music and musician were lost to her. She and Tim should come here sometime, she thought. It would be good to hear some live music in a place like that. She looked at the name above the door: 'Razmajazz'. She'd never remember it after all the champagne she'd drunk. She should take a picture.

She held up her phone and focused the camera on the building with its sign. Then the door opened, and who should step into the night, but Gordon! Pip took the photo without thinking, lowered the phone and looked at him. He managed to make his guard's uniform look dishy, but in smart street clothes he was absolutely gorgeous. The flickering light of the sign caught the planes of his face, lit up his white teeth, and bounced off his gleaming leather shoes.

Only when Pip managed to tear her eyes from Gordon did she notice his date. She was cast from the same mould as Gordon – beautiful, shiny people. She seemed oddly familiar, and Pip wondered where she might have seen her before. She could have been a model, or a hot young actress from Hollywood. Her hair cropped close to her perfectly sculpted skull, her dark skin, her long limbs, her wide and generous mouth. And she was wearing two dresses: a sheer see-through kaftan shift on top of a figure-hugging tunic. On her, it looked like the most obvious and stylish way to wear dresses. She leaned into Gordon as they walked along the pavement into the slight chill of evening. He slipped an arm around her shoulders, and with the other, hailed a black cab.

Pip headed back inside, feeling much better, if somewhat confused by Gordon's sudden appearance. What was an ordinary chap like Gordon doing in a trendy city jazz bar? Where had he got those fancy clothes? The shoes alone must have cost two weeks' wages. And not to mention the date: who was she? And what was a girl like that doing dating someone who was neither rich nor famous, no matter how hot?

'Pip! I was worried about you!' Tim said, hurrying over to her. 'I sent one of the cousins into the ladies' loo to look for you, but you weren't there. Are you okay?'

'I'll be fine. I have a mushroom allergy, remember? I took a pill and went outside for some air. I'll be okay, thank you.'

'That was kind of weird,' he said, after a pause.

She didn't know whether he meant the embarrassing aborted kiss, or her hasty exit.

'Yeah, it was, sorry.' She didn't know what she meant either: the kiss or the exit. 'Hey, I saw something odd when I was outside trying not to die of *champignons*. Check this out,' she presented her phone screen to Tim. 'You recognise this guy? He's the guy from the security camera pics. The guard from my work.'

'That's an extremely strange coincidence. What's he doing there?'

'I don't know. It's a jazz club. A super trendy-looking spot. The entrance must be thirty quid. The drinks are probably twenty each. And the cab? What would that cost? Looks like he's putting his windfall to good use. Not to mention the date. I mean, wow.'

'She is a very pretty young lady,' Tim agreed, in a sweet, respectful way.

'Does she look familiar to you at all? I feel like I've seen her somewhere. She could be a famous person.'

'No. I don't recognise her, but I probably wouldn't. You're much more up on that sort of thing than me. Who's who. Celebs.'

'Well, someone has just secured himself the top spot on my suspect list,' said Pip.

CHAPTER 19

The sunlight was streaming in the window, but Pip couldn't drag herself out of bed. A busy week in her new job, plus the mushroom incident and the knock-out antihistamine, had left her tired. She had got up early for tea and to feed the ravenous pack of cats, then retreated back to her duvet, where she planned to spend most of the day catching up on the celeb news and thinking about her work.

Even though the internet was full of up-to-the-minute gossip about celebrities and royals, Pip enjoyed the paper magazines, with their glossy covers and their big spreads of photos. She bought one a month, two if she was getting a regular pay cheque, rotating through *Hello* and *OK!* and some even less salubrious ones, which she snuck into the house under cover of darkness.

It was so calming, paging through the magazines full of familiar faces, seeing their lives unfold, admiring their clothes and homes, empathising with their disasters, celebrating their new babies, tutting when the poor things were shamed for their cellulite, sitting in stern judgement of their bad behaviour and poor life choices. They were miles removed from her, with their fame and money, but somehow, not so different. Pip finished the article on the supposed fashion war between Meghan and Kate – it must be about the twentieth one she'd read on that topic in the last year, poor girls – and put the mag down.

Most was enjoying the lie-in, purring like a lawnmower and drooling a wet patch onto the duvet next to her. Even the kittens were calm, their tummies full, all snuggled up and asleep in the tangle of fur and sheets. It was fairly blissful. Pip gave them all a stroke and picked up her phone. Now would be a good time to do a bit of research-slash-stalking of her colleagues-slash-suspects.

The more she thought about it, the more suspicious Gordon's behaviour seemed. Maybe she was wrong about him being a mere accomplice; maybe he'd been her man all along. She had the CCTV footage of him outside the museum on a Saturday night, with a woman – probably Arabella. He had money in his account that didn't make sense. And then here he was out on the town at some swanky club with a gorgeous modelly type. That was another thing that was bothering Pip – who was that woman? She felt sure she'd seen her, and recently, too. She took out her phone and looked at the picture she'd taken of the two of them. It wasn't great quality, taken in low light from across the road, but there was enough light from the sign for her to see the woman's face quite clearly.

Gordon had told her before that he wasn't into that 'social media stuff', and it appeared he was telling the truth. An online search found nothing more than a Facebook page that hadn't been updated in two years. Pity. It would have been handy to find a clearly tagged pic of him and the woman.

Pip sighed, and allowed herself to pop onto Instagram. Maybe there would be some pics of the engagement party… Although, thinking about the engagement party gave her an idea. The club, Razmajazz. Did they have a web page?

Clicking and swiping, she found it in minutes. Her blood rushed to her face when she saw that they had posted photographs from the previous night's gig. There was the tall guy, leaning over the double bass; there was the rest of the band, who Pip hadn't seen in her glimpse through the door. And there, at the bar, perched on a barstool and clutching a glass of wine, was the girl Gordon had been with.

Pip sat up, scattering kittens as she did so. 'Sorry, guys,' she said. 'But your mum has just hit the jackpot.'

Because, guess who was tagged in the pic? Gordon's mystery Golden Girl, aka VintageMinx. Pip set to work finding out more about her. VintageMinx was the user name of a minor TV personality called Victoria M – VM, as she called herself. *That* was where Pip had seen her before. Victoria was the co-presenter of a wardrobe makeover show called *New You, Woo-Hoo!* in which a plummy, toothy woman called Trixie showed people how to 'dress for their body' and suchlike. The lovely Victoria was Trixie's side-kick, providing diversity and youth, and a cool eye for – drumroll, please – vintage clothing!

Did it not seem an outrageous coincidence that this woman was known for her interest in vintage clothing *and* that she was hanging out with Gordon, when she was out of his league by about a million miles? Pip had one of those blinding revelations that hit with the force of a religious epiphany. And Pip didn't use the word 'epiphany' easily. What if the Mystery Woman from the Museum wasn't Arabella at all? What if it was Victoria M in that grainy CCTV picture?

She looked at the phone again, examining the blurred black and white photograph. With her hair covered by a beanie and her face turned away, there were frustratingly few details. VM looked to be about the right shape: tallish, slimmish. The more Pip thought about it, the more it made sense: Gordon and Victoria had stolen the red dress from *Pretty Woman*. But why? And where was it now?

CHAPTER 20

Pip spent Monday morning trying to spy on Gordon, which was even harder than it sounded, and it had sounded pretty hard. For a start, she wasn't really sure what she was hoping that he would *do*. Perhaps a scrap of red material would waft out of his pocket, or he'd start whistling the *Pretty Woman* theme song. Detecting was much harder than it looked on TV. Nonetheless, she kept popping out to see what he was up to.

But every time she wandered outside, he was so pleasant and helpful that she felt bad for suspecting him of a crime, even though all the evidence pointed to him. Also, it made it impossible to spy on him.

She was sitting in the small kitchen, sipping a mug of tea and trying to decide what to do next, when Gordon strolled in, chatting on his phone.

'I don't know what to do, Vic,' he said.

Vic? As in, Victoria? As in, glamorous accomplice? Pip perked up.

Gordon was quiet, presumably while Vic spoke. 'Would you?' He was smiling now, as he filled the kettle with one hand. 'I'll message you the address and you can pick it up. Then I can meet you, and collect it from you. That would be amazing – if I don't get it today, there'll be hell to pay, I can tell you that.' He chuckled, as if 'Vic' would know all about that. 'But don't tell anyone, okay?' continued Gordon, putting a teabag in a mug. 'I was supposed to do it myself.'

Pip couldn't believe it. Gordon was standing in front of her, bold as brass, discussing a secret assignment that he was supposed to do himself. It had to be something to do with the dress, it had to. Pip tried to shrink into the chair, sitting as still as a cushion.

'I'll see you at the entrance to the big Starbucks in Covent Garden at two-fifteen,' Gordon continued. 'And you'll have it. And Vic, whatever you do, don't open the bag. You don't want to get creases in the bloody thing, or spills or whatever.'

Silence while Vic spoke, and Pip tried to look invisible.

'Thanks, baby, you're the best,' said Gordon. 'Love you.' And with that, he ended the call, smiled vaguely at Pip and disappeared with his tea.

Bingo!

By 2 p.m., Pip was hidden behind a newspaper in the Covent Garden Starbucks, with a clear view of the door. She sipped a hazelnut latte, and kept her eye on the door, shielded both by the newspaper and a pair of giant sunglasses. She felt like the real deal. A proper sleuth. A woman who knew how to find a dress.

At two-ten, she spotted Victoria's arrival. She was wearing another of her two-dress ensembles – honestly, did the woman not know you could wear dresses one at a time? – and was carrying what was clearly an item of clothing in one of those dry-cleaner bags. It had to be the dress – right there. So close, Pip could almost taste it, except that her mouth was full of latte.

Gordon arrived bang on time. He kissed Victoria on each cheek and, after some talk, took the bag and sauntered away. *Shit.* It had all gone down so quickly that Pip had missed her chance. She slammed five pounds down on the table to cover the cost of the latte, and ran to the door. Then she remembered that she'd paid for the latte at the counter, and stood, dithering for a moment. Five pounds was a lot of money in kitten toys, after all, but dammit – her suspect was getting away.

With a last glance at her money lying forlorn on the table, Pip wrenched the door open and looked up and down the street. Where was Gordon? She caught sight of the garment bag over his shoulder, bobbing atop the crowd like a cork floating in the sea. She set off after him, watching the bobbing black bag, keeping her distance. As she followed him, she realised that he was heading in the direction of the station, and guessed he was going to catch a train. Damn. Tailing someone on a train was notoriously tricky, despite what movie directors would have you believe.

Pip joined the crowd heading to the Tube, dodging the dawdlers, passing the pram-pushers on her long legs, all the while keeping a beady eye on the black bag. As she had expected, Gordon headed into the station. She followed him at a distance. He walked briskly, like a man on an errand, and didn't seem in the least interested in his surroundings or fellow commuters – which was good for Pip. The most difficult time to keep someone in view without being spotted was waiting on the platform. She lurked behind a gaggle of Chinese tourists towards the end of the platform in the direction the train was headed, so that Gordon would likely be looking in the other direction to see if the train was coming.

And here it came, in a blast of warm air. She let Gordon get on first, then headed quickly for the next carriage and stepped in. Pip could see a sliver of Gordon through the carriage windows, enough that she'd notice if he moved. She sat in a state of high tension, trying to avoid glancing at him every couple of seconds. She stared at the ads and the notices. There were polite reminders to do the most ordinary things, like to please take your paper and recycle it. Another encouraged commuters to please move down to make room for others – under which someone had written '*You Git*', which made it quite a lot less polite.

At Oxford Circus, there was a turnover of passengers – people standing, preparing to get off, blocking Pip's view; others on the platform, getting ready to swarm the train. She had no option but to stand up and check whether Gordon was getting ready to exit. He was sitting calmly, the big bag across his lap, looking at his phone. Investigating was extremely stressful, thought Pip. She was quite pleased now that she had lost that BI job. Not that curating vintage clothes was any picnic, as it turned out. But it was nowhere near as terrifying as that month she'd spent waiting tables in Beirut, because Mummy had decided it was 'time she saw how the rest of the world lives.'

The train moved. While Pip considered the various merits and stresses of the jobs she'd had, Gordon gathered up his bag and looked at the door as if he were getting ready to leave. 'The eagle prepares for flight,' Pip muttered to herself. An elderly lady sitting next to her nodded and winked, somewhat disconcertingly. Pip stood up and edged towards the door in her own carriage, with the old lady still watching and nodding. Leaning against the pole, she angled herself so that she could see a faint reflection of Gordon in the glass of the sliding door, but he couldn't see her. The train stopped at Notting Hill Gate. She hung back and let him get out – much to the annoyance of the man behind her who said crossly, 'You in or out, love? Make up your mind.' Clearly, this man had neglected to read the politeness notices. Then off they set, the suspect and his tail, out of the station and up the street.

Pip followed him for five or ten minutes with no trouble, leaving a bit more of a gap when they turned off the main road. It was astonishing how absolutely blind regular people were to their environment and to the people around them, assuming they weren't expecting a tail. When Gordon stopped in front of a residential building, Pip stopped a couple of doors down, her back to him, pretending to scan the names on the bells. When she thought it safe to glance round, she was just in time to see Gordon and his black garment bag swallowed up, the door closing behind them.

She needed to know who he was visiting. It was now or never. She walked quickly towards the townhouse where he'd entered. The building was indistinguishable from its neighbours – well-maintained and solid, petunias in pots in the windows, a big black painted door, a black railing. Pip's nerves were jangling. What if he was simply dropping the 'delivery' and he came straight out? Her heart in her mouth, she walked up to the front door. There were three bells attached to an intercom. Presumably the once-grand house had been divided up, and there was a bell for each flat. She bent down to read the names, hoping against hope that one of them would be familiar, or at least useful in helping her work out what was going on. It was not to be. The plates where the inhabitants' names should be were blank.

CHAPTER 21

The question was what to do next. Someone who lived in one of these flats was the recipient of what was in the garment bag – which had to be the dress. Pip could hardly ring on the bells, at least not when Gordon was inside. She decided to wait him out. When she saw him leave, she would ring the bells and try to find some information about the inhabitants. In the meantime, she'd have to think up a plausible story that would result in them offering their names to a stranger.

Pip made a note of the address on her phone. Maybe she could do some sort of search, find out who owned the building. This seemed like a job for Tim, but she didn't want to take further advantage of his legally dubious computer skills.

She retreated to a bus stop a block or so down, to keep out of Gordon's way. She put her head in her hands, and tried to think about her next step.

'Good day. Has the number seven been past?' asked an old chap in a full three-piece suit, taking a seat next to her.

'I don't know. Sorry.'

'Or the fourteen?' he asked, pulling a gleaming gold watch on a chain from the pocket of his waistcoat.

'I don't know. I just got here,' she said again, looking over the man's shoulder to see if Gordon was anywhere to be seen.

'What bus are you waiting for?' he asked, settling in for a good chat.

'Um,' Pip glanced around for a possible number, but couldn't read the details at this distance. 'I haven't decided.'

'Well I never, that's a first for me,' he said, seemingly delighted at the wondrous strangeness to be found at the local bus stop. 'How will you know?'

Pip's phone vibrated. 'Please excuse me,' she said, with the politeness demanded when addressing an elderly gentleman in a three-piece suit.

She looked at her phone and noticed there were a couple of missed calls from an unknown number, which always made her nervous but usually turned out to be a robocall or some poor telesales rep selling an upgraded mobile phone package.

More frightening, there were text messages from Mummy. Mummy did not believe in messaging, even though Pip had explained that it was merely a system of communication, not a religion or a paranormal phenomenon. She touched the screen with a sigh, knowing that any message from Mummy was something to worry about.

> '*There's nothing to worry about.*' said the first message, ominously.

This message was the last of five. Pip took a deep breath, as if prior to diving into a very cold swimming pool, and started from the first, remembering, as she read, what Flis had said about their mother calling and telling her to tell Pip she'd be home before she had to worry about any dramas.

> '*As I said to Flis,*' the first message read, '*there was a problem with Andrew and the boat. I will be back in England next Sunday night.*'

> '*I know I said I'd be back before the llamas,*' continued the second message, '*but the llamas have arrived early. Can you believe it?*'

Yes, Pip could. It wasn't *dramas* Flis had heard, but *llamas*!

'All you need to do is pop out there and sign the paperwork. Ask them if they wouldn't mind hanging on to them for a week or two.'

'I've emailed you the paperwork and the address. It's all very simple.'

And, now in context, the chilling words:

'There's nothing to worry about.'

A new message popped up while Pip contemplated the llama drama.

'You must go Tuesday. The shipping company is being a bit silly about it. I don't want them to send them back!'

And then, God help her, Mummy had included a llama gif. The llama was wearing a hat. What fool had shown her how to do that?

Pip typed as fast as she could.

'Mummy! Phone me. We need to talk.'

Nothing, not even the blue ticks to show it had been read.

'I have a job. You said that you'd be back. NO LLAMAS.'

'MUMMY!'

'I'm not kidding.'

'*PHONE ME NOW.*'

Mummy had either turned off her phone or was ignoring Pip. This was typical of her mother. Toss in a hand grenade, making out as if it were nothing more perilous than a balloon, then run for cover, leaving chaos and carnage in her wake.

Pip let out a string of muffled expletives, leaving out enough consonants that she didn't alarm her elderly bus stop neighbour.

'Trouble?' he asked.

'My mother,' she said. 'An issue with llamas.'

'Ah,' he said, nodding. 'Llamas can be troublesome, but once you get to know them they make lovely companions. Had a few myself, back in the day. No space for them where I live now, though, or I'd get me one here.' At which, he pointed to the very block that Gordon was at that very moment exiting.

'You live in that house right there?' Pip asked, with as much casualness as she could muster.

'I do.'

'I'm sorry, I haven't introduced myself,' Pip said. 'Epiphany Bloom.'

'Pleased to meet you, Epiphany. What a fine name,' the man said. 'I'm Henry Powell.'

CHAPTER 22

'Henry Powell? You're Henrietta Powell's father?' Pip blurted out. The mad confluence of leads, clues and coincidences overwhelmed Pip's brain. How was it that she was sitting at a random bus stop in Notting Hill next to the father of her boss, whom she had never met?

'I am indeed. Do you know Henrietta?' he said, surprised.

'Yes. I mean, no. Well, I work for her actually, at the museum. But I'm new and I've never met her. When I started last week, she was abroad.'

'Well, fancy that. What a coincidence, you being here outside my house. Morocco, yes. She's still there, I believe. Back on Wednesday, assuming she doesn't take off on some other flight of fancy,' he said, his hand swooping through the air, indicating fancy in flight, presumably.

Pip's brain, meanwhile, was grinding its way through the facts, trying to draw the links. Gordon was the common denominator in all this. But why was he visiting Henry's house? And what was in that garment bag?

Henry seemed to read her mind. 'Henrietta lives here, too, in fact, when she's not off to some horse race or fashion show. I didn't need that big old house all to myself, so I divided it up. I live on the lower two floors – fewer stairs, you know – and she lives on the floor above, and my housekeeper is up on the top. Henrietta thinks it's so she can keep an eye on me and I think it's so I can keep an eye on her. Mrs Kemp knows that she's the one keeping an eye on both of us.' Henry gave a gruff laugh.

If Henrietta was still out of town, what could Gordon be doing here? Delivering the bag to Mrs Kemp, perhaps? But why? Could

Mrs Kemp have some gripe with the family, and be working with Gordon to steal the dress?

'That sounds a nice arrangement,' said Pip.

'It is. Nice garden out the back, too. Not enough room for llamas, though. Pity really.'

Pip laughed. 'Well there's certainly not enough room for llamas in *my* flat. And my lunatic mother seems to have shipped six of them to me from Ecuador.'

'Oh, do tell me more,' said Henry, seemingly delighted at this notion. 'Your mother does sound like a card.'

Why did people keep *saying* that?

Pip sighed and settled in to give Henry the short version of the story of how her mother had fallen for the ridiculous animals when she'd seen them at a petting zoo a few years back. 'Then when she and her… I suppose you'd call him her boyfriend… Well, they travelled to the Galapagos to see the blue-footed boobies. Life's dream, and so on. And Mummy decided to pick up a couple of llamas while she was there.'

Henry guffawed.

'I mean, why not?' Pip continued. 'Other people are buying those woolly hats with the earflaps, or perhaps a little faux Inca souvenir, or a nice fridge magnet… But why not buy six llamas! *Six! Llamas!*' Pip was raving now. Henry was wheezing with laughter.

'Well, as far as I'm concerned, go ahead,' Pip carried on. 'Buy exotic ungulates and ship them to England, no business of mine. Except – and if you knew Mummy this would surprise you *not one iota* – the llamas arrive not after she gets back as she promised, but, due to some mysterious incident with a boat, before!'

Henry by now was wiping the tears from his eyes. 'Ah, what a story,' he muttered. 'What a woman. I do like the sound of your mother.'

Pip took a deep breath and calmed down enough to say, 'Would you like to guess who is now landed with the problem of what to do with half a dozen llamas? Go on, Henry, take a flyer, who?'

Pip explained to Henry – who had now stopped laughing, and was suitably sympathetic – that the llamas had arrived in England and were somewhere in some sort of quarantine facility, or holding cells, or llama refugee camp, or whatever – Pip hadn't had time to look at her mother's email with the paperwork. 'And she needs me to go and sort it out. Tomorrow. I work, you know. It's a new job. I have projects to take care of. And now I have to spend half the day tracking down six llamas through the Port of London Authority and doing lord knows what with them.' She actually felt quite tearful at the thought.

'Let me take care of it,' Henry said, giving her a consoling pat on the shoulder. 'I don't have much to do. Retired, you know. I need a project. You seem like a lovely girl, and almost part of the family, if you work at the museum. And I do like llamas, funny little buggers. I'm sure I can sort it out. I know some of the London llama people.'

'There are London llama people?' Pip asked weakly.

'Oh yes, you'd be surprised. There's a llama sanctuary. A llama fanciers society.'

Pip did not know what to say to that, so she just nodded, rather miserably. She would rather not be having any llama conversations at all.

'And as for the permits and so on, that shouldn't be a problem. I did a lot of exports when I was in business. Plumbing items, that sort of thing. I'll have a chat with the people at the ports, see what I can do on that side of things. You forward that email to me and I'll take care of it.'

'Would you really? Do you think you could?' she asked.

'It would be my pleasure,' he said gallantly.

Pip opened her phone and found the email, which she forwarded to the address Henry gave her, adding her contact details at the top.

A bus came into view.

'Here's the number seven, Henry,' she said. 'Isn't that your ride?'

'I don't think I need an outing this afternoon. It's been such a good chat, and I've got the llama situation to get working on. I think I'll just go home for tea. Fancy a cup?'

'Thanks, but not today. I think I'd better get going,' said Pip, distractedly, her full attention now on Gordon, who was leaving Henry's house, no bag over his shoulder this time. She had absolutely no idea what that man was up to. But one thing was clear. He'd left the bag in Henry's house.

'Actually, you know what, Henry? I think I would like a cup of tea.'

Henry led the way through a wide entrance hall, with stairs up to what Pip now knew was Henrietta's pad. Hanging on the stair railing was the black garment bag, and – Pip's heart beat a little faster – perhaps the red dress. Perhaps Mrs Kemp would soon be down to hide her stolen bounty, and cause havoc in the Powell family.

'I do wish people wouldn't leave things lying around,' Henry said tetchily. 'It doesn't seem too much trouble to take Henrietta's things up one flight of stairs, does it?'

'No trouble at all. In fact, let me do it,' Pip offered, seizing her chance. 'You put the kettle on and I'll run up with it'.

'Would you? Thank you. She doesn't lock the door to her apartment, seeing as it's just us in the building, so you can just pop it in inside. I will reward you with my famous homemade shortbread.'

Pip couldn't believe her luck. She grabbed the bag, feeling the weight of it, the clothing inside slipping around. Definitely heavy enough to be the dress. Trying not to run, she ascended the staircase and opened Henrietta's flat. She took a split second to note, with envy, its generous proportions and wide windows overlooking the back garden. But now was no time to be looking at the décor. Now was the time for solving mysteries. Now was the moment that she would find the dress.

Pip laid the bag down on the sofa, pulled down the zip a little and reached in. Her hand touched a slippery softness, and she caught a glimpse of red. Epiphany Bloom – finder of lost boys *and* lost dresses. Really, it was easy when you put your mind to it. She pulled the zip the rest of the way.

She paused for a moment. Was that footsteps on the stairs? Had Mrs Kemp realised that the dress wasn't waiting for her on the banister? Had she come looking? There was a creak as the door pushed open, and Pip dropped the bag, trying hard to look innocent. A small black cat wound its way around the door, purring loudly, and looked at Pip as if she might be a sardine. Pip let out the breath she'd been holding, and opened the bag.

Her heart sank. Inside were two silk dresses and a bright red jacket. One dress was a silver sheath of an evening gown, the other a yellow day dress, printed with feathers in gold and brown, with an enormous skirt. No red dresses. Just the blasted jacket, with its dry-cleaning tag boldly on display, mocking Pip.

Another dead end.

CHAPTER 23

When Pip arrived at the museum the next morning, her co-workers were gathered in the kitchen. Gordon, Emily and Arabella didn't seem particularly eager to get a start on their work. They were at the table, a steaming mug in front of each of them. Even Arabella, who usually claimed to be too busy to drink tea.

'Hi, Pip. Emily made banana bread,' said Arabella. 'Help yourself.'

Pip made herself a cup of tea, and took a piece of banana bread. It seemed this was the first time they had all sat down together this week, as they were talking about the weekend, despite it being Tuesday. Bloody people, they'd probably talk about it all week. She tried letting their chatter wash over her. Emily had spent the weekend spring-cleaning her bedroom and her wardrobe, using the philosophy of Marie Kondo.

'If an item isn't useful and it doesn't spark joy, you're supposed to thank it for its service and let it go,' Emily explained, to a snort from Gordon.

'You should be out partying at your age, not examining your sock drawer for sparks of joy,' he said.

'You can laugh, but I feel an incredible lightness in my being,' Emily said. 'It's *amazing*.'

Pip feigned great interest in selecting her preferred slice of banana bread from the plate Arabella had put in the middle of the table.

'Anyway, what did *you* do on the weekend? Were you out partying?' Emily asked Gordon, bringing Pip back to the present.

Pip snapped to attention. What would Gordon say about his night out on the town with @VintageMinx? And would he mention his visit to Henrietta's house yesterday?

'Nothing much. Went out for some music on Saturday night, that was nice.'

'Where did you go?'

'Oh just a local place, nothing special.'

Pip knew this to be a lie, but why would Gordon lie about where he'd been? The only reason she could think of was that the Razmajazz was a fancy expensive joint, and the others might wonder where he'd got the money to go to a place like that. A fair question, as far as Pip was concerned.

'So did you have a hot date, then?' asked Emily, with a studied offhandedness that made Pip wonder if she did in fact fancy Gordon, despite what he thought.

'My sister, Victoria,' he said with a laugh.

Wait. What? His sister, did he say? Pip tried to process this, while listening to the next revelation.

'And Sunday was a bit of a write-off. Henrietta texted me and asked me to do some errands for her. She's coming back tomorrow, wants a few things sorted before she gets in.'

'I wonder why she asked you,' Emily said, trying to sound casual, but coming off as affronted. 'She usually asks me to help her with her personal matters.'

'Maybe she knew you were busy tidying your sock drawer,' Gordon said, teasingly. 'Didn't want to disturb you. She asks me sometimes. It doesn't mean anything. Anyway, it wasn't much, just fetching some dry cleaning, dropping it off at her house. You didn't miss anything.'

'So she's back tomorrow,' Arabella said, with a quick glance at Pip. 'So soon. I guess that means we'll see her in the afternoon. Or Thursday.'

'I'm looking forward to meeting her,' Pip said.

'She's amazing,' said Emily. 'You'll love her.'

Pip drained her tea mug, rinsed it, wiped up the stray crumbs of banana bread, then headed for the office. She needed to think. She needed peace.

But peace was not forthcoming. First a voice message from Rosanne, who was as good as her word – *quick-quick!*

'I have sourced the perfect item. Glorious! Early 90s. Iconic dress. Iconic actress. Very pretty, shall I say,' and she gave Pip the address of her office and an invitation to meet at two.

Was this it? Had Rosanne found the dress? Pip felt a prickle of excitement run up and down her spine. It was like that time in the Amazon. The ants… She refused to think about it.

Before she could call Rosanne back to confirm the meeting, her phone rang. It was Henry, with good news.

'I've located the llamas,' he said, all proud and chipper. 'They are safely ashore, no need to worry for their welfare.'

'Thank you, Henry, that's a relief,' said Pip, feeling rather guilty that in all her grumpiness with her mother, she'd never been at all concerned for the llamas' welfare.

'The llama people have arranged temporary shelter, and I've sent over some funds for special llama feed to tide them over. British hay isn't optimum for their guts, you know.'

'I did not know that, but thank you.'

'Gas. No one likes a gassy llama.'

'I imagine not. You are a star, Henry, thank you,' said Pip. She really was deeply grateful. It was so nice to have someone just take a problem off her hands and deal with it. As opposed to, you know, phoning from South America and dumping llama dramas on her during working hours. 'I'll pay you back for all this as soon as Mummy is back,' promised Pip.

'Absolutely no need, dear girl,' said Henry. 'Haven't had so much fun in years.'

Things were really shaping up. She had a lead on the dress. The llama drama was sorted… And here came Arabella to spoil her good mood, pacing up and down, pale-faced and shaky.

'Tomorrow!' she said to Pip. 'Did you hear that? Henrietta will be back tomorrow! You need to get that dress back. What have you found out? Where is it?'

'Arabella, please calm down. I'm making progress.'

'What? What progress? It's been over a week!'

Pip noted that Arabella seemed to have forgotten that she was the one who had created the problem and had, in fact, speedily gone from gratitude that Pip was helping her out, to this being Pip's problem and something at which she was failing. But it certainly was looking less likely that Arabella had anything to do with the theft, given her clear distress.

'While the theft might have been an inside job,' Pip explained, 'I've discovered that there is a criminal underground of thieves specialising in valuable items of clothing: high-end vintage stuff and famous and iconic pieces. I suspect someone like this might be behind the theft, and whoever was on the inside was just a pawn.' She wasn't quite ready to tell Arabella that she was onto Gordon, and possibly Arabella herself.

'Oh, my. That sounds serious.'

'It is. But I've got it under control. I've made contact with a dealer, and we're meeting today.'

'Really?' Arabella had gone from anxious and accusatory, to pathetically grateful. 'Do you think…?'

'Yes,' said Pip. 'I do. I think I've found the dress.'

CHAPTER 24

The dry cleaning had been a disappointment, no question, but Pip refused to be downhearted. She had high hopes for her meeting with Rosanne. Except that Rosanne wasn't at her office when Pip arrived.

'I'm sure she'll be in shortly,' said the receptionist who let her in. 'She said she'd be back at one thirty. I'll see where she is. Would you like to wait?'

They both surveyed the reception area, which was tiny, its only furniture a little table with a kettle and tea things, and a sofa, which was piled with hangers and clothes in clear bags.

'Bit of a mess in here, I'm afraid,' the receptionist mumbled. 'Rosanne has been doing some sorting… A big order…'

Pip shifted the pile along a bit and perched on the sofa. 'No problem, I'm fine here.'

The receptionist was looking at an appointment book that was lying on the desk. 'Let's see. Here we are, Tuesday. So you must be Epi… what does that say? Such terrible handwriting, Rosanne. It looks like Epiphany, but that can't be right…' She angled the book towards Pip, and sure enough there was Pip's name, along with her phone number.

'Epiphany, yes, that's my name. Me. Two p.m.'

The receptionist looked surprised but recovered quickly, moving gamely on. 'I'm Frances; pleased to meet you. Ah yes, I see she had a breakfast with someone. What does this say? Starts with an A, but honestly, she writes like a deranged hornet. Anyhow, doesn't matter. Then she had an appointment at twelve.' She tapped her red-lacquered fingernail against the page, where Rosanne had written in green, in handwriting that looked as illegible as that of a medical school graduate.

'Don't know who Ed R is, but she's sure to be in any moment. Must have been waylaid. London traffic. I'll give her a call, make sure she hasn't forgotten.'

Frances tapped through to Rosanne's contact details on her mobile, and pressed call. She held it to her ear. Pip listened as the faint ringing sound went on and on.

'No answer,' Frances said, apologetically.

'Not to worry, I'll wait.' No way was Pip leaving without seeing Rosanne.

Ten minutes of awkward silence later, during which both women tried to look busy, there was a knock on the door. Pip looked up from her phone to see two policemen standing outside the glass office door, their caps in their hands. Pip knew from the incident with the rattlesnake – which really could have happened to anyone – that policemen only hold their caps in their hands when there was bad news. But what possible bad news could they be delivering to a fashion collector?

Frances threw Pip a look, as if to ask her if she knew what this could be about, and Pip shrugged.

'This doesn't look good,' whispered Frances. There had been a shift in the room: the two women were suddenly connected in the face of this strange development.

'I think we'd better answer, and see what it is,' said Pip, in what she hoped was a reassuring voice.

Frances let the police officers in. 'Can I help you?' she asked.

'We're looking for any relatives or colleagues of Rosanne Roberts,' said the older of the pair, stroking his generous moustache.

'I'm her secretary,' said Frances. 'She doesn't have any close family. Is everything okay? Is Rosanne in some trouble?'

'I'm afraid I have some rather bad news,' said Constable Moustache. 'Would you like to take a seat?'

He indicated the sofa where Pip was waiting, and only then seemed to register her presence. 'And you are?'

'I'm waiting to see Rosanne,' said Pip. 'We have an appointment.' But she already knew that whatever the police were going to say, the appointment wasn't happening.

Frances sat down next to Pip and took her hand as if they were old friends, not recent acquaintances. 'What is it?' she asked the officers. 'What's happened to Rosanne?'

'I'm afraid that her body has been found in the Thames. Our working assumption is that she jumped. Off the bridge just up the road there.' The policeman indicated vaguely out the window.

'Jumped?' said Frances. 'Into the river?'

'Yes,' said the younger policeman. 'No suspicious circumstances.'

'As in...?' said Pip.

'Suicide. Yes. I'm afraid so.'

'Suicide?' echoed Frances. 'Surely not? Rosanne has... had... a zest for life. She'd never kill herself. Never.'

'It's often the most unexpected people, hiding their troubles,' said the younger policeman.

'I realise this is a terrible shock,' Constable Moustache put in kindly. 'Perhaps you should have a cup of tea.'

Pip spoke up. 'It's a rather low bridge, that one, isn't it?' she asked. 'If a person was going to commit suicide...'

'Not thinking straight, I suppose.'

'And into water. I mean, you'd swim, wouldn't you? Even if you were trying to drown, instinct takes over.'

'Maybe she couldn't swim?' said the younger policeman, sadly. 'Not everyone can. My sister, bless her, has never got the hang of it.'

'Of course she could swim,' snapped Frances. 'She went swimming every Thursday.' She turned to Pip. 'What are you saying? Do you think someone pushed her?'

'No, no,' said Pip quickly. 'Why would anyone do that? No, I'm sure these fine officers are right. It just doesn't make sense.'

'Does she have an appointment diary, perhaps?' asked the older policeman.

'She does… Did,' said Frances. 'Here.'

She got up and gave them the diary. 'She had breakfast with someone whose name started with an A, but I can't read it. And then an appointment with a chap called Ed, and I don't know who that is. And now, here's Epiphany, waiting.'

'Indeed?' said the younger policeman. 'Epiphany.' He sounded unsure as to whether this was her name or if she was, in fact, an actual epiphany. 'Can we take this with us?'

'We'll be on our way then,' said Constable Moustache, giving the end of said facial hair a tug. 'Our condolences, again.'

The two women watched the officers leave, and then Frances burst into tears. 'I can't believe this,' she said. 'I can't!'

'I'll make that tea,' said Pip.

Pip stirred sugar into the tea, thinking how awful it all was. The poor woman had been found dead in the river not a mile from where Pip was sitting, on a bridge that Pip herself walked across most days on her way to work.

She handed the mug to Frances. 'Here, drink this. I wonder if Rosanne went to that breakfast? And her previous appointment. Whoever they were, they might be able to tell us what sort of state she was in? Ed, and the person beginning with an A.'

'But I have no idea who they are!' wailed Frances. 'Rosanne had so many friends and colleagues in the business. They could be anyone.'

Pip racked her brain for a solution, but none was forthcoming. She could hardly ask about the stolen dress under the circumstances, so she left Frances to her tea, murmuring her condolences as she went.

Pip had only met Rosanne once, but still... Suicide. It was a terrible shock. Based on her brief interaction with the woman, Pip had to agree with Frances. Rosanne had seemed cheerful and lively and full of plans. She'd been so enthusiastic about Pip's non-existent client and their next meeting. Not at all like someone who would kill herself. Awful, to think she had been struggling beneath that vibrant exterior. Still, to jump off a bridge. What a thing to do. Pip imagined the moment: the lean forward, the feet leaving the ledge, the taking flight. And then the cold and greasy Thames.

But there was something that didn't make sense, no matter how she looked at it. Apart from anything else, Pip simply couldn't believe Rosanne would pick a method of dying that would be guaranteed to ruin her beautiful clothes.

That settled it. She just didn't believe that Rosanne had jumped.

CHAPTER 25

As Pip trudged miserably back to work, a chilly breeze started up, blowing at her skirt, tossing grit into her eyes. She passed the bridge, noting a small knot of people there – a policewoman, a couple of people in plain clothes, but looking official. There was an ambulance parked nearby. Poor Rosanne.

Pip walked into the museum like a zombie. She thought about calling Marlene with the news, but before she could, Madison Price phoned for a chat. Ordinarily, Pip would have got a little thrill from seeing Madison's name pop up – she'd never quite come to terms with the fact that she was sort-of-friends with a well-known American actress – but she was too down to take pleasure in that. In fact, she considered not taking the call, but a sense of guilt overruled her. 'Where are you?' Madison asked, as soon as Pip answered. 'Come by the house. Or let's meet for drinks.'

Hard as it was to imagine, Madison seemed a bit bored and lonely. Weird, you never thought of famous people as being bored and lonely. But she was new to London and didn't know a lot of people, and she often phoned Pip for chats without a care for working hours.

Pip explained about the job and the museum.

'A job. How charming! And in a museum. How marvellous, I adore vintage clothes,' said Madison, in an odd nasal drawl. Clearly she was still practising her English accent for her upcoming role as a young Agatha Christie. 'I want to see it. I'll come to you tomorrow, then. You can give me a tour.'

Another thing about famous people, Pip was discovering, was that they assumed you were available to them 24/7, and that if you did happen to have some other minor activity planned – like earning a living, or some other such trifling nonsense – you would drop it in favour of whatever it was they wanted you to do. Which, inevitably, you did.

'Tomorrow's fine,' said Pip, distracted by her more pressing troubles. 'I'll send you the address. Come at 12.30, I'll show you around in my lunch hour.'

Arabella wasn't anywhere to be found in the museum, so Pip didn't bother trying to fake working. Or even looking for the dress. She kept coming back to the problem of how a grown woman would land up dead in the Thames if she could swim. It was like a wasp that wouldn't go away, like that time in the Serengeti. Pip knew what she needed to do. She needed the comfort of Flis.

As Pip emerged from the Tube station, heading for supper at Flis's house, her phone pinged with the arrival of a message. Despite her bleak mood, she gave an involuntary snort of laughter when she saw the picture on her screen – it was a selfie of Henry with a llama, his face wrinkled into a big smile and his hair all mussed up in the wind, tucked in next to the animal, ridiculous with its narrow nose, its eyes almost on the sides of its head, and those silly long ears.

'Henry, you're a marvel!' Pip exclaimed to herself, causing a newspaper seller to edge away.

She put in her earbuds and called Henry as she walked.

'Great picture, Henry, thank you!'

'Your mother certainly can pick her livestock,' Henry said. 'Fine quality beasts, she's imported. Excellent.'

'Well, I'm pleased they're okay, thank you,' said Pip, who really didn't care if they had five legs each as long as she didn't have to deal with them. 'I didn't know you were actually going to visit the llamas in person. That's very good of you.'

'Oh, yes. If I do something, I do it properly,' Henry said. 'I saw them all settled in at their temporary accommodations at The Llama Haven. Very interesting place. They have alpacas too, of course. And a camel. A few other odds and ends. I looked around a bit and then took the director of the establishment out for a thank-you lunch. A very good day all round, I can tell you.'

'Well I'm pleased,' Pip said. 'And grateful.'

'Never retire, Epiphany, that's my advice.'

'No danger of that for a while, Henry,' said Pip, who had seldom kept a job more than six months, and was ever mindful of the need for a rent cheque.

'Everyone said it would be wonderful, retirement, but when you're on your own, it's not much fun. I never thought Charise would go before me. I was older by a decade. Light of my life, that woman. So bright, she lit up everything.' Henry was settling in for a chat. 'And I loved the business. Oh, I know people snigger that I made my money in the loo, but I tell you, it was a grand life. My father invented a thing that worked better than the thing before it, and it was an honour to represent it around the world. I miss those days.'

'I'm sorry, Henry. Henrietta will be home soon, though. She'll have tales from Morocco, I'm sure.'

'Yes, well, it will be nice to have her back. She's very busy, though, is Henrietta. It's not as if she's playing gin rummy with her old dad. She's at the museum all day, running the shows and things. That takes up a lot of her time.'

That didn't line up with what Arabella said, Pip thought, which was that Henrietta popped in to the museum once or twice a week at most. Presumably, she spent the rest of her time shopping, or lunching, or doing Pilates, or whatever it was that heiress socialites did with their time.

'Anyway, I'm sure she'll pop down to your flat and say hello,' said Pip, in what she hoped was a reassuring tone.

Pip had arrived at Flis's front door. She was momentarily confused to find it egg-yolk yellow, rather than the grey-green it had been just a week ago. But it was definitely the right place – the dreamcatcher in the upstairs window, the turmeric plants in the pots by the door.

'Henry, I've got to go; I've arrived at my sister's house for supper. Tell you what, I've got something to sort out this week, but how about we get together next week? We can go and see the llamas, and this time, I'll take *you* for a thank-you lunch. Maybe we can even play rummy.'

Henry said goodbye and Pip hung up, then rang Flis's doorbell. As usual, minutes went by while no one answered the door, and then Flis appeared, looking flustered.

'The yellow's nice,' Pip said, by way of greeting.

'What?'

'The door, the new colour. It's very cheering.'

'Oh it is, isn't it? I thought we could all use more vitamin D, so I went for that bright sunny colour.'

Pip felt fairly certain that door paint was not how Vitamin D was distributed, but she knew better than to enter into a discussion on this. 'Well it looks good,' she said.

'You, on the other hand, look rather frazzled,' said Flis.

'Long day. And something sad. A woman I vaguely know died.'

'Oh Pip, I'm so sorry...'

'She wasn't a friend; someone I knew from work. A woman who was helping me track down the stolen dress.'

'Still, that's awful,' said Flis as she led Pip into the kitchen, which smelled like bonfire night. 'I burned the aubergines,' she added, waving her hand through the smoke. 'Mummy phoned and I forgot them under the grill.'

'Typical. She sows destruction and misery wherever she goes.'

'Yes, well, she's all in a state. Apparently old GeeCee isn't coming home with her. He's fallen in love with the place and is going to stay and look at those blue boobies forever.'

'I'm not even going to respond to that.'

'What do you mean? Anyway, that's why she was delayed. He wouldn't get off the boat, apparently. Poor Mummy. And she said to tell you thank you for sorting out the llamas,' said Flis. Pip rolled her eyes and said nothing. Flis continued, 'She said she didn't want to phone you herself because you always get your knickers in a knot and she thought she'd give you time to calm down. I probably wasn't supposed to tell you that part,' she said. 'Oh well, I never was very good at keeping confederancies.'

'Or vocabularies,' said Pip. 'And by the way, she told me she didn't phone you about the llamas because you always are funny about things. I probably wasn't supposed to tell you that, either. Shall we have wine?'

Flis fiddled about opening and closing drawers and cupboards for a corkscrew and glasses. You wouldn't think it was her kitchen. Finally, she presented Pip with a much-needed glass of chardonnay.

'So, tell me about your friend who died.'

'Not a friend, Flis. She is – was – a specialist dealer in rare clothing and collectibles. She thought she could find the red dress. In fact, she might have, she was about to tell me. She had a few appointments that morning, and then she was going to see me but…'

'She died.'

'Yes.'

'Cancer?'

'No. Suicide, the police said. But I don't know, Flis. Can a person really commit suicide by jumping off a bridge into the Thames?'

'Well, there are always people jumping off the Golden Arches.'

'People kill themselves jumping off McDonalds? Really?' Pip tried to picture it.

'Don't be ridiculous, Pip. That bridge in Sydney. The big one.'

Pip thought. 'The Golden Gate bridge. In San Francisco.'

'Exactly. People are always offing themselves there.'

'But this is different,' said Pip. 'It was a smaller bridge. And by all accounts, she was a happy woman. I don't know, it doesn't make sense.'

'So, do you think she was murdered?' Flis dropped her voice, as if the murderer might be in the next room.

'No, because who would murder a fashion collector?' said Pip. 'It's hardly like she was a mafia kingpin or something.'

'You're right,' said Flis. 'Fashion isn't a crime. Unless it's a crime of fashion, of course.'

Both sisters chortled, despite themselves. Flis was right, though, thought Pip. Fashion didn't naturally connect with murder or crime. Only, the dress *had* been stolen. And that was a crime. But murder? Could the two things be linked?

'And the people that she saw before you?' asked Flis. 'Any idea who they were?'

'There was a breakfast with someone whose name starts with an A,' said Pip. 'I mean, that could be anyone. And then a meeting with someone called Ed R – which we don't know whether she attended or not.'

'Unless A and Ed R did something together?' suggested Flis.

'But how will we ever know?' said Pip. 'I don't even know where to start with the Ed clue, let alone someone whose name begins with A. It could be anyone.'

CHAPTER 26

Arabella had reminded Pip that today was the day she might finally meet Henrietta, so Pip took a bit of trouble with her outfit, opting for well-fitted charcoal trousers and a green silk shirt with a thin tie that she knotted in a loose bow. She was eternally grateful that she'd updated her wardrobe at the start of that ill-fated job in Singapore. She'd lost the job, naturally – honestly, it was quite unfair, that currency muddle could have happened to anyone, surely it was a major flaw for so many countries to have dollars? – but at least she'd gained a collection of rather glam work clothes to see her through a couple of years.

At the museum, Arabella was desperately trying to look busy and Emily was all a-twitter, like a young maiden awaiting her beau. She was dressed in a maelstrom of boho-vintage-chic, with hanging bits and floating bits and accessories and lord knew what.

'Great outfit,' Pip said. 'You look amazing.'

'Really? You like it?' Emily said, pleased.

'I could never put together an outfit like that. You've got a good eye for it,' said Pip. Both statements were true. As Pip's foray into layered dressing for the engagement party had proved, Pip could only deal with one or two items of clothing at a time. And Emily did seem to have a remarkable ability to put things together – even if there were rather too many things for Pip's taste.

'Arabella thinks Henrietta might be in around lunchtime,' Emily said. 'You must be very excited to meet her.'

Emily certainly had a crush – you'd think Timothée Chalamet was coming over.

'I'm looking forward to it. Shall we go over our ideas for the exhibition?' said Pip. 'Henrietta might want to hear about them.'

'Yes! I was just going through what we've got so far so that we can tell her about our plans,' said Emily. She had started to spread out the pictures that she and Pip had found and printed out – reference photos of the great bands and singers of the era, movie posters, iconic photographs. They had compiled a list of the most popular movies and one of bands and musicians. Then there were the photos of the clothes that Marlene had found. The idea was to decide which personalities to feature, and then try and match up the items they had or could source with the looks they were going for.

Pip, still feeling fragile after yesterday's terrible news, her complete absence of leads, and two large glasses of wine at Flis's plus a smaller one at home, could not bear the thought of listening to Emily's gushing all morning. 'I've got an idea,' she said. 'Why don't we go and see what there is in the storeroom. We can start photographing the pieces we like, and seeing what we can match to our themes.'

'We should do that now,' Emily said, chattering on excitedly. 'That's what the boss likes to see. Initiative. I'll go and get the key from Philip.' She dashed off to find the security guard, and came back a few moments later, jangling a bunch of keys. 'Let's go,' she said, leading Pip past the kitchen to the basement door. She unlocked and opened it, revealing a flight of stairs heading down into the darkness. 'Hang on a mo,' she said, feeling the wall for a light switch. 'Ah. Here we go.'

The stair lights came on, and down the steep steps she and Pip went. A musty smell of old clothes and dust, laced with cleaning fluids and naphthalene, floated up to meet them. It reminded Pip of her days in the school drama club, and that strange storage space under the stage where they'd kept props and where she used to go to with her friends to practise kissing – sucking at the bit of her hand between the thumb and forefinger, pretending that the dishy Daniel Grey, opening batsman for the first team, was the enthusiastic recipient. In later years, they'd gone there to smoke. Mummy had not been pleased at Pip's suspension, but really it was just bad luck; anyone could have set fire to the stage curtains.

When they reached the bottom, Emily turned on another light, illuminating a huge area filled with hanging space and chests and cabinets. The storeroom was a lot better organised than the school prop room. Emily explained to Pip that the clothes were arranged broadly by decade, with various subdivisions within that – particular subcultures and so on. The general store was open for them to look through, but particularly valuable or special items were locked in a separate secure room at the far end. There was also a bank of cupboards, at which Emily pointed and said, 'Henrietta's private collection,' in hushed tones.

'We can get to them if we need to, but we've got plenty to get on with here for now,' she added.

They headed for the seventies. Emily found a clothes rail, and they looked and discussed and sorted and hung up their top picks, until a voice made them both look up:

'So, what is going on down here?'

Poised dramatically at the top of the stairs, the light catching her from below, was a willowy blonde.

'Henrietta! You're back!' exclaimed Emily in delight. 'Are you exhausted from all the travelling? Do you want to sit down? Can I get you a cup of tea?'

You'd have thought the woman had been away at the Russian front for a year, rather than in Morocco for a couple of weeks of sun and socialite-ing, thought Pip.

'How kind. I went for a quick massage and popped by the hairdresser, so I'm feeling almost human,' Henrietta said.

Emily murmured her relief at Henrietta's resilience.

Turning to Pip, Henrietta now said, 'You must be Arabella's new hire. What's your name again? Epitaph, is it?'

'Epiphany. Pleased to meet you. I've heard so much—'

'Epiphany, of course. Extraordinary name. Daddy says he met you at the bus stop. What a strange coincidence. I don't use the bus, so I suppose I wouldn't know. Maybe people are always meeting up at the bus stop. Anyway, he had a lot of gushy things to say about you and your alpacas.'

'Llamas, and they're not actually mine. They're...'

Henrietta had already lost interest in Pip and was surveying the room, taking in the open cupboards and the clothes Pip and Emily had selected and hung on the rails.

'Let's go upstairs,' she said suddenly, and rather decisively. 'And you can tell me what you've been up to.'

'We can show you,' said Emily eagerly. 'This rail is for clothes for the music side of things, and this one's for films. For the exhibition, you know. We were waiting for you before we decided exactly which ones to focus on. I'm sure you'll have input.'

'Yes,' Henrietta said vaguely. 'Of course. Maybe you can send me a list to start with. Shall we go up to the office?'

'Of course, I'll send you the list, and the reference pictures we researched. Pip's got a good contact, and she's found some items that we might want to add to the collection.'

'Who would your source be?' Henrietta lost her air of distraction or perhaps boredom, looking at Pip with renewed interest.

'Marlene Tanaka. I believe you know her,' said Pip. She decided to say nothing about poor dead Rosanne, who she had, after all, only contacted in relation to the missing dress.

'I know her, of course. Did she have anything for us?'

'The seventies and eighties are having a bit of a revival. It's a seller's market, apparently. There's a lot of interest from collectors, and not much stock of the really good stuff. And what there is, is priced quite high, especially the movie pieces,' said Pip, paraphrasing the conversations she'd had over the last few days. 'But, you know, we are working the channels. We'll find some gems, I'm sure.'

Henrietta seemed to loosen, finally. She smiled a beaming smile at the two women. 'Well, it looks like you've both got off to a good start. I'm so excited for the show. Now let's get out of the basement and go through your reference pictures, shall we?'

As they exited the basement, all three of their phones vibrated with the joy of signal returned. Pip had a message from Madison Price – '*See you at 12.30*' – with a smiley face emoji. She'd forgotten all about the arranged lunchtime meet. It was now 12.28, and Pip's newly returned boss was expecting her in a meeting. This was going to be awkward – what should she do? Looking up from the phone, Pip spotted Madison herself entering the museum, accompanied – quite to Pip's surprise – by Matty.

'Pip, darling!' Madison called as she swept through the door.

Henrietta and Emily both stopped dead in their tracks, their phones in hand, their mouths agape. They would both know Madison as Dr Miranda Ray from the TV series *Ray's Hospital Files*. The series had been a perennial favourite, worldwide. And even without the fame factor, Madison was a truly astonishing sight. Pip was still struck every time she saw her by just how luminous she was, how shiny and golden, how tiny and trim; how she channelled old Hollywood glamour alongside a kind of LA cool. Matty was her lanky, boyish double, with his sweep of golden fringe.

'Hello, Pip,' Matty said, giving her a hug, before turning to each of the other women and saying politely, 'Good morning, ma'am.'

Henrietta and Emily had closed their mouths, but still seemed rooted to the spot.

'I invited a friend to meet me for lunch…' Pip started, awkwardly. 'I was going to show her around the museum. In my lunch hour, not in working hours. Maybe I can do that first, and then we can meet later to talk about things. If that's OK?'

'But of course!' Henrietta said, waving her hand to indicate her complete acceptance of all and any suggestions Pip might make. She turned to Madison. 'You are very welcome. I'm Henrietta Powell, the director of the museum. I do hope you enjoy our little collection.'

'Madison Price.' Madison offered her hand. 'I'm sure I shall. I do adore clothes. I have too many, I'm ashamed to say.' She gave Henrietta a charmingly guilty, bashful look. 'And as an actor, I love wardrobe; I'm excited to see what you have here from the movies.'

'Well, we're still building up that side of things; that's what Epiphany is going to be helping us with.'

Madison slipped her arm through Pip's. 'Oh you are in good hands,' she said to Henrietta. 'This woman is a marvel.'

'You sure are, Pip,' said Matty.

It was like some girlhood fantasy, or a very nice dream, of having the coolest girl in the class pick you as bestie and show up all the haters. In Pip's case, it was having a famous celebrity compliment her in front of her new boss, who stood there nodding and grinning at the two of them like a loon. Emily appeared to have been struck dumb.

Arabella came out of her office, drawn by the commotion.

Henrietta turned to Madison. 'So, how do you two know each other?'

Pip cut her off – she didn't want Henrietta to get wind of her sleuthing history until she'd found the dress. 'We'd better get a move on; Madison has a lot to do.'

'Of course, you go along. Can I offer you a water or something perhaps, Ms Price? Send someone for a latte? Arabella could go…' said Henrietta, indicating Arabella rather dismissively.

Madison demurred, graciously.

'Well, enjoy your tour!' Henrietta said. 'Pip, we can catch up later. Any time. When you're ready. Or tomorrow. Take your time.'

'Epiphany. That red dress!' Madison exclaimed, as she turned towards the display area. She stopped, posing dramatically, finger pointing to the dress, her other hand to her forehead. 'Don't tell me that's the *Pretty Woman* dress, the one dear Jules wore. Is it?'

'The very one,' Pip said, her eyes meeting Arabella's.

CHAPTER 27

Pip could always tell when Tim had been home a while, because the cats did not greet her with manic mewling when she opened the door. They were starved for neither food nor attention. If Tim was out when she came back, however, the cats were always mad with delight or hunger – hard to tell really, with both cats and tigers, as she had learned the hard way.

'Hi, Tim,' she called. 'I'm home.'

A muffled greeting came from his room.

Pip dropped her bag down on the kitchen table with a sigh. She was happy to be home. It had been an exhausting day. It struck her that she'd gone from no job (repeatedly), to two. She was doing her 'official' job at the museum, and simultaneously trying to find the dress in secret, on the side. She really wanted to excel at both of them, and she felt reasonably confident that her run of bad luck on the work front was coming to an end.

It helped that Emily was actually pretty switched on, and so eager to please that she worked hard on the 'job' part of the job. As for the missing dress, well: Pip was no longer confident on that front. She'd hardly had time to process Rosanne's death and formulate a new plan.

She put the kettle on. She'd been too busy even for tea, today. Madison had stayed for ages, inspecting the exhibits. She'd been enchanted by the whole thing. 'It's so charming, so quaint, so *English*,' she'd said. Whatever that meant. Probably that there wasn't a rollercoaster attached to it, or virtual reality glasses, or a souvenir store. Even Matty had enjoyed it, pronouncing various exhibits 'cool' or 'dope' or 'sick' on occasion – all complimentary adjectives, strange to say – and then wandering off down the road at some point to get a kebab.

Pip made tea in her ridiculous emergency mug. It was big enough to bathe a baby in and was only pressed into service in direst need. She added a slosh of milk and a half teaspoon of sugar, then sucked the top layer of sweet tea into her mouth. That was better.

She checked on the cats, who were calmly snuggled in their bed. Most lifted her head for a scratch, while the little ones nuzzled and suckled. It made Pip so happy, seeing their sweet little bodies all lined up, snuggled into dear three-legged Most, who she had saved from certain death. Which had cost her that job at the vet's. Totally worth it.

Tim came through, rubbing his hands over his face, in the way that he did when he'd put in too many hours in front of the computer screen.

'Long day?' Pip asked.

'Very. You?'

'Yup. And yesterday I heard that someone I know a little bit has died.'

'Oh wow, Pip. That's awful.'

'It is.'

Tim poured himself a glass of orange juice and the two of them slumped into seats at the table.

'How's your investigation going?' Tim asked, taking a sip of the juice.

'Okay,' Pip said. 'I've done a lot of leg work, got a lot of info, bits and pieces of information and conjecture, but nothing seems to fit. I'm not at all sure. Rosanne was my key, and now she's gone. I'm going to try and get my head around it tonight. Go through my notes. Decide what to do next.'

Her plan for the evening was to work through everything she had found out, and try and put it into some sort of order. When she had been working on the Matty Price case, she had made one of those walls you saw on detective shows, linking suspects and victims and clues with bits of string. Maybe she needed to do something similar this time – lay out everything she had, and see what fitted where.

'Would it help to talk about it?' Tim asked. 'There is literally nothing to watch on Netflix. I reckon hearing about your theories and suspects would be more interesting than rewatching *Mad Men*.'

Sometimes Pip couldn't believe how perfect Tim was. 'You sure? You'd do that?'

'It would be fun. Tell you what, you go and relax and I'll make us a couple of toasties.'

While he clattered about at the work surface, Pip got her notebook out of her bag and moved to the sofa. Was there any more delicious smell in the whole world than melting cheese? Pip doubted it. Maybe the soft neck of a puppy. But there were no puppies to sniff, and Tim was soon coming out of the kitchen bearing a plate of buttery toasted cheese sandwiches. Pip's tummy growled at the sight and smell as she lifted hers to her mouth.

'Ow, ho!' She breathed cool air into her mouthful of molten cheddar. 'Aye, ou ear a ayik…' she added, her mouth full of boiling dairy fat.

'What?' Tim frowned.

Once the cheese was swallowable, Pip repeated herself. 'Okay, so here's the basics.'

'Shoot.'

'You know the first part: I noticed that the red dress wasn't the real thing. Arabella 'fessed up that she'd discovered the dress was missing, and that she'd replaced it with a knock-off because she'd forgotten to pay the insurance premiums. So before Henrietta got back and discovered the loss, Arabella was going to try and find the dress and put it back. Or I was. Am. Hopefully.'

'Got it.'

Pip took a smaller nibble of her sandwich and continued. 'My first big clue was the video. That woman and Gordon. Maybe Arabella.'

'I was thinking about that,' Tim said. 'Are they, like, together? A red hot affair, carried out secretly behind the museum exhibits?' He looked quite excited at the idea. 'Maybe that's what they were doing at the museum.'

'If they are, they keep it well hidden. And Gordon's about twenty years or so younger than Arabella, and about a zillion times hotter – not that that stopped anyone before. But I've definitely never seen anything between them. Not even a stolen glance or a weird vibe in the kitchen. And why would they meet in the museum for a tryst? On the exact night the dress disappeared?'

'Have you confronted Arabella and Gordon?' said Tim.

'I can't until I've got something more solid. Besides, I can't show them the tape, for obvious reasons.'

'The main reason being, I could go to jail.'

'Yes, and, I'd have to look after the cats all by myself,' Pip said, smiling. 'But what if it's not Arabella in that CCTV photograph? Remember at the engagement party, I saw Gordon come out of that fancy jazz club across the way with a hot woman? Totally out of his league, remember?'

'One day, you must fill me in on how the leagues work. But yes, I remember Gordon and the hottie.'

'I traced her – she's a minor television personality and his sister.'

'Nice sleuthing,' Tim said, with an approving nod of the head.

'Thank you. Except that now instead of having one possible female thief-slash-accomplice, I have two possibilities. I'm actually going backwards.'

'You still like Gordon for the perp though?' Tim asked, in a truly terrible New York cop accent.

'Yes. What else could he have been doing at the museum? I saw him with a garment bag, which could have been the dress, so I tailed him to a fancy house in Notting Hill – and guess who lives there?'

'Boris Johnson?'

'No, stupid. Henrietta.'

'Wow, does that mean something?'

'Dead end. He was delivering her dry cleaning.'

'Damn,' said Tim, then added thoughtfully. 'Bit odd though, isn't it? Picking up her dry cleaning? That's the sort of thing you'd do for a good friend, or a lover.'

Pip and Tim took a moment to dig into their toasties, chewing contemplatively. When they were finished, Tim took both their plates to the sink, and then slumped into the sofa again and said, 'Henrietta came back today, right? She didn't notice the dress, I presume?'

'No, too busy schmoozing Madison, who came to visit me. Interesting how celebrities turn people's heads. Henrietta was distracted or jet-lagged or whatever until Madison arrived, then she perked up like nobody's business. After Madison and Matty left, she even invited me to come with her to some fancy award ceremony next week – presumably under the impression that I have some celeb cred. Poor Emily was very put-out.'

Pip felt bad just thinking about the look on Emily's face when Henrietta had said, 'Oh, Epigram, why don't you come with me to the Awards for Humane and Sustainable Fashion next week. I have a spare ticket.'

They sat in silence for a moment, digesting all that cheese, and all that information.

Pip sat up, looking perkier, and continued: 'Anyway, I'm working on another angle. I've been thinking about that motive for the theft – presumably, someone stole the dress to sell it, right? I was wondering about the market for a dress like that. Who would buy it? What would it sell for? So, I did a bit of investigation.'

'Yup. Follow the money, as they say in the movies. What did you find?'

'Well, apparently that sort of thing is quite collectible and the nineties in particular are hot right now. A dress like this would be quite sought-after. Turns out there's this whole economy around it, collectors and dealers, and buyers, of course.'

Tim frowned – quite adorably, Pip had to say. 'But this dress is stolen,' he said. 'It would be hot, to use the parlance.'

'Exactly, so my friend Marlene, who is a legit vintage fashion dealer, put me in touch with a somewhat less legit dealer, a woman called Rosanne. Rosanne didn't say it outright, but she led me to believe she might have the dress, or be able to find it.'

'Ah, well there you go then.'

'Not so fast, Sherlock. There's a problem.'

Tim sighed. 'And that is?'

'Rosanne is the acquaintance who's dead.'

'Dead?'

'The police say suicide. But I don't know, Tim. It doesn't make sense. I think her death might have been suspicious. But the thing is, why would anyone kill a fashion collector? That doesn't make sense, either. None of this does.'

'You'll figure it out, Pip,' said Tim, giving her a pat on her back, like she was a puppy. 'You're clever at solving things.'

Pip sighed. She had a terrible feeling that she wasn't going to be clever at solving this at all.

CHAPTER 28

Pip woke before dawn, and spent half an hour tossing and turning like a sausage in a hot pan. Eventually, she threw off the covers, accepting that her brain refused to let her sleep or to think about anything but two concerns: Rosanne's death, and that elusive red dress. There was only one thing for it – the gym.

'Wow,' said Jimmy when she arrived, pulling his arm up in an exaggerated pantomime of a man looking at his watch. 'House burn down, did it?'

'Couldn't sleep. Thought I'd come and hit something. Or someone.'

'At your service, ma'am.'

Pip headed to the changing room, where she pulled on her workout gear, and the bright red gloves that Jimmy had given her as a gift to celebrate her successful closing of the Matty Price case.

She smacked him about a bit, enjoying her gradually increasing fitness and the way her punches landed with a satisfying thwack where she had intended.

'Would this help me in a real fight?' she wondered out loud.

'For sure,' said Jimmy. 'But I don't want you fighting, Pip. The smart money's on running, you know that right? Punching's for dummies.'

By the time Pip left the gym, she was buzzing with the self-righteous glow of the up-early-and-exercised. *Early rising is the business!* she thought, as she settled into a seat on the half-empty Tube. She'd do it more often. It really wasn't so difficult to get up early, and between the endorphins and the not having to stand the whole way to work while some suit breathed into your neck, it was totally worth it.

Inspired by her success, and mindful of Project New Improved Pip, she stopped at a cute little café near work and bought – not a croissant, no – a shockingly expensive quinoa antioxidant salad, studded with cranberries and nuts. Someone had committed vegetable infanticide to make said salad – the ingredients listed baby beetroot and baby spinach and microgreens. She felt sorry for the microgreens. They'd never got a chance to fulfil their destiny and grow into proper sunflowers or peas or whatever. And what actually was quinoa, anyway? And how did you pronounce it? And why did fashionable food now seemed to be composed almost entirely of the sort of items you might find in hamster food mix?

Putting these pressing questions aside, Pip opened her bag to pop away the salad for later, and noticed her phone glowing and vibrating. She picked it up and answered.

'Good morning, ma'am,' said the female voice on the end of the phone. 'It's Detective Constable Graham here. Is that Epiphany Bloom?'

Getting a phone call from the police was enough to drain the feel-good hormones from anyone's body and replace them with fear and dread and guilt, even if you hadn't done a thing wrong.

'Yes, this is Epiphany,' Pip said, shakily. 'Is everything all right?'

'Yes, ma'am, I just have a few routine questions to ask regarding an inquiry. Would this be a good time to talk?'

Pip agreed and walked over to a nearby bench, where she sat down and rested her gym bag next to her.

The woman continued, 'It's regarding the death of Rosanne Roberts. I believe you knew her. Could you tell me the nature of your relationship?'

Pip took a deep breath, her heart pounding. She reminded herself that she had nothing to hide. This wasn't anything like that time with the fighting fish.

'We're... business acquaintances. I work for a vintage clothing museum, and Rosanne is – was – in the business of sourcing unusual and special items of clothing. I'm looking to purchase new items for our collection, and I made contact with Rosanne because I thought she might have something I was interested in.'

All of which was entirely true, so why was Pip's heart beating so fast, and why did she feel so guilty? She had a brief urge to tell the detective all about the red dress, as well as about the time she'd shoplifted a mascara from Boots when she was fourteen, and to clear up what had happened with Most, just to get everything off her chest and off her plate. But she'd promised Arabella she would keep the dress theft quiet, and besides, Rosanne's death was a completely unrelated matter.

'You had an appointment with her the day before yesterday, I believe,' DC Graham continued.

'Yes, but she didn't arrive,' Pip said, 'because... you know... she... I was at her office when the receptionist, Frances, got the news about her death. So sad.'

Pip realised that from the bench where she was sitting, she had a glimpse of the bridge that Rosanne had supposedly jumped from. She shivered at the strange coincidence. She had a horrible vivid flash of how Rosanne's face would have looked on the way down, the red lipsticked mouth open in fear or horror, the glossy black hair streaming behind her as she plummeted into the cold, grey water.

'And you had met her before?'

Pip gathered herself. 'Only once, briefly. We met just to introduce ourselves, and we were going to meet again the day before yesterday.'

'What was your impression of her?'

'Oh, she was lovely. Well-dressed, of course. A nice, energetic manner. Very enthusiastic about working together.'

The detective did not respond to this. 'Do you happen to know if Rosanne knew anyone by the name of Ed R?' she asked. 'Or maybe a friend whose name begins with an A? We can't read her appointment book, but we've sent it to the handwriting people. We've been contacting the people whose details we *could* read in the book over the last couple of days. Rosanne was due to see this Ed R the morning she died. We'd like to get in touch with him.'

'No, I'm sorry,' Pip said. 'I don't know those people.'

'Edward? Edmund? Do you know anyone of that name? Someone in the industry, perhaps, clothes?'

'No.'

'Ms Bloom, can you think of anything else that might be pertinent to the investigation of Ms Roberts' death?'

'I don't, no. As I said, I hardly knew her.' Pip paused. Why was DC Graham so keen to find out these things? Maybe the police were no longer so sure it had been suicide, either.

'Um, Detective Constable Graham?' Pip said. 'The policemen who came to Rosanne's office said it was suicide? Or do you suspect…?'

The detective answered as if reading from a script. 'That would be for the coroner's office to determine, ma'am. They're doing an autopsy as we speak. Right now, the matter is still open. As I said, these are just routine inquiries at this stage.'

'Might she have been murdered?' asked Pip. 'Is that what you're saying?'

'Not at all, Ms Bloom,' said Detective Constable Graham. 'We're just making inquiries.'

But Pip wasn't sure that she believed her.

*

Pip had hardly settled at her desk after her busy morning of gym and police interrogation, when her phone rang again.

'Is this Epiphany Bloom?' said a man's voice.

'I just spoke to your colleague,' said Pip, presuming this was another police officer. Harassment, that's what this was. It was like being back in Beirut, when the coffee mugs had gone missing in the restaurant.

The man ignored Pip's comment. 'I believe that I may have access to an item that is of interest to you,' he said. 'An item, shall we say, of famous provenance. An article, shall we say, that is life-changing.'

Wonderful. A lunatic salesperson. That was all she needed.

'I have insurance, thank you,' she said, ready to hang up.

'Oh, for the love of God,' said the man. 'Are you or are you not interested in buying an item from an iconic movie?'

This wasn't the police and it wasn't a sales call. This was a diamond, falling straight into her lap. *Hallelujah!* sang Pip's internal choir. Was it possible that a miracle had verily occurred, and the dress was going to be delivered unto her, just like that? She really, really hoped so. She could use a break on this stupid case. Detecting was such hard work.

'Oh,' said Pip. 'Yes, yes. I'm definitely interested. Spill the beans, what's the deal?'

'I would prefer to discuss the details in person,' said Mystery Man. 'We must meet.'

No time like the present, thought Pip.

Mystery Man presumably felt similarly. 'I have an opening today,' he said, as if he were flicking through his calendar and had happened upon a spot.

'I can meet you at Le Bistro at noon,' Pip said. 'Do you know it? It is just round the corner from the Museum of Movie Memorabilia and Vintage Costumes.'

'I know it,' he said. 'I'll see you there at twelve.'

'Where did you say you got my number?'

'Noon,' he said, ignoring her question. 'Until then.'

It did seem a bit like a spy movie, lurking behind a menu on a red velvet banquette in a bistro, awaiting a stranger who might have information. As Pip sat there, she replayed their conversation. Who was this man? How did he know she was looking for something? Where had he come from?

'Ms Bloom, I presume?'

Pip looked up to see a man with a shock of silver white hair standing beside the booth. He didn't even crack a smile at his own rather amusing rhyme. Pip got to her feet as best she could, hunched over awkwardly in the booth, her knees pressed to the underside of the table. In this position, she was at eye-level with the man standing at the end of the table. He had probably the most perfectly shaped eyebrows she had ever encountered. They were like the McDonald's arches, rendered in individually placed hairs. It was uncanny.

'Yes, Epiphany Bloom. And you are?'

'De Range,' the man said, sliding into the opposite seat. 'A pleasure to meet you. I've heard so much about you.'

Pip sat down. She hated people who only used their surnames in introductions. It seemed so mad; so narcissistic. Still, she mustn't get distracted.

'About that, how did…?'

'A mutual acquaintance,' de Range said, with a flick of his wrist.

'I see,' said Pip, realising this must be Marlene. 'I wouldn't want to compromise our mutual friend. But before we get into any negotiation, I would like to hear the particulars of the item that you say you can source for me.'

'Ah, tell me a bit more about what you are looking for,' de Range said, 'and then I will ensure that I have the correct item in mind. I believe that our… contact… said that money was no object?'

'For the right item,' said Pip.

'You tell me what you want, and I will make it happen.'

Pip thought for a moment. She couldn't come out and name the dress. She had to narrow it down, but not so narrowly as to name it.

'My client is a fan of the early nineties romcoms,' she said, eventually. 'She wants an item that sums up the era – something iconic, really – that anybody would see and immediately identify as symbolic of the glamour of Hollywood.'

'I see,' said de Range. '*Any* costumes, or does she have a preference?'

'Dresses,' said Pip. 'She likes evening dresses best. So…' She was running out of adjectives. Symbolic. Iconic. Dear God, what more were there? 'Nice evening dresses,' she finished, weakly.

'Evening dresses, well what if I told you that I could get you the gown to top all gowns?' said de Range. He paused dramatically.

'Oh for goodness' sake,' said Pip, tiring of the charade. 'I want the red dress Julia Roberts wore in *Pretty Woman*.'

'Well, who wouldn't kill for a Julia Roberts dress?' de Range said, with a little laugh. 'Epiphany, I'm on it. Give me a day or two, and I'm sure I'll be able to source what your client desires. And both of us will do well from the deal.'

'Wonderful,' said Pip. But inside, she was less sure. This man didn't actually have the dress, he was going to source it – whatever that meant. He could just be a chancer. She couldn't afford to stop looking.

CHAPTER 29

Was it odd that she'd snuck out of the flat without telling Tim where she was going? It wasn't as if they kept tabs on each other; Pip could come and go as she pleased. It was no business of his, but she felt unaccountably weird about telling Tim that she was going on a day out with Jimmy.

For the second time in just over a week, Pip had had to get together an outfit for an unusual outing. This time, she was off to the races. In the course of her celebrity scrolling and her avid perusal of the glossies, Pip had seen the get-ups at Ascot and the like. Well, she wasn't going to wear a giant hat shaped as a rose, or one of those odd little ones that perched on the side of the head, made of bits of wire and feathers that gave no protection from the sun at all. It was a beautiful spring day, so she had decided on a pretty sage green sundress with a print of little white flowers, strappy white sandals, and a straw hat. She'd even found a ribbon to tie around the hat and give it a cheerful – one might say, *racy* – look.

Jimmy had certainly scrubbed up well. Pip realised that before this, she'd only ever seen him in workout gear and trackie bottoms. He went for fancy sports brands and he looked good in them. But, she discovered, he looked just as good – maybe even better – in regular clothes. His perfectly cut linen jacket showed off his good shoulders and narrow waist, and the cloth was a shade of grey that matched up well with Pip's frock. She caught a glimpse of the two of them in a glass shopfront they passed on their way from the train, and noted with satisfaction how good they looked together, even if she was a whisker taller than him. Jimmy caught her eye in the reflection and smiled.

'You look great,' he said. 'Thanks for coming. I'm happy to have your company.'

'I'm excited,' Pip said. 'I haven't been to the races in years. I think I last went when I was a kid. My friend's dad used to take us to the local track sometimes. He'd give us each five quid to bet with. I won once, made twenty-five pounds – probably the most exciting event of my eleventh year.'

'Well, maybe you'll get lucky today. The most exciting event of your thirty-fifth year.' They both blushed at the unmistakable – if unintended – sexual innuendo.

'I'd be keen to have a flutter,' Pip said. 'You'll have to show me how it all works. My friend's dad used to do it for us.'

Once they'd made their way to the VIP boxes, a huge ox of a man greeted them, engulfing Jimmy in a crushing manly embrace, accompanied by the kind of back-smacking that would evict a chicken bone from a trachea, or restart a stopped heart.

'Donavan, this is Pip. She's a client. And a friend,' said Jimmy.

'Well she looks better on it than I do!' the man replied, with a roar of laughter that shook his giant frame. 'Make yourselves at home. Help yourselves, go on. Don't hold back.' He gestured towards a buffet table laden with trays of food, a bar area, and groups of tables and chairs. The suite had a glass front and a balcony overlooking the track.

'This is so cool, thank you, Donavan,' said Pip. 'Last time I was at the races, I was a kid. We didn't have snacks like this, though. We got pies from the chip shop.'

Donavan gave another roar. 'Ha! Same here. I remember those pies. Nothing better. But we might as well have smoked salmon while it's going. We can go for a pie later if you're still in the mood.' With which, he tossed a small salmon-filled pancake into his mouth.

'Pip wants to try her hand at betting,' Jimmy said. 'Donavan, what tips can you give a first-timer?' Turning to Pip, he explained, 'Donavan has some experience in this regard. And, some success too, I hear.'

'Oh, yes!' shouted the giant. 'You've come to the right bloke. I'm a gambler through and through, I'm afraid. Runs in the family. They either land up in the gutter or the private suites. So far, so good, far as I'm concerned, but time will tell and life is long.' He had a good loud chuckle at the idea of himself joining the gutter dwellers in the family, then picked up a piece of paper. 'This here is how you study the form. Look here. These are the races and the times, and this is the list of horses for each race. You want to look at each horse and how it's done in the last few races. The good punters, they look at the race conditions, the track, the distance and so on. It's very scientific.'

'Okay…' Pip said, looking down at the columns of words and figures – it all looked rather like maths homework. 'The way I used to do it was, my friend and I would go down and look at the horses and pick the one we thought looked prettiest. We'd point it out to her dad and he would put five quid on that one for us.'

Another rumbling thunder of chuckle from the host. 'Good method!' he proclaimed. 'Can't fault it.'

'That doesn't sound at all scientific,' said Jimmy. 'Everyone knows that the best way to pick a horse is to look for a name you like.'

'Another excellent way of picking a winner!' Donavan bellowed, giving him a thump on the back. 'You stick with that!'

A group of guests arrived, and Donavan excused himself to go and crush and bellow at them. It was a bit of a relief.

'What a great guy,' said Pip.

'He is,' said Jimmy. 'Absolutely hopeless in the gym. Just look at the size of him! But he's got a heart of gold.'

They helped themselves to plates of tiny treats and went out to the balcony to observe the crowds. Things seemed to be getting up steam for the start of a race. They could see horses milling around at the start. People were gathering at the railing. An announcer was giving information about the horses.

'Okay, practice round. Pick one,' Pip said to Jimmy, gesturing towards the horses as if she were offering him one to take home.

'That black one. Number six,' he said. 'No contest. She's a winner – just look at those legs.'

Pip found the horse on the racing sheet. 'Number six. Ah, Jacob's Ladder, and she's a he. Just FYI.'

Jimmy laughed. 'I know my horseflesh. Your turn, smartypants.'

'That one over there, the brown one who's just going into the starting stall thing. Nice and shiny. He or she has poise, look how calm it is.' She looked at the sheet. 'Number nine. Chicken Dinner.'

'What a daft name.'

'No, it's not. There's the saying – Winner winner, chicken dinner. Well anyway, that's the winner. For sure.'

The horses assembled and took their places. There was a pause, like an in-breath, and the starting gun fired, sending them flying, hooves pounding, bits of earth spraying behind them.

Pip and Jimmy lost sight of their picks almost immediately in the mass of brown and black. As they thundered down the straight, the pack spread out. Pip spotted hers in a group of front-runners, the jockey in emerald green, urging him on. She yelled encouragement, jumping up and down with excitement.

'There's mine, coming up behind!' Jimmy shouted. Jimmy's horse was gaining ground, the jockey's red shining against the darkness of the sweating horse.

For a few paces they were in a group of four or five, bunched up. Then Pip's horse made a break for it, followed by Jimmy's, hot on his heels.

'Go, go!' Jimmy yelled.

The horses thundered towards the finish, seemingly neck and neck. Pip and Jimmy linked arms and clung to each other in anticipation.

'And the winner is… Number six, Jacob's Ladder.'

'I won!' Jimmy shouted.

Donavan came out, beaming. 'Go on! How much did you have on him?'

'Um, nothing,' Jimmy said sheepishly. 'We didn't get round to betting. Just, you know, for fun.'

'For fun?' Donavan roared. 'No such thing! Get out there and put your money where your mouth is!'

'I can't believe how exciting that was,' Pip said to Jimmy, when the ringing in her ears had subsided. 'Come on, let's go and check out the crowds and put some money on the next race.'

It was good to be out of the private suite and into the crowd of punters. Everyone looked just lovely, happy to be out and about in the warm weather, and dressed up nicely in their spring clothes. Okay, well not everyone – there were a few grave errors of judgement – was that a parachute that girl was wearing? Or a tent, perhaps? And clearly, some of the punters had not had Pip's foresight to google 'what to wear to the races'. If they had, they would know that 'do not wear ridiculously high shoes' was one of the top tips, and then they wouldn't be sinking into and tottering on the soft turf, aided and abetted by a glass of Pimms.

Pip picked another horse by her prettiness method, deciding on a very lovely honey-coloured beast with a blonde mane.

'Isn't she pretty?' she asked Jimmy. 'She looks like Jennifer Aniston. I see she's called Kerry Dawn.'

Jimmy picked by his method – names, deciding on a great big bay called Rocky Road.

'Rocky. A boxing reference,' he said. 'That's a good omen.'

'I think it's an ice cream reference,' said Pip.

Jimmy went off to place their bets, whistling 'Eye of the Tiger' loudly.

The starter's gun went and the race before theirs started. Pip could hardly see the horses, but she could hear the crowd urging their chosen ponies on. The shouting swelled to a crescendo as they neared the finish, then subsided. Winners pumped their fists and shouted 'Yes!' Losers – more numerous – groaned or sighed. Pip heard one woman nearby say, 'Oh, Jesus Christ, he didn't even come close. What am I going to do? I'm finished now.'

That voice. Pip knew it from somewhere. She turned round to look.

It was Henrietta.

CHAPTER 30

'Okay, the bets have been placed. Let's go and get ready to see the start of the race,' said Jimmy, coming up with the tickets in his hand. 'Time to watch Rocky Road romp home ahead of old Blondie, or whatever her name is… What are you doing there, behind a pillar?'

'Ssshhh…' said Pip, peering round to see what Henrietta was up to.

Henrietta was in a meltdown, a piece of paper crushed in her fist. She frantically brushed the fringe from her face, smudging her mascara. Was she crying? Pip couldn't hear what she was saying, but she seemed to be raving at her companion, a man in a linen suit and a straw hat. He had his back to Pip, comforting Henrietta, his hand on her shoulder. Henrietta pushed his hand away and waved the crumpled paper at him. Then she lurched forward and buried her face in his chest. It was mildly ridiculous, like one of those silent movies where dramatic physical movements – raised fists, aghast faces – had to convey the action.

Pip had no desire to be involved in any drama of Henrietta's. She needed to get out of there without being spotted.

'What are you doing?' Jimmy asked again, bemused.

'Trying to avoid someone,' Pip said. 'The crying woman over there. She's Henrietta. My boss. Poke your head out. Is she still there?'

'Yup. Looks like someone lost their shirt,' he said, peering round the pillar. 'Henrietta is not happy.'

'What's happening now?'

Jimmy was like the David Attenborough of drunken race goers, keeping up a running commentary in a hushed stage whisper: 'Uh oh, she's blubbering over some poor bloke's nice jacket… Oops, now she's tripped. Or more of a stumble, really. I think she might have had a few drinks before the horsies. Not an unusual occurrence on race days. But she's back on her feet, now – yes, good, she's stabilised. Now she's fiddling nervously with her necklace – I think that's a starfish, if I'm not mistaken…'

'Stop that!'

'You asked.'

'Is she looking this way?' Pip asked.

'Nope, head down. She's fumbling in her bag now. Probably looking for a tissue. Or a Xanax. Or perhaps a gun.'

'This is not funny, Jimmy,' Pip hissed.

'I reckon we're safe now. Let's make a dash for it,' said Jimmy, who was clearly enjoying himself tremendously.

'Okay, let's do it,' Pip said. She edged out and peered round, ready to go – just as Henrietta turned towards her. Their eyes met, Henrietta's swimming in confusion.

'Empathy?' Henrietta slurred, perplexed, prompting a delighted snort of laughter from Jimmy. 'Empathy? Empirical? Is that you?'

Pip sighed. 'It's Epiphany. Epiphany Bloom. Hi, Henrietta.'

The bloke who had been holding up the drooping Henrietta swung round.

'*Gordon*?' Pip said, in amazement.

'*Pip?*' he said, in equal amazement.

'Hi.'

'Hi.'

'Uh, this is my friend, Jimmy,' said Pip. 'Jimmy, Henrietta. And Gordon. Friends from work.'

'Good to meet you,' Jimmy said.

There was a long and awkward pause, punctuated by Henrietta's sniffs. Jimmy saved them from the agony. 'Well, we should get going. Pip! Come on. Better get over there or we'll miss the start of the race. Enjoy your day,' he said politely to the other two, taking Pip's arm.

'Bye, then,' said Pip cheerfully, as if Henrietta wasn't snivelling into a tissue and pulling nervously at her silver necklace, her drunken panda eyes darting back and forth, and Gordon wasn't staring balefully at them as they left. 'Good luck with the gee-gees. See you Monday.'

'Good luck with the gee-gees?' Jimmy asked once they were out of earshot, breathless with pent-up laughter. 'The gee-gees?' He doubled over in mirth.

'What the heck was I supposed to say? That was the only horse-related slang I could think of,' Pip said defensively, punching his arm. '*Stop laughing!*'

'Can't… help…' he wheezed. 'Empathy!'

'That's Empirical to you,' Pip said, hysteria bubbling up inside her to match his.

People were shooting sideways glances at them. They got their breath back and made their way to a spot where they could get a glimpse of the track, and a good view of the screen.

'What the heck was going on there? What was all that about?' asked Jimmy, as the horses and jockeys milled about before the race. 'I'm guessing she lost a big chunk of change.'

'It certainly looks like it,' said Pip. 'She's from a very wealthy family, so I'd have thought she would be okay money-wise, but maybe not.'

'And what's with the guy? Gordon?'

That was Pip's question exactly. The man turned up everywhere! What the heck was he doing here? With Henrietta?

'He works as a security guard at the museum,' Pip explained. 'In fact, he's one of the suspects in the mystery of the missing dress.'

'Do you think they're an item?'

Pip considered this. They had seemed… Friendly, at least. Intimate, maybe. Lovers? Who knew? 'I don't know, Jimmy. It's all very strange. I need to think.'

'Well, save that for later. Keep your eyes on the screen now. The gee-gees are about to go for a trot. And my boy is looking *fine*.'

Pip's eyes were on the screen, but her mind was on the case. Her ideas and questions were like the thundering horses circling the track. She could focus on one, then it slipped behind another. Then another idea came up from behind, but before she could give it her attention, it was round the corner and out of sight. The actual horses were just a clump of moving legs and tails. She had no idea where hers was, or Jimmy's. She needed to get out of here and think.

'You got it!' Jimmy yelled in delight.

'What?' she asked, confused.

'Your horse won! Blondie. Kerry Whatever.'

'She won? That's fantastic. I am rich! At last! Yachts! Cars! A house in France!' Pip enthused, flinging her arms about dramatically.

'Yes, all of that. Let's go and get your winnings.'

With a very handy two hundred pounds in her pocket, Pip headed back with Jimmy to the private suite.

'Pip won!' said Jimmy. 'Her pretty horse won, I should say.'

'Ha-ha! The triumph of beauty,' boomed Donavan, delighted. 'Let's celebrate. Champagne all round.'

A waiter came over with a tray. Pip took a glass, clinked with Donavan, and took a sip. Delicious, cold and sparkling. But Pip needed to keep a clear head: she had work to do this evening.

CHAPTER 31

Pip arrived home exhausted from the long day: the sun, the excitement, the champagne. And the few days previously had been just crazy-busy at the museum. She needed time to sit and think.

The cats had other ideas, as cats do. Most butted her hard head against her, looking for love, or at least a stroke – and supper, of course. The kittens were getting big and boisterous. Pip knew they would have to go to new homes soon – Flis had already said she wanted the black one, but Pip needed to find homes for the other two. Add that to her to-do list.

The tortoiseshell was tightroping it across the back of the sofa, ready to pounce on the grey on the cushions below. The grey, meanwhile, was peering over the sofa arm with wildness in his yellow eyes. A big rumble was brewing, that was for sure.

The sound of Pip opening the cupboard was enough to stop the kittens in their tracks. Whatever their beef was, it was forgotten. They skittered into the kitchen to mew and yowl for supper. Never was there a more pitiful and pathetic sound than that of kittens who had been without food for – what, an hour or two?

Pip dropped a handful of pellets into their saucer and gave Most her supper up on the windowsill, where the greedy little kittens couldn't reach it. For herself, tea. Lots of milk and a good spoon of sugar. She'd sworn off sugar as part of her self-improvement plan, but she needed the energy.

Pip got out her notebook, smiling at the dolphin and the rainbow. Jimmy was a sweetie. But now was not the time to mull over her romantic life. Or, more accurately, her lack thereof. Her plan was to go over her notes, looking for references to Gordon, and highlight them. She felt sure he was key to the whole mystery, but how? She hoped something in her notes would jog her memory. She'd hardly sat down to begin, though, when Tim came home.

'Hey, nice dress. Where have you been?' he asked.

'I went to the races, of all the strange things. Guess who I saw?' Pip filled him in on the Henrietta/Gordon sighting, speaking quickly, before he could ask who she had gone to the races with. She didn't want to have to explain things.

'That's a seriously strange coincidence,' said Tim, when she'd finished.

'Yes. I'm going back over everything I know about Gordon. See if I've missed anything.'

'Good idea. I'm here if you want to bounce things around.'

'Thank you. It really helps to talk things through. I'll call you when I'm ready to chat.'

'Listen, Pip, I had another idea, based on what you said the other day. What about the potential buyers? Who would want to own a dress like that?'

'Collectors of movie memorabilia. And, I guess, other museums and tourist places.'

'And Julia Roberts mega fans,' Tim said.

'I hadn't thought of that. But you are right. That would be a good target market for the thief to find a buyer.'

'Tell you what, while you're going over your notes, I'll check out the internet, see what I can find out about JR crazies.'

There followed a peaceful interlude of tapping and clicking on the keyboard, the whisper of turned pages, the tractor-like purring of Most. Pip felt her eyelids drooping. It was close to eleven.

'Tim, I'm going to turn in. Can't keep my eyes open. Let's pick this up tomorrow, if you're keen?'

'Sure,' he said, without lifting his eyes from the screen. 'I'm busy with something… Going to keep going a bit… See you tomorrow.'

Pip slept like Tutankhamun in his tomb and woke on Sunday morning to sunlight streaming into her room. Weird, the sunlight smelled like bananas, her dozy brain observed. Both yellow. Like Flis's front door and Vitamin D. She stretched and groaned, and her mind gradually unfuzzed. The banana scent was still there.

'Breakfast!' Tim called through the door, giving it three sharp knocks. 'Banana pancakes and fresh leads for your investigation – get 'em while they're hot!' Someone was in a good mood.

'Coming!' Pip got up, pulled on a sweatshirt over her pyjamas, and stumbled eagerly to the kitchen for breakfast.

'Wow, those look amazing!' she said. And they did, all golden with crispy brown edges, bits of banana showing through, and glistening with syrup.

Tim set out two plates, knives and forks, and a cafetière of coffee. He offered Pip the dish of pancakes.

'You are amazing!' she said. 'Is there no end to your talents?'

'Sadly, yes. Pancakes and hacking. Those are my key skills.' He shrugged. 'You've seen the best of me.'

'I doubt that,' she said, and immediately felt embarrassed. Why did everything she said to Tim take on a slightly creepy flirtatious air?

'So, on the subject of my talents, I sent you a few links that might help,' he said. 'I've been snooping around the Julia Roberts fan pages on Instagram and Reddit. She's a popular lady.'

'No doubt about it,' said Pip. 'People love Ms Roberts.'

'So it seems there are official fan pages – PR and fluff, basically: lots of glam photos, snippets of "news",' he put down his fork to do air quotes, indicating just what he thought of that sort of news.

'And then you have the fan sites,' he continued. 'People who love a certain singer or actor or whatever start their own groups. These are unofficial groups, nothing to do with the star, or their management. Just run by the fans.'

'Tim, you are speaking to an incorrigible fangirl, remember? I've been on more than a few of those.'

'Yeah, so I had the idea of lurking around a few forums, seeing what people were talking about. There was a bit of chatter on one about her movie memorabilia and someone mentioned clothes. Nothing specific. Nothing about the red dress. There are a few threads with people trying to sell things.'

'So if Gordon – or whoever – was trying to sell the dress, he'd likely go that route?'

'I didn't get as far as taking a look. You can check out the links, read the chatter and then see what was going on.'

'That's a good idea. I'm going to look through my notes on Gordon again, and then I'll tackle that. Thanks.'

'Well, hope it helps. Want the last of the coffee?'

Feeling much restored after a good sleep and a giant plate of banana pancakes, and a giant cup of coffee, Pip gathered up her second cup and the kittens and headed back to the sofa with her notes, to pick up where she'd left off.

'Where's that pic? The one of Gordon and the woman, from the CCTV camera?' she asked, sorting through her papers on the coffee table.

'There it is,' Tim said, pointing to the corner of the photo peeping out from a nest of papers, magazines and pencils.

'Thanks,' she said, and picked it up distractedly.

'Have you managed to find out anything more about the two of them? Their relationship, I mean? Arabella and Gordon?'

'No,' said Pip, looking at the picture again. 'But from what I saw at the racecourse yesterday, it's possible that Gordon has something going with Henrietta. So I'm starting to think the relationship between Gordon and Arabella might just be business.'

'The body language, though,' Tim said. 'When I look at this photograph, I can't help but think there's something between them. The way the woman leans into him. It's very… sexy.'

'Oh my God!' said Pip, snatching the photograph from his hand. 'I can't believe I didn't see that before!'

'What?' Tim asked. 'What can you see?'

'The necklace,' Pip said, pointing to the chain around the woman's neck. 'The pendant. What do you see?'

Tim peered in. 'Is it a star?' he said, squinting.

'It's not a star, it's a starfish,' Pip said. 'And that's not Arabella. It's Henrietta.'

CHAPTER 32

It didn't make sense. According to Arabella, Henrietta had already been on her way to Morocco when the dress disappeared. The dress was stolen on Saturday and Henrietta had left on Friday. Or at least, she'd said she had. She could have lied to everyone, Pip realised; told them she was leaving earlier, so that she wasn't under suspicion when the dress disappeared. Pip felt in her bones that she was onto something. That she might actually be about to solve the mystery of the red dress.

'That was the necklace Henrietta was wearing at the races,' Pip told Tim. 'I noticed it because she kept playing with it – fiddling, you know, in a sort of nervy way. That's her in the picture, sneaking in at night. Henrietta stole the dress, with the help of Gordon – possibly her lover, but definitely her accomplice.'

'Well, it certainly looks that way.'

Pip frowned. 'But there's just so much that doesn't add up.'

'Like the question of why she would do it,' Tim said. 'Why would Henrietta steal a dress from herself?'

'That's the one question that's always easy to answer,' Pip said. 'For the money. I suppose she stole it to sell, or to claim on the insurance. Or both.'

'Isn't she from a super wealthy family? You said her grandfather was some kind of electrical industrialist.'

'Plumbing. Yes. But just because there's money in the family doesn't mean she gets what she needs. Or wants. As I should know.'

'True,' said Tim. 'Maybe she's got expensive tastes. The clothes. The travel.'

'Or there's another possibility. Gambling. She was at the races and she looked very distraught. Maybe she'd bet big. Maybe that's just the latest of a string of losses. It could be that she's got herself into trouble.'

Tim nodded thoughtfully. 'Okay, so here's another question. She takes the dress, leaving the mannequin empty. And when she gets back from her travels almost a month later, she finds a replica dress on the model. What does she think happened?'

'Who knows? But she can't ask anyone, because if she enquires about the fake, she'd have to admit to taking the real one.'

'You're right, many questions.'

'And only one person who can answer them,' Pip said. 'Time to talk to Henrietta.'

Pip sipped on her now-cold coffee, thinking about how she could approach this with Henrietta, and idly clicking on the various links that Tim had sent her – links to Julia Roberts fan sites and discussion groups. She began to fall down a social media rabbit hole, clicking on this and that, learning surprising theories about Julia, and not coming up with a plan. Pip pulled herself up short. This was typical of her, and she needed to stop. She needed to come out of the social media web and back to reality. She took a last glance at her phone, where she'd clicked through several links to what appeared to be some sort of vintage clothing website. There were various articles and links, and then what appeared to be a list of classified type ads in the right-hand column. She was about to log off when something caught her eye. 'Tim,' she said, 'I think I've found something.'

Pip read it out loud: 'Iconic Julia Roberts-slash-*Pretty Woman* movie piece. Authenticity guaranteed. Serious buyers only.'

She looked at Tim. 'It doesn't say which dress, but it must be our dress. The whole thing is just too much of a coincidence, don't you think?' She read it again. 'Do you think this could be Henrietta, trying to sell the dress?'

'Does the ad have a name?'

'No. Just contact details. It must be her though, surely? The timing works.'

'But really, she's selling the dress on eBay?' Tim said, with mock disdain. 'She's an amateur; she has no idea how to go about selling high value, niche stolen goods.'

'Well, I suppose she couldn't go straight to one of the dealers. They would all know her.'

'True. And individual collectors might be hard to identify.'

'But are we sure it's her? I mean, maybe they were at the museum for some other reason, her and Gordon, that didn't have anything to do with the dress. I don't want to go and accuse her and let the cat out of the garment bag, so to speak, and then find out it wasn't even her. Especially as this de Range chap also claims that he can get it. He could even be the one advertising it.' Pip lapsed into thought for a few moments, before continuing, 'It would be great if there was a way I could check out this ad before I go and confront her. The thing is,' she said, tapping her lip with her finger like she imagined a real detective might, '*I* can't answer the ad, because if it *is* Henrietta, then it will tip her off. Give her time to make up some story.'

'True,' Tim said.

'But you could?' said Pip, raising her eyebrows. 'Would you do that for me?' She gave him what she hoped was an endearing look that he couldn't refuse.

'Of course.' Tim shrugged in a particularly charming, boyish way, and Pip had to stop herself from reaching over and kissing him.

'It's perfect,' said Pip. 'She's never heard of you.'

'You mean, you haven't talked about your charming and good-looking flatmate at work?' Tim teased.

'Well, not to her, I haven't,' said Pip, before realising this sounded like she had chatted to other people about his charm and good looks. Suddenly they were both blushing.

'Okay,' said Tim, reaching for his phone. 'What should I say?'

'Ask her what she's got to sell.' Pip thought for a moment. 'Tell her you're only interested in dresses; see if she'll give you the details.'

Tim tapped away a bit.

'Done,' he said. 'Now we wait.'

Pip scratched the tummy of the grey kitten that was lying stretched out on his back between her thighs. 'Look how long he is,' she said to Tim. 'He almost reaches my knees. It makes me sad that they're growing up so fast.'

'I suppose you'll have to start thinking about where they'll live,' Tim said, gently picking up the tortoiseshell kitten and holding it up to his face. 'We will have to find you loving homes,' he told the cat, pressing his forehead to its tiny furry one.

'I know, I just love them so much,' Pip said, stroking her thumbs over the pink pads of the kitten's paws. 'I can't bear the thought of them going, but I know I need to get on to sorting it out. Flis will take one, so that is nice. At least I can visit. I'll be its aunty.'

'Ask around the office, there might be someone there who would like a kitten.'

'Good idea. As soon as I've got this red dress thing sorted out. I've been delaying the inevitable.'

Tim's phone pinged. He reached for it and swiped it open. 'Well, that was quick,' he said.

'What does she say?'

'The message reads: "Thanks for your enquiry. Let's just say I have *the* iconic dress. I would prefer not to discuss the specifics here. Let's meet. I can show you what I have."'

Tim and Pip looked at each other and smiled. 'Well, she doesn't say that it's the red dress,' Pip said, 'but I must say, it does sound like we've got what we need. What next?'

'We meet. Or rather, you do,' he said, tapping his screen.

Another ping.

'Bingo!' he said. 'She's just sent me an address and a time to meet tomorrow afternoon. Says we can chat first, then view the merchandise. I'll forward it to you.'

The message arrived on Pip's phone. She read it, and excitement coursed through her body. The suggested location was the coffee shop two blocks down from the museum. And the writer said to look for a blonde woman sitting in the far corner. It *must* be Henrietta. Pip had done it. She had solved the mystery of the missing red dress. Now, to confront the thief!

CHAPTER 33

'Epigram!' Henrietta said, in astonishment. 'It's you!'

It was no wonder that Henrietta was surprised to see Pip. Just fifteen minutes earlier, they'd both been at the museum. Henrietta had popped into Pip's office to remind her about the Awards for Humane and Sustainable Fashion the next night before muttering something about a doctor's appointment and dashing out. Pip had waited five minutes, before leaving herself.

'Yes, me,' said Pip, looking down at her. 'Although, my name is Epiphany.'

'Well, it's very nice to see you,' Henrietta said, regaining her poise. 'But I'm waiting for a friend, so perhaps we can catch up some other time. We'll have a nice natter at the awards tomorrow, eh? Enjoy your coffee.' She turned pointedly to the menu, lifting it to her face to block her view of Pip.

'I'm the one you're waiting for,' Pip said. 'I'm the buyer.'

Henrietta lowered the menu. 'But, I thought…'

'I know everything,' said Pip, rather stretching the truth. 'I know you stole the *Pretty Woman* red dress from the museum.'

'What on earth are you talking about?' Henrietta said, making one last attempt at outrage. Her eyes shone with manufactured fury. 'I am the director of the museum. And your employer, I might add. How dare you accuse me? And besides, the dress is there in the museum, in full view of everyone. Now, please leave before my friend arrives.'

'Chap called Tim you're waiting for, is it?' said Pip. Henrietta blanched. 'My flatmate. I didn't want to tip you off, so he sent the message. Sorry, Henrietta. There's no friend, or buyer – only me.' Pip sat down at the table and waved a waitress over to them. 'Cappuccino, please,' she said. 'And for you, Henrietta?'

'Water,' Henrietta said quietly, all her bluster gone. Pip felt quite sorry for her, but steeled herself – the woman was a criminal, after all.

They sat without speaking for what felt like a long time. Pip was determined to make the awkward silence trick work again. She wanted to wring the facts out of Henrietta. It was crucifyingly difficult, though, not saying anything.

'I was desperate,' said Henrietta, finally cracking under the strain. 'I would never… I love the dress; it was my mother's most treasured possession. But I was in too deep, and it was the most saleable, most valuable item in the museum.'

The waitress put a glass of water in front of Henrietta, and a coffee in front of Pip. 'Anything to eat?' she asked. 'We have fresh cheese scones?'

'No, thank you,' the two women said in unison.

'Tell me what happened,' Pip said, firmly, as the waitress left. 'From the beginning.'

'My father has got pots of money, but he keeps me on a pittance,' Henrietta started bitterly. 'He believes that "work develops character" and that "it is a source of great personal reward". He has about a million trite sayings on the subject, but overall, he doesn't think it's good for me to get everything I want. And he has no idea how expensive it is to keep yourself decently clothed and entertained in a city like London. I live in his house, of course, so there's no rent to pay, but honestly, my monthly allowance would barely cover a Kate Spade handbag.'

Pip certainly understood the strain of a stingy parent, but she had seen Henrietta's pad – provided by Henry – and it was hard to feel any sympathy for her. Pip had to pay her own rent and she certainly didn't have a Kate Spade handbag, but she'd never been tempted into a life of crime. (Stealing Most from the vet didn't count.)

Henrietta seemed keen to unburden herself. 'Anyway, I was doing all right, making do between the allowance and my salary. I'd learned to live within my means, even though it was not easy, I can tell you. And then I discovered the horses.'

Ha! Pip had been right. She wanted to shout, 'Knew it!' but she restrained herself to more encouraging nodding and agreeable humming.

'The first time, I went along with some friends and I took a bit of a gamble on the trifecta. I won big. A thousand pounds or so. It was so easy. And so fun and exciting. For a while…' Henrietta took a sip of her water and waved for the waitress. 'Double espresso,' she said, before turning back to Pip. 'I was winning a bit, but not as much as I was losing,' she said. 'To start with, it was just every now and then. But it escalated. And then something else happened.'

Henrietta seemed unsure whether to say more, but Pip employed the silent treatment, again to good effect.

'So, around the same time, I got a new boyfriend. He's great, lovely manners, very good-looking, adores me, but he's got absolutely no money.'

'Gordon, I presume. So you gave him some walking-around money, did you?'

Henrietta looked at her. 'How do you know so much? Who even *are* you, anyway?'

'Just finish up your story and I'll fill in from my side,' said Pip. 'So, you and Gordon…'

'Well, yes, so I gave him a bit of cash, just to buy some decent clothes. I can't go around town with someone in an H&M pullover, can I?'

Pip gave that question the benefit of the doubt and treated it as hypothetical.

'I was already on a tight leash,' Henrietta continued, 'and I was losing a bit more than I was winning, and giving Gordon a few hundred here and there. A few months in, I was in trouble. I went to Daddy to ask for a loan. I couldn't tell him about the gambling – or that I was dating the museum's security guard. He told me to show some initiative and sort out my problems myself. So I stole the dress.'

A confession! Pip felt like jumping up and pumping the air with her fist. She had cracked it!

'I decided to fix the problem,' said Henrietta, defensively. 'Like Daddy told me. I would sell the dress, get what I could for it – that would be mine to keep – *and* claim on the insurance, so the museum wouldn't lose out.'

'This probably wasn't what Henry had in mind,' Pip said. 'In terms of initiative.'

'Well, obviously not,' Henrietta said, looking miserable. 'I feel absolutely terrible about it, I really do.'

Pip looked at her with some sympathy. 'You made a mistake. It happens. Tell me how it all went down, then we can see if we can fix this.'

'Do you think we can?' Henrietta said, brightening visibly. 'Would you help me?'

'Tell me the rest of the story, then we'll see.'

'I got Gordon to help me. For company and support, and to help with the dress. Do you have any idea how difficult it is to get an evening gown off a mannequin?'

Pip had been around the block a few times, but no, she didn't have any experience undressing mannequins. Undressing performing hamsters, yes, from when she'd been the assistant in that ridiculous 'magic' show. But not mannequins. 'No,' she said.

'Well, it's very difficult. The dress is slippery, and of course the mannequin is stiff and not very compliant. Anyway, Gordon helped me get the dress off the model and then take it away. He knows all the museum security systems, so that was helpful.'

'Not quite as knowledgeable as you'd hoped. I got security camera footage from the offices across the road. It shows you and Gordon going into the museum that Saturday night.'

Henrietta paled at the mention of hard evidence. She rested her forehead on her fists. 'Oh, God. I'm in the most awful trouble,' she said. Then added, 'But what has this all got to do with you?' Her face suddenly hardened. 'Are you something to do with the police? Or are you working for Daddy? Is that why he met you at a bus stop? I *knew* that sounded fishy!'

'No, no,' Pip said, hastily, not wanting to get Henry in trouble, especially since he'd been such a hero in the llama drama. She explained to Henrietta how she had come to be involved with the missing dress, although leaving out Arabella's part in it: her chance visit to the museum with Flis, how she'd spotted the fake dress at her interview, and how her accidental background in investigating disappearances had led to her looking for the real dress.

'How *did* the fake dress get there?' Henrietta asked. 'I couldn't believe it when I got home from Morocco and saw it there. The plan was that while I was away, Arabella would find the dress missing and report it to the police, and when I got back, I'd be all surprised and devastated and file an insurance claim. But instead, there was the dress!'

Pip thought carefully before she answered. She knew she was about to betray Arabella's confidence, but she couldn't see that Henrietta could take the moral high ground. And the truth, as she knew too well, would eventually come out.

'Arabella forgot to pay the insurance. That dress wasn't insured. She was terrified that you would be furious and she'd lose her job. She replaced it with a replica, and asked me to try and track down the original. I have a bit of experience with finding missing things,' Pip said, wondering if describing a teenage boy as a 'thing' was strictly accurate. 'Speaking of which, where is it? Where did you put the dress?'

Henrietta sipped at her now-cold espresso and gave Pip a steady stare. Pip knew that she was feeling her out, trying to decide whether she could trust her. Pip settled her face into a relaxed, friendly mask that anybody would feel comfortable confiding in.

Henrietta had made her decision. 'I'm not going to tell you,' she said, leaning backwards triumphantly, her arms folded, her cold gaze on Pip.

CHAPTER 34

She wasn't stupid, Henrietta. She knew that the dress was the only leverage she had, and she was damned if she was going to give it up just yet. Even as Pip's brain was in full spin, trying to find a way forward, she took a moment to admire the other woman's tactics.

'I understand your position,' Pip said, in her calmest, most reasonable voice. 'You need to find a way to get out of this tricky situation and get everything back to normal.'

Henrietta thawed a little, and nodded.

'You don't want any legal problems.'

Henrietta shook her head fervently.

'And you want to avoid any trouble with your father.'

She nodded in enthusiastic agreement.

'And you don't want to give up the dress until this is all smoothed over and you feel safe,' said Pip. 'Is that it?'

'That's exactly it,' Henrietta said. All the cold-eyed swagger had gone out of her and she regarded Pip with a hopeful, pleading expression. 'That's all I want. For this whole mistake to go away.'

'I think I can make that happen,' said Pip, with a quiet confidence that, in truth, she didn't feel. 'Let's talk this through. I can help you, but you have to be completely honest with me, okay?'

More nodding from Henrietta.

'Where is the dress?'

Henrietta only hesitated for a fraction of a second.

'In the basement storeroom at the museum.'

It was all Pip could do to keep her face expressionless and her mouth from falling open. All this time, it had been literally under her feet! No wonder Henrietta had been so eager to get Pip and Emily upstairs when she'd arrived and found them in the storeroom. Pip took a moment to think about the implications of the dress still actually being in the museum.

'Thinking of this logically: legally, the dress is still on the premises.'

Nodding from Henrietta.

'Which means that one could argue that the dress hasn't actually gone anywhere. I mean, if it was put into storage by the owner herself, it hasn't, in fact, been stolen, wouldn't you say?'

When Henrietta smiled, it was as if the sun came out. 'That is *exactly* what I would say!' she gushed, grabbing Pip's hand. 'You're right, Epitome. You are absolutely right!'

Pip sighed. 'Just call me Pip, please. Anyway, all we have to do is put it back. We'll square it with Arabella. You can deal with Gordon, make sure he's on-side with this. Which I'm sure he will be, given that he was an…' She was about to use the word 'accomplice', but caught herself just in time and let her sentence tail off.

'Oh Pip, thank you,' said Henrietta. 'You've saved the day. I'm so, so grateful.'

There was still something nagging at Pip.

'Do you know someone called Rosanne?' she said. 'A clothes dealer?'

'Rosanne? Rosanne?' Henrietta looked vague. 'No, not that I can think of, but I meet so many people. Why?'

'She's dead,' said Pip. 'And it looks like murder. I just can't shake the feeling that it's something to do with this dress. But I guess I could be wrong.'

'Are you accusing me of murder?' Henrietta's eyes bulged so much, Pip feared they might fall out.

'No, no, not at all,' she reassured her. Maybe this nagging feeling in her gut was misplaced, and Rosanne's death was nothing to do with the dress. She hoped fervently that she was wrong, and that Henrietta's antics hadn't resulted in the death of an innocent woman. She tried to put it out of her mind. The police were on it, after all, and her task right now was to wrap up this matter of the dress. She smiled at Henrietta. 'I'm glad we've sorted out this minor misunderstanding. And, the way I see it, no harm done.'

They smiled at each other, as if both pleased with a good outcome, although frankly, even if Pip was wrong about Rosanne's death, she thought Henrietta was getting off rather too lightly. A rap over the knuckles – perhaps from Henry, or the cops – would be well-deserved. But it wasn't Pip's place to restore justice or to dole out smacks to spoiled brats. Her job had been to find the dress, and that she had done. Now she could carry on earning her salary, without lost red dresses weighing her down.

Henrietta shifted in her seat. 'There's just one more little thing,' she said.

The words struck ice into Pip's heart. *No! No little things,* she wanted to shout. *Little things are where it all unravels. Little things are where it all goes pear-shaped! Do not come here with your little things!* Pip's life was a long list of disasters that had started with 'one little thing'. However, she asked, patiently, 'What is it?'

'I had made contact with a buyer. Before I heard from you. He's coming to see me at the museum; he wants to see the dress. But it's okay. I'll just tell him that the dress is no longer available.'

Pip was relieved. This was easily fixable, as 'little things' go.

'Okay. Not a problem. Phone him and cancel. Tell him the dress is not for sale. Now, we'll go back to the museum. Tell Arabella and whoever is on security that they can leave early, and when everyone has left and the place is closed, we will go and replace the fake dress with the real one.'

'That's a good plan, but this dealer is coming at quarter past five.' Henrietta picked up her phone from the table and scrolled through. 'There's a message from him here somewhere. Ah, there it is,' she said, and pressed a button to call the number, holding the phone to her ear. She waited. 'No answer,' she told Pip. 'It's already half past four, so he's probably on his way to the museum now. Don't worry. I'll go and meet him. You can hang about a bit, I'll get rid of him quickly, and then we'll do the old switcheroo on the dress.' She picked up her handbag (which really was very gorgeous and might well have cost a month's wages – or allowance, if you were fortunate enough to receive such a thing, thought Pip), all perky now that she was no longer in trouble.

Pip sighed. It had been a long day. She didn't feel like waiting around for some meaningless meeting to be wrapped up before they could put the dress back in its rightful place. But there was nothing else for it.

By the time they got back to the office, it was nearly five. Emily was leaving as they arrived. Arabella had already gone. Henrietta batted her eyelids and told Philip that she knew how hard he worked, and that there was no need for him to stay when she intended to work late. True to form, Philip looked mildly affronted didn't make anything of it. The boss had told him to go, so he would go.

'I would love to see the dress,' Pip said. After all, she had cleverly found the thing, even if it had been there all along. 'Shall we go and take a look?'

'Of course,' said Henrietta. 'We've got a few minutes. Let's go and get it out. We can bring it up now, and when the dealer guy has gone, we'll quickly pop it on the mannequin.'

They locked the front door and unlocked the door to the basement. Henrietta switched on the light and led the way down the stairs, before unlocking the door into the little private storeroom Emily had pointed out to Pip. She took another key and opened a big cupboard.

'Oh, wow,' said Pip, when she caught sight of the dress. It really was a sight. So red. So familiar.

'It's marvellous, isn't it?' said Henrietta, bringing it out into the light, where it glowed like a ruby. 'I'm so glad it's still here. I can't believe I ever thought to get rid of it. Thank goodness we've sorted this whole mess out, Pip. Honestly, I'm very grateful. And you know, I've decided I'm just going to sell some of the smaller pieces that Mummy left to me personally, which should be enough to clear the debt. I hadn't wanted to sell my own special mementos, but now I see that it would be the right thing to do.'

'Well, I'm pleased too,' said Pip. 'Come on, let's get it upstairs. Your guy will be arriving soon.'

As the two women got the dress to the top of the stairs, the bell rang. They lay the dress down on the sofa. Henrietta went to unlock the big main doors of the museum and turn her buyer away. Meanwhile, Pip went to her office to keep out of the way. She would check whatever emails had come in that afternoon while she'd been out, deal with what she could, and wait for Henrietta to tell her the coast was clear.

'See you in a minute, good luck!' she said, closing the door of her office.

Pip really had meant to check her emails, but it just seemed so boring after the excitement of the day. Emails could wait until tomorrow. After all, she had solved the mystery and found the dress. She deserved a bit of downtime. She put her feet up on the desk, inserting her earbuds in her ears, having decided to listen to her chilled old-school playlist while she trawled Twitter and Instagram for celebrity news and gossip, fashion pics, memes and silly jokes. Really, if you thought about it, this was all part of her job.

CHAPTER 35

Pip woke with a dry mouth and a wet cheek, the clear belting voice of Beyoncé ringing in her ears. What was going on? Where was she? Slowly, she realised she was on her desk, lying in a damp pool of her own drool. Pip pushed herself up and gazed around her office. She must have dropped off. She hoped she hadn't been snoring. Thankfully, she was alone, so there were no witnesses to her embarrassment. Only Henrietta would be on the premises now, and she was getting rid of the would-be buyer so that they could replace the fake dress with the original.

Pip thanked Bey for her service, turned her off and took out the earbuds. Her phone told her it was nearly six o'clock. Where *was* Henrietta? Surely she should be done with the dealer by now – all she'd had to do was to apologise and shoo him out. Pip opened the door a crack to see if she could spot Henrietta or hear voices. Nothing.

Pip tiptoed down the passage and went in search of Henrietta. The main foyer, where she'd last seen her going off to answer the door, was empty. The front doors were closed. No sign of Henrietta. Pip quickly went through to where they had placed the dress on the sofa, and her blood ran cold – Henrietta wasn't the only one missing from this scene. Where was the red dress? Pip ran over to the sofa to see if perhaps it had slipped to the floor, or if Henrietta had laid it out somewhere else. There was no sign of it. It was gone. Again.

Pip sat down on the sofa and rested her head in her hands in despair. She had solved the mystery and found the dress – for a total of one hour! She had no idea what to do next. But she had plenty of questions. What was going on? Where was the dress? And where was Henrietta?

'Oh, bloody hell,' she muttered to herself. 'She must have sold it to that dealer.' It was the only explanation that made sense – he must have offered Henrietta a big sum, and she'd changed her mind. And then Henrietta had skipped out on Pip. She had sold the dress and done a runner.

But then again, thought Pip, Henrietta had seemed so keen to sort out this whole mess quietly. Why would she go back on their arrangement, and steal the dress – again? She knew that Pip could just point the police in her direction.

Pip sighed, rose from the sofa and headed back towards her office to fetch her phone to call Henrietta. Her number was one of those that Arabella had stuck up over her desk. It was perhaps unlikely that Henrietta would answer, but she was going to try anyway. As she passed the kitchen, however, she heard a muffled banging. Rats? A door left open on an appliance, banging in a draught? She'd better go and have a look.

From behind the door, she heard a voice: 'Help! Pip! Let me out!'

Pip froze.

'Henrietta, is that you? Are you stuck?'

Pip ran to the door and grabbed the handle. She rattled it and pulled. 'I can't open it. It's locked!' she cried in a panic, before noticing that the key was in the door. She unlocked it and wrenched it open. A dishevelled Henrietta stumbled out.

'Are you all right?' Pip asked. 'What happened? How did you get locked in the kitchen with the key on the outside?' She couldn't grasp what was going on.

'The buyer… The one I was meeting,' Henrietta said, breathless from the exertion of the banging and panicking. 'He pushed me… He locked me in…'

'Who? Why? What happened?'

Henrietta calmed down a bit and told Pip the story.

'As soon as he arrived, I told him that another buyer had already paid, and that the dress was no longer available,' said Henrietta. 'I said that I tried to call, so he wouldn't waste his time, but hadn't been able to reach him.' Henrietta took a breath, and continued.

'He was furious. He said that he was a dealer and had a buyer. That I was a chancer. Was I taking him for a fool? That sort of thing. Spitting mad,' said Henrietta. 'And then he just walked through the museum as if he owned it, with me trying to call him back. He spotted the dress lying on the sofa, where we had put it. He went over and inspected it and kept saying how perfect it was, how beautiful, just right. He asked if I was absolutely sure it wasn't for sale. I said no. That there had been a misunderstanding, and then… Then he…'

'Did he give you his name?' Pip said, breaking in. She was already trying to work out how she would find the red dress – for the second time.

'He didn't. He was a small guy, petite, but very pushy and quite – I don't know – quite scary, sort of creepy. Charming at first – a bit too charming, almost – until he got angry. He seemed to calm down when he'd seen the dress. He asked if he could have a glass of water. I said okay, and he followed me to the kitchen, and before I knew what was happening, he'd shoved me as hard as he could through the door, and locked it. It was awful,' Henrietta said, clearly sorry for herself. 'My phone was on the outside. I was banging and shouting for simply hours, where *were* you?'

'Not hours,' Pip said, defensively. 'A few minutes at best. But the dealer. Didn't he give you a name or contact details when he answered your ad?'

'He answered my ad, but it was from one of those accounts that doesn't have a name.'

Pip rolled her eyes, on the inside. Great idea, hawking stolen goods online and then meeting up with someone with no name. What could possibly go wrong?

'Didn't he give you a name when he phoned? Or when he arrived?'

'I didn't catch it properly. I thought he said "Enrage", but I can't be sure. It seems like an odd name.'

A suspicion that had already been forming was now becoming more concrete.

'And what did he tell you about what he did?'

'He said that he was a dealer in movie memorabilia and costumes. He had a special interest in the eighties and he was particularly looking for dresses. He said he had a serious buyer, someone with money, someone who was in a hurry to buy right now. A major Julia Roberts fan.'

Pip was pretty sure she knew who this keen, rich, Julia-loving buyer was. In fact, Pip thought she might know who this desperate and dodgy dealer was, too.

'What did he look like?' she asked Henrietta. 'Did he, perhaps, have lots of silver-white hair?'

'How did you know?' Henrietta asked, looking at Pip in astonishment, as if she'd picked the ace of spades in a magic card trick. 'He did! He had the most unusual white hair. And the most perfectly shaped eyebrows you ever saw.'

CHAPTER 36

So de Range – not Enrage, as Henrietta had misheard – was trying to track down a dress to sell to Pip, who was trying to track down the same dress to put back where it belonged! This was a situation that could make your head spin. And it did. Pip had to explain it three times before Henrietta got her head around it all.

'So, just to make sure I understand: this de Range character phoned you out of the blue?'

'Yes,' said Pip. 'It was all rather hush-hush. My friend, Marlene, must have given him my details, although she was very reluctant. First, she put me in touch with the woman called Rosanne, who was murdered. And then de Range contacted me.'

'And then he found me,' said Henrietta.

'Yes. I guess he searched the places online where he knew he might find, let's just say, items of dubious provenance. And with the Julia Roberts angle, he would have been able to search, and he would have found you quite easily.'

'Why don't we just phone him?' Henrietta said. 'Tell him we know what's what, and that he'd better give that dress back.' She picked up her phone, found his number, and pressed call. 'I'll just tell him to bring the dress back, or I'll call the police,' she said.

'Maybe we should just call the police first,' suggested Pip. What was it with these women and not calling the police?

'No!' Henrietta almost shouted this. 'No. If they ask too many questions, it will get back to Daddy that I tried to sell the dress. He will be so disappointed in me. We need to sort it out ourselves.'

Pip wasn't convinced by the idea of inviting an actual thief back to the museum – it hadn't exactly gone well so far – but what else could they do? The whole question of whether or not it was a good idea was, however, moot.

'It says that the number isn't available,' said Henrietta. 'Maybe he's run out of battery.'

'Or,' said Pip, 'maybe he's ditched the phone. He's probably been using a burner all along, if he's the sort of person who deals in stolen goods. And locks women in kitchens. That's a sure sign of being a burner-phone-type. We should wait for him to call me, instead. Think about it. He thinks he's got this great find that he can sell to me for a fortune. He'll be just *dying* to call me and get the deal in process and the money in the bank. You mark my words. My phone will be ringing before 10 a.m. tomorrow. Guaranteed.'

And with that, Pip's phone lit up on the table next to them. The two of them stared at it in wonder. Had they summoned de Range from the ether?

Apparently not. 'Mummy' flashed up on the screen, and Pip's mother's personal ringtone began to sing out – the stirring 'Ride of the Valkyries'.

'Wagner?' Henrietta asked, in a stage whisper.

'Long story,' said Pip, fiddling with the phone to shut it up. 'It was a joke. Not a very good one. My mother is, um…' She couldn't get into a discussion about Mummy right now, but one thing that this phone call told her for sure was that her mother was back in the country. An ache started up in the base of Pip's skull as she considered the inevitable complications that would be coming her way in the next few days. She suspected that those complications would be trotting towards her on cloven hooves, covered with shaggy wool, and making baaing sounds.

She sighed, and said to Henrietta. 'Let's call it a night. As soon as I hear anything from de Range, I'll let you know.'

'You'll do more than let me know,' Henrietta said, her eyes glistening with anger. 'That man pushed me, locked me in the kitchen, and stole my dear late mother's most treasured possession.'

Pip restrained herself from pointing out that Henrietta herself had stolen her dear late mother's most treasured possession, and would cheerfully have passed it on to de Range for cold hard cash if Pip hadn't intervened. People's ability to delude themselves never failed to amaze her.

'I'm going to come with you and confront him myself, Epiphany,' Henrietta added.

Well, she'd finally got her name right, but still, Pip wasn't keen to have her along on a sting operation. 'I don't think that's a good idea.'

'You don't think I can handle some sleazy little fashion weasel?'

'I'm hoping there won't be too much handling to do. I will wait for him to call, and then I'll ask to come and see the merchandise. When I see the dress, I'll tell him that he's busted and that we have witnesses and CCTV tape – which we will, by the way, from across the road. The deal on the table will be that if he gives the dress back, we won't press charges.'

'What on earth do you mean, we won't press charges?' asked Henrietta, flinging her arms out in a dramatic gesture of disbelief. 'We most certainly will. I won't let that man get away with this... this... outrage!'

'You said yourself you didn't want to go to the police,' Pip reminded her. 'There's rather a lot of background to this whole situation that is, um, rather difficult to explain. The details, you know. How the dress went missing in the first place. How de Range came to be here. It might look...' Pip struggled for the word – 'suspicious' came to mind, but that wouldn't do – and settled rather lamely on, '...odd. As you said, your father could get wind of it all.'

'Oh yes, Daddy.' Henrietta seemed not to grasp that her own behaviour was criminal too, and had set the whole thing in motion.

But she wasn't quite ready to dismount from her moral high horse. 'No police. But I want to be there when it all goes down.'

Pip sighed. She knew she'd have to relent. Henrietta was, after all, her boss.

'OK, then,' she said. 'I'll wait for the call, make an arrangement with de Range, and we'll go together.'

'Excellent! How exciting!' said Henrietta, clapping her hands together in glee. 'I've never been on a sting operation before. This will make a great story at parties.'

Pip intended for the so-called sting to be entirely unworthy of a dinner party story – simple, low-stress and incident-free. Was that too much to hope for?

CHAPTER 37

If Pip were a gambler herself, and if she'd made a bet instead of just a prediction, she would be in the money right now. Ten a.m. on the dot, and here was de Range, on the phone.

'Elliot de Range here. I'm pleased to say that I have good news for you.'

Finally, a first name.

'I have the item we spoke about.'

'Gosh, that was fast work,' said Pip. 'I'm impressed. I can see I've come to the right man.'

'As I promised, I get things done.'

'How did you manage that?'

'Well, I can't say exactly, it's a matter of confidentiality,' de Range said reluctantly. What he meant, of course, was that this was a hot item. Stolen.

'I can assure you that my client is interested in such an item only for her own personal collection. She has no interest in showing it or selling it. What I mean is, you can count on her discretion, regarding its source. To be clear, you have the red dress?' said Pip.

'When Elliot de Range says he will bring the goods, Elliot de Range brings the goods.'

'My client will be delighted. I can't wait to show her the dress.'

'I will send you a picture as soon as we finish this phone call. And we will arrange for a viewing of the real item. I assure you that you will not be disappointed.'

'Excellent. As soon as possible.'

'But surely you would like to know the price? Confirm our financial arrangement?'

Damn, Pip had forgotten that part of the negotiation. Seeing as she wasn't planning on giving him any money at all, just grabbing the dress, it had slipped her mind.

'Of course. What are you thinking?'

'It is a very special item. A once in a lifetime opportunity to own an iconic piece.' Honestly, he sounded like a timeshare salesman trying to flog a monsoon week in Tenerife. 'And, as you can imagine, the price tag will reflect that.'

'Understood.' She shifted the phone to the other ear. Would he get a move on and just make a plan already?

'Well, I've priced similar items – nothing *nearly* as special, of course – to determine the value.' De Range hesitated. Pip could almost hear the cogs of his brain whirring. He was wondering what he could get away with. Greedy bugger. He hadn't even paid for the dress. He'd stolen it. He was looking at pure profit.

His nervous, heavy breath came down the phone as he prepared to deliver the figure. 'A hundred thousand pounds,' he said with a rasping exhalation.

Good lord, that seemed a bit steep for a stolen item. It didn't matter to Pip anyhow, given that no one would be paying, but she thought she should at least make a pretence at negotiation.

'Ah, gosh. That is a high price tag. Not to say the dress isn't an absolute treasure, but my client was expecting something rather lower priced, given the private nature of the acquisition, I suspect. Given that this is the start of a collection, and there will be ongoing business for you, perhaps we could factor that into the price?'

'Should we say ninety, as a gesture of goodwill, going forward?' de Range said smoothly. 'And of course there's another five for yourself, over and above whatever your arrangement is with your client. A little gesture of friendship, just between us.'

With a wistful thought to her non-existent cut of a non-existent deal that would be kept from her non-existent client – five thousand pounds would come in *very* handy – Pip agreed. 'Now, when can I see the dress?'

It was agreed that Pip would show the forthcoming photograph to her client, discuss the price, and thereafter – assuming no problems from her client – they would arrange a viewing.

'I will need a deposit in order to show the dress. A token of trust,' said de Range. 'Fifteen per cent would be appropriate.'

Pip set to work dividing by fifteen and timesing by… No, *timesing* by ninety and *dividing* by… Hang on, first you would do fifteen times… Sister Carmelita had always said maths would come in useful one day. Pip suspected that negotiating a deal with a thief wasn't what she'd had in mind. Anyway, it was ninety divided by… Her brow furrowed, her fingers twitching.

'Let's round it off and call it thirteen thousand pounds,' de Range said, helpfully, assessing the silence correctly.

'Of course,' said Pip. 'That shouldn't be a problem.'

'Let's meet tonight,' de Range said. 'The sooner the better, wouldn't you say?'

Pip could not remember when a man had been quite so eager to make a date with her. She was about to agree, when she remembered that she'd agreed to go to that awards thing with Henrietta.

'Unfortunately, I have another arrangement this evening,' she told de Range. 'An awards event that cannot be moved.'

'I don't suppose your arrangement is the Awards for Humane and Sustainable Fashion?' de Range asked.

'Yes, I think that's what she said,' said Pip. 'I'm going with, um, a friend.'

'Well, what do you know? The venue is very close to where I keep my merchandise. Not more than five minutes away. I could meet you there and drive you to the dress.'

Pip thought for a minute. It wasn't ideal. For one thing, Henrietta couldn't come with her. Pip would have to go alone, in his car. She didn't love the idea.

'The dress is ready and waiting,' de Range said. 'You can view it tonight, and pay the deposit. After that, all I will need is the full price, and it's yours.'

'Okay,' she said, trying to ignore the fluttering of misapprehension in her stomach. He only planned to show her the dress, not hand it over. But once he saw Henrietta and realised that they were onto him, he would surely give it up.

'Excellent!' he said.

It was all arranged. They went over the details. De Range would send photographs of the dress. Pip would speak to her client to arrange the cash deposit (she hadn't had a moment to dwell on the thorny question of how she'd pull *that* one off). At 9 p.m., when the actual awards part of the evening would be over, she would meet him at a particular corner outside the venue and the two of them would go together to fetch the dress.

'Sounds like a good plan,' Pip said. 'I'm sure there'll be no problem.'

As it turned out, that was very far from the truth.

CHAPTER 38

'You okay, Pip?' Philip asked. 'You look a little stressed. Are you' – he dropped his voice – 'worried?'

Pip was at the kitchen table, staring into her tea and looking at the pictures that de Range had sent through, wondering how she was going to get her hands on thirteen thousand pounds. And fretting about whether de Range was trustworthy. I mean, obviously he wasn't. He'd stolen the dress, and all but attacked Henrietta. But was he trustworthy – within the context of a criminal dealing in stolen items? And was he dangerous? And would he give her the dress as promised?

Once she had put the phone down on de Range, she'd realised that this whole set up was actually quite complicated, not to mention risky. It had the makings of one of those situations where afterwards everybody would say, 'But Pip, what *were* you thinking?'

And then there was the question of how much to tell Arabella. Henrietta didn't know that Arabella knew about the dress, and Arabella obviously didn't know that Henrietta was involved. Who to tell what? The problem had been avoided in the short term, as Arabella had phoned in sick, but would certainly reappear. As problems tended to do.

'Oh yes, I'm fine,' she said to Philip, now. 'I've just got rather a lot of tricky things on my mind.'

'What sort of things?' Philip asked.

'Oh, you know, money and trust issues and transport and practical problems and fear. The usual.'

'Can I try and help you with that?' Philip asked. His voice took on the sing-song quality that had sent her to sleep the last time. 'The thing is,' he continued, 'most anxiety and stress comes from thoughts of the future, the unknown. If you can be present in the here and now, you can release your body from the cycle of worry. There are a few techniques I've been working on that I find help me to stay in the moment. They have been really helpful to me. Close your eyes.'

'I don't know, Philip,' Pip said. 'Remember last time.'

There was a moment's silence while they both remembered.

'No visualisations this time,' Philip said. 'This is more about being present through the senses. Give it a try. I really feel it will help.'

Somewhat reluctantly, Pip agreed, just because he was so kind and helpful and she didn't want to seem ungrateful. And she actually was very anxious this time, so it couldn't hurt.

'Good.' He smiled and sat down opposite her. 'Now, I want you to focus on your senses. I'm going to ask you some questions, but you don't have to answer out loud. You just have to focus fully on each answer in your head, okay?'

She nodded.

'Now, name to yourself one thing you can hear.'

The annoying hum of the fridge. What was that rattle? And why didn't someone fix it?

'Now, think of one thing you can smell.'

The gross odour of the breakfast burrito that someone had recently microwaved. Egg and spices in the morning. It made Pip's stomach turn.

'Now, focus on one thing you can feel in your body.'

That would be tension in her neck from the stress of having to get the damn dress back from an actual criminal. It felt as if a giant was resting his massive paw on her left shoulder.

'Now, what can you taste?'

The dregs of the too-milky tea she had been drinking before Philip had interrupted her with his shooey-whooey nonsense.

'And finally, one thing you can see.'

She opened her eyes and looked into Philip's kind eyes, and his broad, calm face, free of anger or stress, full of concern and care. She smiled.

'I see you,' she said. 'I really do feel better, Philip, thank you.'

She did – for about five minutes. But back at her desk, she started to worry about all the things she had to do to get ready for tonight. Starting with the money. Henrietta pleaded poverty, but who knew what the situation was, really? Pip hoped she could come up with the deposit. She needed to be able to at least pretend to have the deposit to get access to the dress. Pip herself was a non-starter for the money. She had been considering downgrading to single-ply loo paper before she'd won the two hundred pounds at the races. Where on earth was she going to drum up thirteen thousand pounds?

As if on cue, Henrietta arrived. Pip had messaged her to tell her about de Range's call, asking her to get to work pronto so they could sort out the details.

'Oh hello, Pip,' Henrietta said, breezing into the office with two coffees in a cardboard tray. 'I brought us lattes. Double shot, to help with the planning.'

Emily popped her head into the office. 'Hello, Henrietta,' she said, brightly. 'I thought I spotted you coming in.'

Had been waiting in eager anticipation with eyes glued to the door, more like, thought Pip, reaching for a cup.

Emily eyed the coffee tray. 'Oh, and you went to Bean There. I love Bean There!'

An awkward silence hung in the air as the three women surveyed the two coffees.

'Are you two talking about planning the exhibition?' Emily continued gamely. 'I have a little time. Should I join you? Because I've had some ideas.'

'Oh no, we're not talking about that,' Henrietta said with a dismissive wave. 'Pip and I have another thing going on. Nothing you need to concern yourself with. We'd better get on with it, it's quite time-sensitive. And important. I'll let you know if I need anything.'

Before poor Emily had got two steps down the passage, Henrietta was gabbling on excitedly to Pip, 'So, you were right! Ten a.m. on the dot, you said, and there he was. Clever you. You knew he'd come crawling. Isn't this thrilling? Now, how are we going to trap him; what's the plan? Will I need a disguise, do you think? I had in mind something chic but practical, Mata Hari meets Lara Croft, with perhaps a touch more verve?'

Pip cut her off. 'We can discuss wardrobe later, but for now, let me fill you in on what I've agreed with de Range.'

'That snake!'

'Well, yes. But at least he's our snake now.'

Pip explained about the deal – that she would bring him the deposit and he would take her somewhere nearby to get the dress. That they would meet at nine outside the venue, and Henrietta would have to follow them, keeping track of Pip via a location app on her mobile phone.

'First things first, you're going to need to come up with thirteen thousand pounds for the deposit.'

Henrietta looked aghast. 'Thirteen thousand pounds? Where on earth would I get thirteen thousand pounds? I told you, my father is as mean as a Madrid madam.'

Whatever that meant. When Pip had accidentally roomed with a madam in Madrid, she'd seemed very nice. Pip gave herself a shake. No time to get distracted by her memories.

'Can you borrow it from someone? It's just temporary. We'll get it straight back.'

Henrietta looked downcast. 'If anyone was willing to lend me that sort of money, I'd have asked them long ago. Probably have, in fact. We wouldn't be here if I could get my hands on cash like that, Pip.'

'How much cash can you lay your hands on right now?' Pip asked.

'I guess four hundred pounds, maybe five hundred at a pinch.'

It was remarkable how little cash really rich people actually had. Pip knew this from her time working on the superyachts. Rich people had been forever bumming smokes off deckhands, or Maseratis off other, richer people. They'd thought nothing of stiffing you on the tip whilst wearing thousand-pound sunglasses.

'OK, so you've got five hundred-ish and I've got the two hundred that I won at the races.' Pip was pacing now, trying to get her brain going. It seemed to work, because she suddenly remembered a scene from a movie with a suitcase full of newspaper cut out to look like money. 'I tell you what we'll do,' she said to Henrietta. 'We'll photocopy some bills, and put a layer of the real ones on top. I'll tell de Range I won't hand over the deposit until we have the dress in hand. I'll just open the bag and give him a quick flash of the notes.'

Pip got a pencil and paper and worked it out, after a few tries. If they used fifties, they would need two hundred and sixty bills for thirteen thousand pounds.

'What do you say we give Emily this job?' Pip suggested. 'I've got the two hundred in my purse, so she can copy those. We'll need a smallish bag to put it all in. We'll pack it in snugly so de Range can only see the top ones. You get a bag and get what you can from the cash machine, and we're good to go.'

Emily, of course, was thrilled to be of service. Pip called her in and Henrietta told her that the money was needed for a shoot they were working on. Emily started to pepper her with questions, but Henrietta blew her off. 'I can't chat now, I have errands to run,' she said, making to leave the office. 'Important errands for the thing I'm doing with Pip. I'll tell you some other time.'

Henrietta turned as she got to the door. 'Hey, Pip, what are you wearing for the do tonight? Would you like to borrow something? I've got loads of clothes. My backup clothes cupboard is downstairs. I can't fit everything into my flat; the dressing room is minute. Anyway, you can help yourself if you like.'

She reached into her bag and pulled out a key on a key ring shaped like a fifties dress, black with white polka dots. She handed it to Pip. 'Emily can show you which cupboard. Just take whatever you want.'

Pip eyed Henrietta's svelte frame and wondered exactly how she expected Pip to jam her considerably taller body into her clothes. But it didn't do to be ungrateful, especially to your boss. She'd learnt that the hard way. She smiled and thanked Henrietta. 'It will be a big help, not having to go home to change. There's so much going on here,' she said.

'Exactly, we have a lot to sort out. Ooh, I've got a fab idea. I'll book us both for a blow-dry at the place I go to down the road. They always fit me in. Three thirty, OK? That should give us time.'

'Um, sure, OK. You're the boss,' said Pip. It really was no wonder Henrietta was in such financial trouble, with her lattes and blow-dries, but Pip was not going to say no to a free session at the hairdresser.

'What fun! Girls' outing. I can't wait,' said Henrietta, shivering with excitement and putting her arm through Pip's for a squeeze. She was acting like they were going to a hen party. Had she actually forgotten that they were actually going to try to get back a dress that Henrietta had stolen, by double-crossing an actual criminal and possibly putting themselves in actual danger?

'Right, let me phone and book those blow-dries. We've got to look our best. After all, it's a big night,' Henrietta said, with a huge conspiratorial wink. 'A very big night.'

Henrietta swept out of the room, with Emily looking wistfully after her.

CHAPTER 39

The ka-chunk, ka-chunk of the photocopy machine finally came to a halt. Twelve thousand five hundred pounds in fake notes. A loud, rasping, schick-schick sound replaced the ka-chunk. Emily must be using the guillotine to slice up the notes. Pip reckoned that her head would be on the block in two ticks, if Emily had her way. She had a big-time crush on Henrietta. Henrietta, meanwhile, seemed completely unaware of it, and blithely unconcerned about stamping on the poor devoted girl's feelings.

Emily came in with the notes and sullenly put them on Pip's desk.

'Thank you,' Pip said. 'Sorry about this morning. It's just some little project that Henrietta needs my help on, and she wants to keep it a bit under the radar for now. I hope you understand. It's not very creative, or she would have asked you. I just know she wants to keep your talent focused on the seventies exhibition, which is much more important. And forward-facing, you know.'

'Sure,' said Emily, unconvincingly unconcerned. 'So, you want me to show you the cupboard?'

'I would, thank you. And Emily, would you do me a favour? Do you think you can help me select something to wear? You've got such style.' Honestly, mollifying Emily was becoming exhausting. But Pip knew from her brief time as the personal assistant to a top FBI hostage negotiator that nothing broke down resentment quicker than a well-placed dash of flattery.

'I'm very busy with Arabella being off sick, but I guess I could make a bit of time,' Emily said, and then added, looking at her watch: 'In fact, I suppose now would be okay; I've got a gap. What look are we going for? What exactly is the function?'

'An evening thing. Henrietta invited me to go along. Fashion awards.'

Emily's eyes widened. 'Oh yes. The Awards for Humane and Sustainable Fashion,' she said.

Pip nodded.

'Those awards are just so important. Humanity. Sustainability. Such a good cause, and so hot right now; I'm sure *everybody* will be there. It's going to be at The Waiting Room, right? I read that. So amazing, I'd love to go there. And this is so perfect, you wearing something from Henrietta's wardrobe. Reuse, recycle, upcycle; that's all the rage, you know. None of this nonsense of commissioning a new dress for every occasion.'

Which Pip had literally never done, except when Flis had got married. Pip tried not to think about the bridesmaid's dresses that she and their cousin Charlotte (a foot shorter than Pip, and a stone heavier) had been talked into. 'Maypole dancer with a romantic modern twist,' had been Flis's description. Pip had burned the photographs.

By the time Emily flung open the big double-door closet that housed Henrietta's backup clothes, she had warmed up considerably. Her hands moved briskly through the hangers, and she made little 'ooh' and 'aah' noises. Within minutes, she had reverted to her usual gushy self.

'Oh my word, look at this… Ah, this would look great on you… Not that, it's too small… Isn't this coat amazing? I saw one like it at Paris Fashion Week. I suppose it might just fit, you could try… And those boots!'

'Nothing too tight or too fussy,' Pip said. 'I want something that lets me move. Something I can run in.'

'Run? Why would you want to run when you're going to an awards ceremony?'

Fair question. 'Er, I don't know. If I'm a bit late? Or there's a fire, maybe?'

Fortunately, Emily was easily distracted by the clothes. 'Eeek! Is this a Gaultier? Yes I thought so… Here, hold this… Argh! The colour! Too small, though.'

After a good deal of gasping and squealing, followed by the regular announcement that a particular garment was too small, Emily had a selection of outfits that might actually be persuaded to fit Pip. Pip selected a lovely flowing green sheath that hung and slithered over her body. On Henrietta, it was probably floor length, but it reached to Pip's calves, and the stretchy fabric meant that it looked great, despite not being exactly the size intended for Pip's body. She gave a high kick and found the dress pleasingly unrestrictive. An outfit that brought out the colour of her eyes, while giving her room to take a man down if she had to. Perfect.

Emily gave Pip a quizzical look, but pronounced the dress, 'Stylish, without trying too hard.'

Henrietta returned to the museum in her party attire – a black, high-necked A-line chiffon number, which even Pip could tell was worth as much as a small second-hand Mini. She had a perfect little bag for the cash, and another perfect, bigger one full of make-up and jewellery.

'Looks great on you,' Henrietta said, when she saw Pip in the dress. 'You should keep it. It's so long and loose on me that I've never really worn it.'

Emily looked as green as the dress.

'Well, it's thanks to Emily,' Pip said. 'She chose the outfit for me. She's got a good eye.' Pip didn't think she'd ever used the phrase 'good eye' as much as she had in the last two weeks, not even when she'd worked briefly as a receptionist for an optometrist. That accident with the eye drops could have happened to anyone – how was she supposed to know that they were flammable?

'She has got a good eye, hasn't she?' Henrietta said, as if this was the first time it had occurred to her. Emily glowed. Pushing a jewellery pouch towards Pip, Henrietta said, 'There are some pretty jade earrings in here somewhere. They might go well with the dress. Try them.'

Henrietta and Pip went back to the office to stuff the perfect little bag with the notes. It was surprising how little space such a large wodge of fake cash took up.

'Here we are, stashing the cash,' said Henrietta, with a laugh. She seemed to be having a marvellous time. She was treating the evening's activity as if it were a cross between a girls' night out and a murder mystery evening, with a sprinkle of dressing up and a dash of intrigue. She seemed excited at the chance to teach old de Range a lesson, but completely unaware of the potential danger of the undertaking. Rather, she saw it as an opportunity to enjoy some larks and get some stories to regale future dinner companions with.

Henrietta looked down at her watch, which appeared to be lightly encrusted with diamonds. 'Ooh. It's hair time! Let's go.'

They pushed the cash stash to the back of the filing cabinet and headed out for the hairdresser. Henrietta, of course, went to one of those insanely expensive, ridiculously over-designed salons that Pip would never usually set foot in. But oh my, what a head massage that shampooist gave. Pip felt her cares and worries – and there were many – fall away as the strong fingers caressed her scalp. The blow dry left her looking sleek and shiny and, well, rich. Henrietta did, too, although she always looked that way.

With a quick pass by the office to fetch the cash before heading out on the town, they waved goodbye to Emily and headed out.

'You look fab,' said Henrietta.

'You too,' said Pip. 'Now let's go get that dress.'

CHAPTER 40

It was rush hour, and the traffic was insane. It would have been quicker to get the Tube than to drive, but Henrietta needed the car so that she could follow Pip and de Range to the undisclosed destination, where the two women would confront de Range and make off with the dress. Pip ran her through the plan one last time. It was a simple one, but the most important thing was that de Range didn't see Henrietta before the confrontation. That would send him into a spin. If he saw Henrietta with Pip, the whole plan would fail – he'd know that he was being set up.

'Yes, yes, I know,' said Henrietta impatiently, moving out of her lane, which was going at one mile an hour, into the right-hand lane, which was going at one point one miles an hour. She repeated Pip's instructions back to her. 'I won't come out of the venue until I know that you're on your way. Then I'll be right behind you.'

She swung back into the left lane, eliciting a volley of hooting from the car she'd cut in on. 'People are really rude,' she said, snippily. 'He can see I'm in a hurry.' And she switched back again. A fresh crescendo of hooting.

Pip tried not to stress about the traffic, or Henrietta's driving, or the evening ahead, but it wasn't easy. Her heart was racing and her tummy was doing a jig. Oh, for Philip with his visualisations, or Flis with her turmeric candles. Still, at least she looked nice, with her smooth hair and her silky green dress.

*

There was an actual red carpet. It was a small one, admittedly, and a little frayed around the edges, but when Henrietta took Pip's arm and swept up to the door, Pip couldn't help but feel a thrill. It was like all the red-carpet footage she'd ever watched on television since she was about nine years old. There was even a journalist of sorts, a slight, red-haired man in a hunting vest with millions of pockets, holding an iPhone as a microphone, and slung with cameras. He was taking pictures and asking people about their dresses. He recognised Henrietta at once, and zeroed in on her.

'Who are you wearing?' he asked, putting the iPhone to her face.

Henrietta did a bashful, fake-modest thing and said, 'Oh, hi, Brad. This old favourite? It's a little something I got from my mum, the actress Charise Adderley. She loved it so. Would you believe Audrey Hepburn wore it once? I thought, what a special occasion to wear it, in honour of a cause so close to my dear mother's heart.'

Pip was amazed. Henrietta was usually all over the place, but here she was delivering this moving little anecdote which Pip was one hundred per cent sure had been prepared in advance, without so much as a pause or a hesitation.

Brad was lapping it up. 'Wow, that's a true heritage piece.'

'You're so right. Reuse, recycle; that's where it's at, Brad. True vintage wear. Fifty years old!' Henrietta said, with a charming smile and a tinkling laugh.

'And you?' he turned to Pip. 'Who are you wearing?'

'This is something I borrowed from a friend,' Pip replied, looking to Henrietta for guidance.

'Balenciaga. 1975, if I'm not mistaken,' Henrietta said, taking Pip's arm – the one that wasn't clutching their sack of cash. 'Well, nice to see you, Brad, we'd better get inside. Please come by the museum sometime soon, and we'll chat. There are big plans afoot.'

Inside, they fell upon the champagne which was proffered from a silver tray at the door.

'To justice!' Henrietta said loudly and dramatically, clinking her glass against Pip's and taking a swig.

'Only one glass,' Pip reminded Henrietta. 'We need our wits about us.'

'Of course!' Henrietta downed the glass and took another.

They circled the room of beautiful people. Pip knew not a soul, but Henrietta was in her element, moving from one group to the next, air kissing, complimenting, laughing her tinkling laugh. She introduced Pip as her dear, *dear* friend, and squeezed her arm companionably.

The MC called the room to attention. On a screen behind him was a projection of a version of an Erté magazine cover for *Harper's Bazaar*, in the distinctive deco style. Pip recognised it at once. A woman in a blue dress scattered with stars stood on a staircase. In the original, there were three white planters with red flowers tumbling from them. In this version, the planters were full of old clothes and rags, tumbling to the floor, dripping with black stuff – oil, presumably. Effective, if not very subtle.

The MC – a poor woman's Benedict Cumberbatch, was how Pip would describe him – welcomed everyone, and gave a little speech about how fashion was ruining the planet and killing the polar bears, but also about how amazing and wonderful and vital fashion was. Not an easy job. As he spoke, the image on screen alternated with three more: all Erté covers for *Harper's Bazaar*, all altered to incorporate messages of waste and destruction, while also being stylish and rather lovely.

As the MC launched into a description of the awards, Pip was transported back to her school days and the prize-giving ceremony that had ended each year. The clever, compliant swots had walked back and forth to the stage, claiming the silverware. Once, when she was about ten, Pip had won something herself – most improved netball player, it had been; marginally improved from a base of zero ability and no effort – and had been so unprepared to hear her name that they'd had to call her three times, while the girls next to her nudged and pushed her to her feet.

It was rather like that when Henrietta's name was called tonight. It hadn't occurred to Pip that Henrietta was in the running for an award until that moment. Henrietta did a good job of being surprised and overwhelmed, touching her hand to her chest and mouthing, 'Who, me?' She was glowing when she came back to Pip with a plaque made – they had been told – out of a recycled wardrobe salvaged from the wreck of the *Titanic*. Pip wasn't one hundred per cent on board with the Titanic symbolism, but the plaque looked great, and Henrietta was delighted to be awarded 'in recognition of her contribution to heritage fashion'.

The MC was wrapping up, and Brad was making his way over in their direction.

'So well done! I'm thrilled for you. I'm going to go now,' said Pip, checking the time. 'I'm meeting de Range in five minutes at the corner. Give me two minutes on top of that, then come and follow me.'

'I'll be there,' said Henrietta, helping herself to another glass of champagne. Catching Pip's look, she said, 'Just a sip. I won, darling. It's a celebration. Don't worry, I'll be right behind you. Promise. Make sure your location sharing is on.'

Pip checked her phone for the zillionth time. Location sharing was on.

Brad had reached them by now, and was asking Henrietta a long and fawning question about fashion and heritage and sustainability, and her great contribution to humanity. Pip tightened her grip on the sack of cash and leaned in to Henrietta. 'It's on; keep track of me. I'm out of here. See you there, wherever "there" is.'

CHAPTER 41

Elliot de Range was on the corner as arranged, leaning against a car, his silver-white hair flashing alternately purple and red under the blinking neon lights of the Raj of India restaurant behind him.

'Hello,' Pip said.

'Good evening,' de Range said. 'How delightful you look. I am most eager to show you my find. I think you'll be delighted. You have the deposit, I take it?'

Pip indicated to the bag. 'Of course, as agreed,' she said.

De Range reached for it. Pip unzipped the bag, but kept a grip on it. 'I'm sure you'll understand that I want to hold on to this until I see the merchandise.'

She felt like she had been transported into some bad made-for-Netflix series about drug dealers.

'Thirteen thousand pounds,' she said, holding the bag open so that the clean, new, legit fifties caught the red and purple light. 'It's all here, and the rest has been arranged. I'll have it transferred to you as soon as I've seen the dress.'

De Range peered in and caressed the notes gently, then withdrew his hand from the bag. Pip closed it quickly.

'Marvellous,' he said. 'I'm sure we'll make your client a very happy woman. The car's right here.' He held his keys up and touched the remote control to unlock the doors of the low, sleek Mercedes.

Pip got in next to him and texted Henrietta:

'Leaving now.'

The car slid out of the parking place. As Pip gazed out of the window, hoping for a glimpse of Henrietta heading out to follow her, she was sure she saw Emily. What could she be doing here? The poor girl must have come to check out the red-carpet procession and keep an eye out for her Big Crush, Henrietta. Unless it was just someone who looked very like her?

'Where are we going?' Pip asked de Range, trying to sound curious rather than petrified. 'It's all very mysterious.'

'Apologies for all the secrecy, but I'm afraid it's my policy. You can't trust anybody these days. I deal in valuable merchandise and you wouldn't believe how many thieves and ruffians I've had try to get their hands on it. Not that I think you're a thief or a ruffian,' he added, reassuringly. 'But it's shocking, really, how little you can trust most people.'

Pretty rich, coming from a man who had proved himself both a thief and a ruffian, stealing the dress and manhandling Henrietta.

'I quite understand,' Pip said. 'You need to protect yourself and your business. No offence taken.'

He smiled, eyes on the road. 'It's quite close,' he said. 'Not far to go now.'

Pip eyed her phone. No word from Henrietta. She was probably driving, so she couldn't text. She looked in the side mirror to see if she could catch sight of the car. Nothing.

'This is just a little storage space I keep,' Elliot said, drawing the car into a narrow alleyway that led to a roll-up metal door. 'Good to have somewhere in the city for times like this, when I need to keep items on hand to show clients.' He turned off the car and said, 'Shall we?'

Pip had been expecting an elegant shop, or perhaps even a flat. Not a storage facility in an alley. This was starting to feel like the time that the tuk tuk driver had tried to kidnap her in Bangkok. And there was still no sign that Henrietta was following. Pip thought, with a sinking heart, of all the champagne she'd seen Henrietta drink.

Pip took her time getting out of the car. The timing was going to be very tricky. She didn't want to get into a confrontation with de Range before Henrietta arrived – *if* she was even coming. Pip didn't know how de Range would react when she told him she was onto him and was going to take the dress – and the money, or report him to the police. He didn't look very tough – he was certainly no Jimmy – but he was a criminal, after all. She would prefer not to confront him alone, and especially not in some warehouse in a secluded alleyway with no way of escape.

Pip closed the car door and walked slowly after de Range. He unlocked a number of locks and padlocks on the storage unit and pulled the roller up. Behind the roller was what looked like an old shop front with a glass door. He unlocked that, and felt along the wall for a light switch.

'Ready?'

Pip nodded.

'You are going to be blown away. I can hardly look at it without getting tears in my eyes!' he said, holding his hands together over his heart, as if this were some cheesy musical and he was about to sing. He turned on a light, then stood aside to let Pip in.

Pushed against the walls were big cardboard boxes, antique furniture and stacked frames. The interior of the room was filled with racks and racks of what were presumably clothes, covered in cloth to keep the dust off. And in the centre, on a mannequin, was the bright red *Pretty Woman* dress.

'Oh, it's magnificent,' Pip said, quite genuinely struck, yet again, at how beautiful it was. 'This is really the actual dress? From the movie?'

'The real thing,' he said. 'As worn by the glorious Julia Roberts herself.'

The two of them surveyed the dress in admiration.

'It's perfect,' Pip said. 'I'm sure my client will be delighted with it.'

'Do you need to get in touch with her?'

'No. I have her authority to purchase. How would you suggest we proceed with the handover?' she asked, stalling for time as she glanced down at her phone. No message. Where on earth was Henrietta?

'Very simple. As long as the deposit's all in order, I could deliver it to you during the week.'

'I would rather take it now. Otherwise, I might never hear from you again.' Pip laughed in what she hoped was a this-is-a-joke way, rather than an I-don't–trust-you-because-you-are-a-criminal way.

'I have far more to lose,' said de Range, with a smile.

Pip sighed, and nodded. 'I suppose that's true.' Once Henrietta arrived, and de Range realised he was busted, it wouldn't matter who was supposed to get what, when. The threat of the police would surely make him give up his plan.

De Range looked at her expectantly, eyeing the bag. Pip didn't move. Every second she delayed was a second closer to Henrietta's arrival.

De Range reached out his hand. On his pinkie was a large signet ring that looked like it would be quite handy in a fight. His initials were engraved next to a small ruby: EdR. Or was it Ed R? Pip felt light-headed. Ed R, the name in Rosanne's appointment book, the last person to see her alive. It hadn't been Ed R at all: it had been EdR – Elliot de Range. What was it he had said when they'd first met? *Who wouldn't kill for a Julia Roberts dress?*

Elliot de Range was Ed R, the last name in Rosanne's appointment book. The person she'd seen before she died. Rosanne hadn't committed suicide. Rosanne had been killed. The only question was why. And now the murderer was holding out his hand, waiting for Pip to hand him a bag of cash. Photocopied cash. Once she handed it over, if he looked inside and realised it was fake, she was done for. She hesitated. But had no other option but to give him the bag.

De Range snatched it from her, his greedy little eyes gleaming. 'Excellent,' he said. 'So that's all arranged. Now you just need to give me an address. And get the rest of the money, of course.'

'That won't be a problem,' said Pip weakly, hoping against hope that he wouldn't check the cash. If he didn't see the fake notes, she could at least get away from this dark and isolated storage unit, and come up with a new plan. Because he would discover the fakes soon enough, and there would be no delivery of the dress. And then Pip would be back to square one, and two hundred pounds poorer, with two disappointed bosses.

'Shall we go?' she said. 'I've seen the dress, and I'm sure my client will be delighted. It's getting late, and I need to get back. People will be looking for me.' She said the last part in a slightly high-pitched voice. Best to get going as soon as possible. With no Henrietta to back her up, Pip didn't feel safe. If de Range saw the fake notes, she wasn't sure that she would make it out of this warehouse alive.

'Yes, let's go,' he said, opening the bag and slipping his hand in, feeling the notes. Pip looked on, frozen. She saw on his face the moment his fingers felt the transition from the bank notes to the photocopy paper. There was an instant of confusion, then rage. She turned to run, but she hadn't gone three steps when she felt the full force of him land on her back, taking her down, down, down to the concrete floor. And then, nothing.

CHAPTER 42

Her eyes fluttered open. The light was terribly bright. She closed them again. There was a pounding in her head, and what felt like something damp on her face. Was it blood? Pip tried to move her hand to touch the liquid, but her arms wouldn't move. Struggling towards consciousness, she tried to work out what was going on, but her head felt as if it was filled with thick mud.

She pushed the pain and the pounding aside. She needed to focus. She needed to remember what had happened. Ed R. Elliot de Range. The dress. The money. No Henrietta. The hard fall on the concrete floor. She opened her eyes. There he was, in front of her. With a gun.

'Ah, I see you are awake,' he said, peering into her face. 'Well, well, well. We do find ourselves in a bit of a pickle, don't we, Epiphany? If that's even your real name. What to do, what to do?'

'Let me go,' Pip croaked, pulling against the ties that held her to a wooden chair, her hands tied behind her. She knew this scene from a thousand movies. It did not generally end well.

Elliot crossed his arms, the gun resting loosely in the crook of his elbow. 'So you thought you could come and take a valuable, iconic dress from me, did you? You thought you could scam me and run? Well you don't know Elliot de Range, I'm afraid.'

'We can just call off the deal,' said Pip. 'You keep the dress. We forget this ever happened.'

Elliot ignored her and continued his musing, 'I must say, I'm very disappointed. Very. It was all going so very nicely. I'd found the dress, found a buyer. Got that pesky Rosanne woman out of the picture.'

'You killed her, didn't you? You arranged to meet her and source the red dress for her, and once you had whatever information you needed, you pushed her off the bridge.'

'You are less stupid than you look,' he said. 'But not clever enough to cheat Elliot de Range. As for that woman, she brought it on herself. She tried to blackmail me, stupid bitch! Just because she'd stumbled on some of my… shall we say, more controversial finds. The cheek of it! Well, I sorted *her* out very nicely. And as a bonus, no cut for her!' He laughed maniacally at his own sick joke.

'Now, I'm afraid, it's not going nicely at all. In fact, it's going very, very badly for you,' he said, reaching for a scarf. He flourished it like a magician, snapping it mid air before taking it between his two hands and stepping behind her to put it over her mouth.

'Hhnmf… *Mmmhff*!' Pip did her best to yell, but produced nothing more than a strangled and muffled whimper.

'This isn't some two-bit operation that you can trick with a bag of fake money,' de Range continued, tying the gag behind her head. 'This is an international syndicate. I have partners. Bosses, even. There is a lot of money at stake, you know. *A lot.* And I'm not going to jeopardise it all over some silly girl and a dress.'

He looked at her, sneering. He seemed to be considering his options. Pip turned her head and looked hopefully towards the door. She strained her ears for the sound of a car, or footsteps. Nothing. She was all alone.

'You're coming with me, and I'm going to make you disappear. Or my associates will. I'm not one to get blood on my hands. Or my clothes.'

In all the scrapes and perilous situations she'd been in before, Pip had never really believed that she wouldn't escape unscathed. She'd known she would always make a plan, or argue her way out of trouble, or be rescued by some kind soul or a random act of chance. But now her good luck had run out. She was in terrible danger. She whimpered into her gag, and felt tears come to her eyes.

'I know, I know,' de Range said, patting her shoulder. 'It's very sad. Tragic. It's hard for me, too, you know. If I didn't have to kill you, we could have been friends. We could have made good money together. But you had to go and try to steal my dress.'

'It's not yours, it's mine,' came Henrietta's steely voice from the doorway.

Pip had never been so pleased to see anyone in her life. Not even that time when Brad Pitt had popped into the gelato shop she'd been managing in Marbella, looking hot enough to melt the entire stock, and had ordered a blood orange sorbet.

'You!' de Range said, turning the gun toward Henrietta. 'What are you doing here?'

'I came to get my mother's dress back,' Henrietta said, walking into the room. She looked completely calm. For a spoilt society girl, she had nerves of steel. Probably went to one of those horrible boarding schools where you had to fight for your share of gruel as some sort of character-building thing. Pip certainly knew all about that.

Before de Range could react to the surprise arrival of Henrietta, they all heard footsteps approaching. As one, the three of them looked to the door.

Emily was silhouetted against the door, framed by the street lights filtering in. 'Henrietta, I've brought you…' she started, and then stopped, taking in the gun trained on Henrietta, and Pip tied to a chair.

'Henrietta!' cried Emily, and then to de Range: 'You leave her alone.' She stamped her foot like an angry child. And then, somewhat as an afterthought, 'And her,' gesturing towards Pip.

De Range stared at the new arrival in shock. 'Where did you come from? How did you get here? And why?' he said to Henrietta, waving his gun. And then he pointed it at Emily, 'And who's that? This isn't some sort of tea party.'

'We're partners, me and her,' Henrietta said, gesturing towards Pip. 'We set you up. Emily here is our friend, although I'm not quite sure why she's here. But still. We're the backup. And you are in serious trouble.' Henrietta looked very fierce, for a woman with a gun pointed at her.

De Range looked from Henrietta to Emily, his attention drawn away from Pip. It was one thing disposing of one nosey woman, but three? He stood staring at the new arrivals, his gun moving from the one to the other, unsure.

It was now or never. Pip took the opportunity and swung her right leg up in a powerful swing kick. It connected hard with Elliot's hand and he gave a yelp of pain. A shot rang out and the gun clattered to the ground.

Pip looked around in terror – no sign of blood, no one on the floor writhing in agony, or dead, thank God. No one had been hit. The bullet was probably lodged in some priceless Chinese chest or a stolen Picasso.

She gave de Range another kick for good measure, a good hard one, just like she'd learned at Jimmy's Glove Box, her chair teetering dangerously with the force of it. She didn't see where the kick landed, but de Range exhaled heavily with a loud, 'Ooof!'

Seeing him momentarily incapacitated, Emily and Henrietta both lunged at the gun, knocking heads in their attempts to grab it before de Range got up. They both looked dazed, but thankfully de Range wasn't going anywhere quickly; he was bent over, winded, or hurting, or both.

Now was the time to take him on and put him out of action, but Pip was stuck to the chair like an idiot. She tipped herself forward onto her feet, carrying the stupid chair on her back like a tortoise with its shell, and pivoted. A chair leg smacked into de Range with a resounding crack. Pip turned to see him clutch his jaw and go down. She wished Jimmy were here to see that move; he would be so proud. She then sat down on the chair, pinning de Range inelegantly to the ground beneath it, like a butterfly pinned in a display case. The chair was over his chest, one chair leg on his jacket, one of Pip's feet on his arm. He was cursing and threatening, his free arm flailing at Pip wildly, smacking at the only bit of her he could reach, her left thigh. If someone would just come over here and untie her hands, she'd be pleased to give him one back.

Emily came up behind her, and had the presence of mind to pull the gag down from Pip's face – a rather lovely red and gold Hermès scarf, she noted.

'Henrietta, come and help!' Pip yelled.

'Henrietta!' Emily shouted. 'Now would be good!'

But Henrietta was still holding the gun and was staring at it as if it were Excalibur pulled from the stone. It was as if she didn't even hear them. She seemed to be in shock.

'Lower that gun, Henrietta. Put it down nice and gently; we don't want anyone to get hurt,' came a man's calm voice. Pip swivelled in the chair and saw Gordon, his eyes on Henrietta.

'Gordon? What are you doing here?'

There was no time for exchanging pleasantries. De Range was squirming and pushing at the chair, trying to escape. Thinking unusually quickly, Emily sat on Pip's lap for extra weight and reached behind her to try and undo the ties, but the whole edifice was rocking wildly, the two women listing and pitching as if they were on a boat in a storm.

'Gordon! Help! Get over here!'

Gordon, who had been tending to Henrietta – who was completely fine, in absolutely no danger at all – dragged himself away.

'Oh, yes sorry,' he said, putting the gun he'd taken from Henrietta into his waistband and coming over. Planting one foot heavily on de Range's chest, he held the chair steady while Henrietta untied Pip's hands and helped her and Emily up. Gordon reached down, sending the chair clattering to the floor, grabbed de Range by the collar and hoisted him to his feet.

De Range knew he was done for. Four against one were not the kind of odds he was going to take. Especially in view of the fact that they now had the gun. Pip and Gordon worked together, trussing him up in the chair Pip had so recently vacated, tying him down securely with a selection of ties, scarves and belts rifled from his collection.

'Not that one,' de Range hissed, at a certain point. 'It's a genuine Gucci snakeskin belt, you philistines.'

Pip ignored his complaints, but Gordon gave a snort of laughter. 'Oh, these ladies have you good and proper,' he said cheerfully, pulling up a chair of his own, as if they were two blokes having a chat over a beer. 'Must be pretty embarrassing, getting your arse handed to you by some women from a dress museum. Big, tough criminal like yourself.'

While Pip phoned the police and told them where they were, Emily had pulled out her phone and was snapping pictures and selfies.

'Is this the time, Emily?' snapped Henrietta.

'Do you have any idea how many likes this will get?' said Emily, standing up for herself for once. 'This is going to make me.'

Gordon double-checked the ties on Elliot, while Henrietta strolled around the room. 'Pretty sure that's the Picasso that was stolen from Sotheby's before the auction in February,' she said, indicating a picture in the corner. 'And that is definitely the royal wedding gown that went missing from the V&A.'

'You will all be hearing from my lawyers,' said Elliot. 'This is an outrage. You are trespassing on my private property. The damage you've caused… And the emotional pain… There will be a civil suit. Millions, it'll cost you. Millions.'

'You be quiet,' Pip snapped. 'You'll have plenty of time to talk when the police come. I phoned them and they're on their way. I think they're going to be very interested when they realise that you're the mystery man that Rosanne Roberts met on the day that she was murdered.'

De Range turned on a dime, from threatening to wheedling. 'Let's not be hasty, now. I feel sure we can sort this out between us, without resorting to the authorities. We will just tell them there was a small misunderstanding. If we work together, I can make this very beneficial for you. There's a great deal of money to be made; more than enough to go round…'

'No deal. Now shut up or you get the Hermès gag.'

With de Range quiet again, Pip turned her attention to Henrietta and said angrily, 'Where were you? You were meant to be right behind me. I could have been killed.'

'Pip, I'm so, so sorry,' she said. 'I had a bit of trouble with my car… The pavement… A tyre burst. That second glass of champagne, I'm afraid. Or maybe the third. I phoned Gordon, because I knew he was waiting to meet me nearby, the darling. He came to the rescue, changed the tyre quick as a flash and drove like the blazes. Did you know that he used to drive one of the royals around, and one time he…'

'Enough,' Pip said. 'Stop talking. You're giving me a headache. There's nothing more tedious than people's ridiculous pasts.'

'Um, the headache might be from the giant bruise on your forehead,' said Emily. 'It does look rather bad.'

Pip touched it tenderly. It felt puffy and grazed.

'I've got some arnica in my bag, I think. I use it for my spots.' Emily searched through a small sack of lipsticks and pencils, producing some wet wipes and a tiny tube. She wiped blood from Pip's face, then squeezed out some gel and dabbed it onto the wound. The bruise hurt like hell when she pressed it.

'But if you came here with Henrietta, why did it take you so long to arrive?' Pip asked Gordon. 'Where were you?'

'Parking the car,' said Gordon, morosely. 'It's yellow lines all over. I had to go round the…'

'And what are *you* doing here anyway?' Pip asked Emily, suddenly realising that this hadn't yet been established, as useful as Emily was proving to be. The girl blushed and stammered. 'Speak up,' said Pip, who was rather low on patience by this point. It had been a very long evening, and while she had escaped certain death, she still had a pounding head. 'Spit it out.'

'I followed Henrietta from the venue.'

'Well, what were you doing there?'

'I just wanted to see everyone arrive – the red carpet, you know, the fashion, the people. And to see the two of you arrive all dressed up, after I'd helped you with the outfit and everything. So I waited outside. And then afterwards, I just hung about. There were people coming in and out. It was interesting. I saw you leave, and then I saw Henrietta and Gordon, and I knew you must be going somewhere. I figured it was an after-party or something, so I got into a taxi and followed you. I shouldn't have. I feel very silly now,' she said, looking at the floor.

'Pathetic,' said de Range.

'Shut up, you,' Henrietta said, and then to Emily, 'I'm glad you came. We needed the help. You saved the day.' This wasn't quite true, but Emily looked so pleased that Pip decided to let it go.

'It's true. Thank you,' said Pip, to the blushing girl. 'And you too, Gordon.'

'Anything for my Henrietta,' said Gordon, with what could only be described as a bashful smile, aimed at Henrietta. 'The police will be here soon, thank goodness.'

Henrietta and Pip exchanged glances. They needed to get their stories straight for the police.

At which point, there was a hard knock on the door and a shout. 'Police! We're coming in!'

CHAPTER 43

'Lloyd, Llewelyn, Polly, Billy, Sally and Ellen,' said Mummy, pointing to each llama in the paddock in turn.

Ridiculous names, thought Pip. Arbitrary. If she had a llama she'd call it Shama. Shama the llama. Obviously. Or Dalai Llama, although that had probably been done. She certainly wouldn't have gone with just any old name, like Sally.

'Excellent names!' cried Henry, clapping his hands. 'Clever use of the double l. As in, llama.'

'Ah, so pleased you got it,' Mummy blushed and looked up at him from under her wide straw hat, which she had trimmed with fresh flowers for the picnic. 'You'd be surprised how many people don't.'

Pip nodded knowingly, as if she had got it, too.

'Now take me through which one is which again?' Henry asked with genuine interest.

'Well the boys are a bit bigger, and then they all have their special features. If you look at Lloyd – he's that cheeky fellow there on the left, you can see he has a slightly deviated septum…'

Pip wandered away from the paddock, leaving her mother and Henry to an in-depth discussion of each beast's unique markings, personality, quirks and heft. She walked round to the opposite side of the pond to join Gordon and Henrietta, who had established themselves on a blanket under the old oak tree, and were unpacking a picnic basket. Crispy baguettes and a large gooey brie were already languishing on a board, begging to be eaten.

Tim and Jimmy were working in unlikely synchronicity, setting up drinks on a table behind them, putting champagne in an ice bucket, and fetching glasses from Mummy's house. The kittens were asleep in a basket. Pip had insisted they come to the picnic party, and they were tired from the drive.

Henrietta pulled out a box of chocolates and offered one to Pip. 'Hey, birthday girl. Have a choc. How are you feeling? Your head looks much better,' she said.

'I feel one hundred per cent fine. It was good to rest up, though.' Pip hadn't been at work since the incident. Henrietta had insisted she take the rest of the week off to recover.

'It didn't look that restful,' said Tim. 'You've been interviewed by every major paper, it feels like.'

After Emily had posted her photos on Instagram, about three minutes after the police had finished questioning them, a media frenzy had, indeed, ensued. Pip had become the hero of the hour – to Emily's distress. Pip had told the various reporters a somewhat edited version of how they'd found themselves tying up a master criminal in his warehouse in order to reclaim the red dress Julia Roberts had worn in *Pretty Woman*. She and Henrietta had had to fudge some details for the press and for the police. Henrietta, as the owner of the dress and the director of the museum, had put the dress on the market. Rosanne had offered to assist. Elliot de Range had come to view it and then stole it. They simply edited out the first disappearance of the dress, amongst other details.

Pip had told Arabella a similar story. As far as Arabella knew, Henrietta had taken the dress to show to a possible customer, and had been so busy with her Morocco plans that she'd forgotten to put it back. It had all been a big misunderstanding. No harm done – until de Range had decided to steal the dress. Pip wasn't entirely sure that Arabella had bought the story, but she seemed to be willing to put it behind her.

People had been intrigued by the story – the Hollywood star angle, the fashion angle, the three girls from a museum taking down a criminal – and the story was being syndicated all over the place. It had gone viral within days.

Gordon handed Pip the *Sunday Mirror*. 'Have you seen this one?' he said. Pip saw her own face staring back at her. In the picture, which took up nearly half the page, she was standing behind de Range, who was tied to the chair, his face furious, his mouth open in a snarl. Henrietta was on one side of him, Emily was on the other side – one hand on his shoulder, restraining him, the other taking the selfie. Pip was looking straight into the camera, blood dripping down her face from the gash in her forehead. It was an extraordinary photograph.

'Pretty cool, hey? This is the full story, and an exposé about de Range and his bunch of crooks. Look inside, it runs over two pages.'

Gordon opened to pages six and seven and there it was: not only their escapades, but everything the police had uncovered since their adventures at the warehouse. It turned out that de Range had been the frontman of a web of criminals specialising in collectibles, artworks, memorabilia and rarities.

'Take a look, Mrs Bloom,' Gordon said, passing the paper over to Pip's mother. The llama fanciers had dragged themselves away from the livestock and come to join the party, sitting companionably side by side on two canvas beach chairs. 'The police have been trying to bust the ring for ages. And your daughter has done it.'

'I haven't been Mrs Bloom for decades,' Pip's mother said to Gordon. 'Please call me Magnolia.' She looked at Pip. 'I must say, Epiphany, this is quite remarkable.'

Pip glowed, despite herself. It was just so nice to be the centre of Mummy's attention. Well, the centre of her admiring attention, to be precise. She did have some experience of being the centre of her attention for other reasons.

'But I still don't quite understand how you got to be in the business of finding missing things. First the boy, and now the dress.' Pip's mother frowned, as if someone was keeping something from her.

'Neither do I, Mummy. It was just a strange set of circumstances. Luck or chance, or something.'

'Chance, and natural talent,' said Henrietta. 'You just have a way of seeing what's going on and fixing the problem.'

Again, not something that Pip generally heard. She was, historically, more in the business of *causing* the problem. She tried not to run through a list of examples in her head, but to instead enjoy the flush of success, and the love and admiration of her family and friends.

'And there's another piece of good news I need to tell you,' said Gordon. 'It's not in the paper; Philip found it out from one of his old cop contacts. When the police raided the warehouse, they found a load of valuable stuff that had been stolen or reported missing. Rewards were offered on some of the pieces. You and Henrietta are going to get some dough.'

'Really? That would be very handy, wouldn't it, Henrietta?' said Pip. 'Any idea how much?'

'It would be thousands. Possibly many thousands.'

The conversation about the reward money was cut short by the arrival of Flis. She dashed in all a fluster, trailing her husband and the kids.

'Goodness, I'm sorry we're a bit late. I was about to leave and I saw the most enormous caterpillar, it was staring at me in this very strange way and I realised it looked very like someone I know, so I...'

'Oh, that's OK,' interrupted Pip. 'You're not that late. We weren't in the least worried.'

It was hardly surprising – there had never been an occasion, in the whole history of family occasions, where Flis was on time.

'I've got lovely snacks. Camelia, bring out the tofu treats please, and those delicious cauliflower kebabs. Harry, go and help Daddy get the elderflower kombucha out of the car.'

When everyone was settled, Emily came out of the house bearing a huge cake, candles blazing. Arabella followed her with a large gift box.

Jimmy started everyone singing 'Happy Birthday' in a surprisingly good alto, while Tim poured champagne into flutes and handed them round.

Pip blew out her candles and made a wish. For once in her life, she didn't know what to wish for. She had so much to be grateful for. Her friends and family. Her success at work. The kittens, who had given her so much joy and would soon be heading to loving homes – one with Flis, one with Henrietta and Henry.

While Emily got to work cutting the cake, Arabella handed the present over with a smile.

'Happy birthday,' she said. 'Here's your gift. I think you'll like it.'

Pip lifted the lid, and lifted layers of tissue paper to find a red dress.

'It's not the real thing,' said Arabella. 'But it's close enough. If anyone deserves it, you do.'

Pip stood up and held the dress against her, and gave a twirl. Emily snapped a picture.

Everyone laughed and clapped, and Tim popped another bottle of champagne.

As she took a sip, Pip's phone rang in her pocket.

'Take it,' said her mother. 'It's probably someone wishing you happy birthday.'

Pip handed her cake plate to Jimmy and fished out the phone. Unknown number. She would usually ignore it, but today she was so full of optimism, she decided it must be good news.

'Hello?'

'Hello. Is that Epiphany Bloom?' The voice on the end of the phone was American. Female. Oddly familiar.

'Yes.'

'Epiphany, hello. This is Julia Roberts.'

A LETTER FROM KATIE

Dear reader,

Katie Gayle is, in fact two of us – Kate and Gail – and we want to say a huge thank you for choosing to read *The Museum Murder*, the second Epiphany Bloom cosy mystery. If you enjoyed the book, and want to keep up to date with all Katie Gayle's latest releases, just sign up at the following link. Your email address will never be shared and you can unsubscribe at any time.

www.bookouture.com/katie-gayle

We hope you loved Pip's adventures, and if you did we would be very grateful if you could write a review and post it on the site where you bought the book and Goodreads. We would love to hear what you think, and it makes such a difference in helping other readers to discover Pip too.

You can find us in a few places and we'd love to hear from you. Katie Gayle is on Twitter as @KatieGayleBooks and on Facebook as Katie Gayle Writer. You can also follow Kate at @katesidley and Gail at @gailschimmel.

Thanks,
Katie Gayle

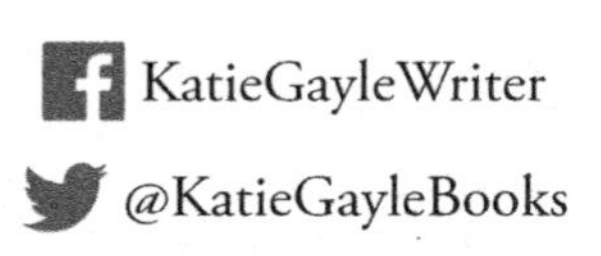